"I am not a child!" Cynthia screamed, pushing with all her might at his hands.

Nick's fingers flexed and tightened. "You're childish enough to do something stupidly reckless, so I'd say you're childish enough to be turned over my knee."

"You just *try* it."

His gaze flicked to her straining arms. When he spoke again, he leaned close, his voice dropping to stroke over her skin. "You think I wouldn't?"

Nick's eyes narrowed. He looked at his right hand as it slowly tightened to a vise on her wrist.

"Nick . . ."

His gaze slid to her lips. And then his mouth descended.

For a brief moment she didn't understand what part this played in their argument. And then her body reported to her mind what was really happening. Nick was *kissing* her. Just as she'd hoped. Oh, sweet mercy . . .

She'd imagined this a thousand times and a thousand more. She'd thought Nick's lips would brush softly, a gentle taste, a breath of love across her cheek. She'd never once considered he would kiss as if he were needy. As rough as James, even. But better than those stolen kisses with James Munro. Infinitely better . . .

Books by Victoria Dahl

TO TEMPT A SCOTSMAN

A RAKE'S GUIDE TO PLEASURE

ONE WEEK AS LOVERS

Published by Kensington Publishing Corporation

One Week As Lovers

VICTORIA DAHL

ZEBRA BOOKS
Kensington Publishing Corp.
http://www.kensingtonbooks.com

ZEBRA BOOKS are published by

Kensington Publishing Corp.
119 West 40th Street
New York, NY 10018

All Kensington titles, imprints, and distributed lines are available at special quantity discounts for bulk purchases for sales promotion, premiums, fund-raising, educational, or institutional use.

Special book excerpts or customized printings can also be created to fit specific needs. For details, write or phone the office of the Kensington Special Sales Manager: Attn. Special Sales Department. Kensington Publishing Corp., 119 West 40th Street, New York, NY 10018. Phone: 1-800-221-2647.

Zebra and the Z logo Reg. U.S. Pat. & TM Off.

ISBN-13: 978-1-4201-0482-0
ISBN-10: 1-4201-0482-9

First Printing: August 2009
10 9 8 7 6 5 4 3 2 1

Printed in the United States of America

This book is for my editor, John.
Thank you.

Acknowledgments

First, thank you to my readers. I can't tell you how much it means to hear from you. I hope you enjoy Lancaster as much as I have.

Thank you to my boys for being so wonderful. I couldn't be more proud. And to my husband, who truly believes in me. You're the best and I couldn't do it without you.

As always, thanks to my agent, Amy, for being an ally and a friend.

And boundless appreciation to my critique partner and friend, Jennifer. You understand me, and that's priceless. We're living the dream!

I also want to acknowledge Thomas Campbell for providing the bit of "maudlin poetry" quoted by Lancaster on the beach. Your words fit Lancaster's mood perfectly.

Last but not least . . . Thank you to my editor, John. In a moment of uncertainty, your words meant so much.

Chapter 1

London, Spring 1846

Nicholas Cantry, Viscount Lancaster—known to friends, family, and every single person in the *ton* for his unerring charm and constant good humor—was furious. His vision blurred faintly at the edges, and his teeth ached from the pressure of being clenched together, but as he made his way through the crowd of the waning dinner party, people still offered him smiles. If they thought anything at all, perhaps they wondered if he had a touch of dyspepsia. Certainly, they didn't suspect him of anger.

He was, after all, an ornament. A pleasant way to pass the time. A fairly harmless fortune hunter. And that was the way he liked it. No one ever looked past his humor and goodwill. No one looked deeper. He could hardly regret a reputation he'd taken pains to cultivate.

But finding his fiancée spreading her legs for another man had ruffled even Lancaster's carefully groomed façade. The hateful things she'd screamed at him hadn't helped his temper. Neither had the knowledge that he could not simply turn and walk away.

"My good Viscount Lancaster!" a voice trilled from his left. Lancaster stopped in his tracks, spun toward the petite matron, and bowed in one fluid motion.

"Lady Avalon," he murmured over her offered hand. "A light in my dismal evening."

"Oh, pah." She giggled, and smacked him in the shoulder with her oversized fan.

"Lady Avalon, I had no idea you'd returned from the country so early. Fleeing an ill-thought affair, are you?"

"Lancaster, you are *scandalous.*"

"Only occasionally. You are acquainted with Mr. Brandiss?" He gestured toward their host and resisted an urge to massage the tight pain from the back of his neck.

"Oh, yes. Mr. Brandiss may be a merchant, but he's as much a gentleman as any peer of the realm." She leaned a little closer. "I've also met *Miss* Brandiss. What a beautiful bride you've chosen, Lancaster."

Beautiful, yes. And treacherous. And surprisingly loud when backed into a corner.

But he only inclined his head in modest agreement.

"Lovely," Lady Avalon continued, "and a very smart alliance. I told everyone you would do quite well, and you have."

"Yes, Miss Brandiss was willing to overlook my fearsome face and thread-worn title for a chance to get her delicate hands on my apple orchards. They're quite profitable."

"Ha! If you'd had a fortune, young man, you'd have reigned as the bachelor king for a decade. It takes a barrel of charm to be seen as a decent catch even in your straits. Very impressive, Viscount. Mr. Brandiss is a stickler when it comes to his little Imogene."

"Quite," Lancaster managed to grind out past a smile. "Now if you'd be kind enough to excuse me . . ."

"Oh, yes! I'm sure you'd like to get back to that darling fiancée of yours."

He turned, but not quickly enough to avoid another whack of her fan. The whalebone cracked against his arm, and Lancaster imagined his nerves as taut wires, popping with just that sound as they snapped apart.

Darling fiancée indeed. He'd thought her darling enough until a few moments ago. He'd thought her demure and shy and as pretty as she was intelligent.

"Demure," he growled as he moved out of the crowded hall and closer to the front door. He'd made it past the densest of the crowd, but he wasn't free yet. Mr. Brandiss himself stood near the door, bidding farewell to the first of his guests to leave.

He'd not be as easy to fool as the rest of these people, and he was the last man Lancaster wished to speak with right now. Martin Brandiss was shrewd, smart, and almost preternaturally astute. Though perhaps not where his daughter was involved.

He edged past the cluster of Brandiss and his guests without notice, but there was no way to escape completely. He had to request his greatcoat and hat, had to wait for his coachman to be summoned. Lancaster hardly even winced when he felt a hand slap his shoulder.

"Off so early, sir?"

Lancaster made himself chuckle as he turned to shake his future father-in-law's hand. "I've an appointment at my club, I'm afraid, but it was a truly delightful evening. Your wife is an estimable hostess."

"Never worry. She insisted that Imogene participate in all the planning. She'll make a fine viscountess."

"I've no doubt." She'd managed to pretend affection for a suitor she hated; Imogene would play the part of Lady Lancaster with aplomb.

A sudden idea sparked. If she backed out, he would have no choice. The decision would be beyond his control. The wedding could not go forward. "Mr. Brandiss, are you certain she is eager for this match?"

Brandiss's bushy white brows slowly lowered until Lancaster could hardly see his eyes. "What do you mean?"

"I mean . . ." His neck burned with strain, but he managed to look merely concerned. "Your daughter has been quiet these past weeks. Since the betrothal dinner."

"Imogene is an obedient girl," Brandiss answered, his voice hardening to steel. "She is happy with this betrothal, milord. She knows her duty."

Her duty. Yes, she had screamed something about duty while her lover tried to shut her up.

Duty. Despite the circumstances he'd still hoped for something more.

Instead of shouting at the man that his daughter was nothing close to happy, Lancaster inclined his head. "Of course. Please convey my farewells to your wife and daughter. As always, it's been a pleasure."

"Milord," Brandiss replied with a cursory bow. Yes, as Lady Avalon had said, Brandiss was every inch the gentleman despite that he was a glorified trader. Lancaster had been disappointed at that, actually. He'd hoped he was marrying into a warmer, more relaxed family. But they couldn't afford to relax. They were a family on the rise; eccentricities, scandals, and even pleasure in life could not enter into the equation. Lancaster was merely a factor in the mathematics of society and wealth. His feelings did not come into play at all. He'd been foolish to imagine they should.

The springs of his carriage were in serious need of repair. Lancaster wondered how much longer they'd last as he stepped onto the street and heard the low groan of protest echoing from the underside of the box. The ride was uncomfortable but at least it was no longer embarrassing. His groom had solved the problem of the peeling crest by scraping it off entirely and repainting the door. Obvious sign of poverty gone in a few strokes of a brush. If only the rest of the problem could be solved so easily.

"Milord," his butler murmured as he bowed Lancaster inside. The young man's face was unlined, his brown hair unmarred by even a hint of gray. In other words, he was far too young to be a viscount's butler, but his services came cheap and he was eager and intelligent. Of course, at twenty-five, Lancaster himself was a bit young to be a debt-ridden viscount. He and Beeks had youth in common at least.

"Beeks," Lancaster offered as he swept out of the dark and into the hall. "Having a pleasant evening, I hope."

"Yes, sir. Very pleasant. Lord Gainsborough has arrived, sir. I've placed him in the White Room."

Gainsborough. Damnation. He wasn't in any position to cheer the old man up tonight.

"Sir? Shall I tell him you've arrived home?"

"No," Lancaster snapped, then immediately softened his voice. "No, I . . ." Hell. However unhappy he might be, he couldn't bring himself to send the lonely widower away. "Just give me a moment, Beeks. Trials of pleasant society and all that. Quite exhausting." He tossed his hat and coat to Beeks and strode down the hall toward the study. The brandy snifter awaited him on a small table next to his desk. Lancaster poured a glassful before he even took a seat.

The small stack of correspondence tipped from its pile when he collapsed into the chair. Lancaster picked idly through it as he made quick work of the glass of brandy. A brief, friendly letter from a woman who'd been his lover for a short time. A scrawled note from the Duke of Somerhart, curtly confirming that he and his bride would attend the upcoming nuptials, though he implied that only the duchess was actually *pleased* to attend. Lancaster managed a ghost of a smile at the thought.

Two creditors' notes, of course, though they'd gotten friendlier since his betrothal to the daughter of London's richest silk importer. Still, he dropped them immediately in the waste bin, then thought better of it and retrieved them to sit on the corner of his great-grandfather's desk as a reminder. He was not free, and he could not afford to forget.

His father had inherited an estate teetering on the edge of ruin and had quickly tipped it straight over the chasm. Not that he'd bothered to inform his heir of the matter. Perhaps he'd thought his son too young to worry over such things. But in the end, Lancaster had inherited at twenty-three.

He poured himself another glass of brandy and picked up the last letter.

It came from the housekeeper of Cantry Manor, the smallest of his estates and the only self-sustaining one. God, he hoped it wasn't bad news about the sheep. Cantry Manor was the one estate he didn't worry over; he'd never even visited in the past decade. Lancaster downed another gulp of brandy and slit open the letter.

Throat burning with liquor, he read the words, his brain not quite understanding the meaning of them. They didn't make sense. But he read the letter again, and his heart sank as reality reared its ugly head.

I regret to inform you . . . I know you were once close to her . . .

Miss Cynthia Merrithorpe was dead.

Sad news. Very sad. She could not have been more than one-and-twenty. What had killed her? An accident, a fever?

A sigh broke free of his throat. She'd been only eleven the last time he'd seen her, just before he'd left Cantry Manor behind. He hadn't seen his young neighbor since, so why did his gut feel suddenly knotted up with grief?

His fingers dug into the mess of his dark blond hair and pressed into his scalp. Perhaps it wasn't memories of Cynthia twisting his gut. Perhaps it was more that the letter was a sign that his world was on the descent and likely to continue in that direction.

You thought it could get no worse, foolish mortal, some wicked god was chuckling from above. Or actually . . . perhaps, *Your troubles cannot be compared to poor Cynthia Merrithorpe's, selfish man.* Lancaster felt chastened at the thought.

She'd never married. Never left Yorkshire. A short and lonely life.

He'd thought she would have grown into an attractive young woman. Thought her wise gaze and stubborn chin would fit a woman's face better than a child's. He must have been wrong. She'd died a spinster. But she'd been so lively in her youth. Honest and open, country-free and peaceful. Nothing, for instance, like Imogene Brandiss.

He grimaced at the thought and tossed back the last inch of liquid in the glass.

No, Miss Imogene Brandiss knew nothing of honesty, though the terrible things she'd shrieked tonight had seemed honest enough. *A real man doesn't look to a woman for money! A real man works for it! Have you ever done one real thing in your sorry life?*

Some weight inside him, some weight that had been slowly adding to itself over the past months, finally made its presence known. It pulled at his bones and tendons, threatening to collapse his body in upon him. Threatening to collapse his whole world.

Too much had gone into this, the plans were too far forward. His family's creditors had retreated to await the bounty brought by his marriage to an heiress. If he called off now . . .

He pictured crows picking at his eyes and knew he had no choice.

Something dark and overwhelming breached the surface calm he always displayed to the world. Something black and trembling with strength. Lancaster recognized it. He'd been well acquainted with it all those years ago. Rage. Fury. And fear. All of it coiled so tightly together that it seemed to have formed some heretofore unknown emotion. There was only one way to deal with it.

Rubbing a hand over his numb face, Lancaster took

a deep breath. He ignored the harsh buzzing in his ears and tried to summon his customary smile. It didn't take hold the first time, nor the second, but eventually it felt in place on his lips, and he tugged the bell pull next to the desk.

A few minutes passed, though the buzzing stayed.

"Milord?"

"Please have a light supper sent to the White Room for Lord Gainsborough and inform him I shall be in for our chess match momentarily."

"Of course," the young man answered with a bow.

He would project good cheer, offer a happy evening for a man still grieving his dead wife, and pretend not to notice the darkness writhing inside his own soul. His smile slipped as Beeks turned away. The buzzing was only growing louder. "Wait."

"Milord?"

"I believe . . ." Lancaster started, the idea forming as he spoke. "I've received word . . ." The buzzing began to recede, so he rushed on. "A neighbor has died. I'll need to travel to Yorkshire to pay respects. It's only right."

Beeks nodded.

"You'll need to pack, of course, and make my excuses to Miss Brandiss's family." Eager as he was, Beeks was not predictably knowledgeable.

"How long do you expect to be gone, milord?"

The sound rushed back into his ears, louder than before. He shook his head, looked at the letter. The weight pulled him down, pressing him into his seat. The beast writhed against the pressure. How long? He'd say his wedding vows to an unwanted wife in only two months.

"Six weeks, I'd think."

"As you say, sir. And you'll leave . . . ?"

Now, he wanted to bark, but he didn't, of course. He only squinted thoughtfully and tried to tamp down the need to flee. "Tomorrow morning, I suppose."

"Yes, milord." Once Beeks had departed to start the frantic packing, Lancaster gave the letter one last glance, allowing himself the luxury of a few more deep breaths. He only needed a little time. Marriage would not be the worst thing he'd ever done for his family, after all. Not by far.

Once the surface of his soul was calm, Lancaster walked from the study and stepped into the White Room with a grin. The broad-faced man standing in front of the fireplace raised his head and his sad mouth broke into a smile. "Lancaster! It's bloody good to see you."

"And you as well, of course. Have you prepared for our match?"

"Prepared?" the older man snorted. "By dulling my wits with whisky? 'Tis the only preparation I need for a chess match with you."

Lancaster inclined his head. "Then I have you exactly where I want you, Gainsborough. I shall strike when you least expect it, pounce upon you like a doxy on a drunkard. Or a debutante on a duke, I suppose."

"Oh!" the old widower chortled, holding his gut against the laughter. "Oh, by God. You do cheer me up, young man. Every single time."

Lancaster chuckled and glanced toward the mantel clock. Twelve hours more and he would make his brief escape.

Chapter 2

Spring may have begun its arrival in London, but it hadn't yet touched the coast of Yorkshire. Freezing rain drummed against the carriage roof and tinged the air with ice, despite the brazier hidden beneath the seat. Lancaster watched his breath form mist before him, and marveled that he'd planned to stay here for six weeks.

They'd just passed the village of Neely, where he'd spent so many hours of his youth, so they were nearing Cantry Manor.

His family had abandoned their smallest estate when they'd moved to London ten years before. He'd never returned, had never even thought much about it, despite all the years spent here during his adolescence. It was cared for by Mrs. Pell, the housekeeper, and the rents were just enough to support the nominal upkeep. No thought required.

But of course, it was deeper than that. He did not like to think about his time here because that led to other memories, other histories. . . . It was a testimony to just how desperate he'd been to escape London that he'd given no thought to the demons that might be exhumed here.

I am a man now, he told himself as he shifted in the hard seat. *Not a boy to run from nightmares.*

Just as anger began to rise like bile in Lancaster's throat, the coachman shouted something and the carriage began to slow. They'd arrived. Old Mrs. Pell would be out to greet him in a matter of moments.

For the first time since he'd departed, it occurred to him that Mrs. Pell would be grieving. Cynthia Merrithorpe had spent hours in her kitchen every day. Sometimes it had seemed as if she'd spent more time in his family's home than her own. If she hadn't been following Lancaster around the estate, then she'd been in the servants' quarters, trailing after Mrs. Pell like a shadow. Poor woman probably felt as if she'd lost a daughter.

The carriage slowed to a stop, sliding a little before the coachman controlled it. Within seconds, the door opened to a blast of rain; clearly Jackson didn't want to remain in the sleet any longer than necessary.

"Looks dark, milord. No one about."

"Lovely. Well, I'll let myself in, Jackson. You get the horses settled, then come 'round the kitchen for something hot."

"Yes, sir. My thanks, sir."

Lancaster steeled himself against the shock of the frozen rain before he stepped to the ground and dashed toward the wide front doors. He made it to the faint shelter of the doorway, but Jackson was pulling away before Lancaster realized the doors were bolted tight against him.

"Christ." A niggling suspicion that had begun to bounce around his head suddenly became solid and real. Beeks had neglected to inform Mrs. Pell that the viscount would soon be in residence. He could only hope that the housekeeper hadn't decided to take this week to visit her younger sister in Leeds.

"Well, there's no help for it," he muttered, and stepped back out into the deluge. By the time he made it around the square bulk of the manor, he was soaked through and half numb with cold. But the knob of the kitchen door turned easily in his hand, and then he was rushing into warmth and glowing light.

"Adam," a familiar voice called from the darkness of a short hallway, "if you're dripping rain all over my floor, you'd best be planning to clean it up. I'll not—"

When Mrs. Pell stepped into the kitchen, she looked up and gasped in surprise. Her shock did not turn to horror until Lancaster spoke.

"Good evening, Mrs. Pell. It seems my man in London has neglected to inform you of my imminent arrival. But here I am, all the same."

"Nick?" she whispered, causing a little shock to course through his veins. No one had called him Nick in years.

"Yes, it's me. Nick. Returned from the—" He caught himself just in time, and cleared his throat. "I apologize for catching you unawares, Mrs. Pell. I know the past two weeks must have been difficult for you, and now I have come to add to it."

She'd yet to recover; her lips were still parted in shock, her skin pale, and he'd begun to fear she'd simply fall over, though she looked as sturdy as ever. The laugh lines around her eyes had deepened certainly, her hair had gone grayer, but she wasn't as old as he'd remembered. Youth had a way of inflating age, it seemed. "Mrs. Pell?"

She blinked, and that finally seemed to release her from her trance. "Milord," she gasped, and fell into a slow curtsy. "Milord, I apologize. Please forgive me. I—Let me put the water on for tea, and then I'll open the library for you, if that will do for a few moments. I'll need to make up your bed and . . ."

"I'm sure the library sofa would be just lovely for the night, if—"

"Never say so!" she gasped. "A bare hour, sir. That's all I need." She snapped into motion, and the teapot was on the stove and warming before he could form another sentence. A blur of calico and white cambric flashed by, but Lancaster managed to snag one trailing end of an apron tie and tugged hard enough to distract her.

"Mrs. Pell."

She stopped, but she didn't turn toward him. She stood frozen, hands clasped tight in front of her, wisps of gray hair drifting from her coiled braid. Her shoulders rose and fell in deep, rapid breaths.

"Mrs. Pell, I want to offer my condolences. I know how close you were to Cynthia. Her death must have been a terrible shock."

Her breathing hitched, and he was sure that she would cry. He was reaching out to wrap a comforting arm around her when she nodded and stepped away. "Yes, sir. Thank you." A brief glance over her shoulder showed eyes bright with tears, but she blinked them away. "You are as kind now as you always were, milord." She brushed her hands over the apron as if she were dusting off flour. "Come now. Let's get you settled in the library so I can brew the tea."

"Hm. You wouldn't happen to have any of my father's special whisky about, would you?"

Her face creased into a familiar smile. "Only for medicinal purposes, sir. But you're clearly on the verge of catching your death. I wouldn't want that on my conscience."

"You're an angel sent from heaven, Mrs. Pell. The best housekeeper a man could hope for."

The smile that had taken over her face fell away, and she dropped her clutched skirt and turned. Lancaster had no choice but to follow. Any questions he had would wait until the morning.

A half-filled cup of tea. An empty glass tumbler. The crumbs of a vanished bit of bread and cheese. These things lay scattered over the long table.

She drifted closer.

A man was stretched out along the dark green fabric of the sofa, his feet crossed at the ankles, hands folded over his flat stomach. A strange visitor. A stranded traveler. Or . . .

No.

The cool air of the room pressed her white gown to her legs when she stopped in shock before him. It could not be. Not now, not when he could no longer help her.

But the golden waves of his hair were undeniably familiar in the flickering light of the fire, as were the fine straight line of his nose and the gentle curve of his mouth. She did not need to see the color of his eyes to know it was him.

"Nick," she whispered, the word falling from her unwilling mouth and stirring his eyelids.

She backed away, but not before his eyes opened, just for a moment, then lowered again in sleep.

Cynthia Merrithorpe turned and ran, disappearing

into a dark shadow in the wall. If the man woke behind her, she did not know and did not care.

Nicholas had returned, the answer to her girlhood prayers . . . and she could not allow him to stay.

"What have you done?" Cynthia whispered as soon as Mrs. Pell stepped foot into the attic.

The housekeeper jumped, already shaking her head. "Nothing!"

Cyn clutched her arm. "You wrote to him, asked his help!"

"I did no such thing, missy. And how did you know of the viscount's arrival?"

"*Viscount,*" she muttered, irritated as ever by his new status in life. He'd been no more than a tall, humble boy when she'd known him. A tall, humble, handsome boy with impossibly sweet brown eyes. "I saw him," she finally admitted.

Mrs. Pell looked doubtfully toward the tiny round attic window.

"No, I was worried when you did not bring tea. I feared you'd fallen ill. I had no idea I'd stumble over a grand lord asleep in the library."

"Tell me you didn't!"

"What?" Cynthia chewed thoughtfully on her thumbnail.

"*Stumble* over him!"

"No, of course not. He didn't see me." Hopefully.

"Well, for the love of God, no more sneaking about. Stay in the attic. Surely he'll leave soon. If he finds you here, he'll toss me out on my rump without a reference."

"He would not."

"And stop biting your nails. It's not ladylike."

Cynthia snorted at the woman's priorities. "You just told me to stay in the attic. I'm hidden away like a leprous mistress. Hardly ladylike."

Mrs. Pell nodded in distraction, but then her eyes focused on Cynthia's woolen stockings and thick robe. "It's not fair, what's happened to you," she said, as she'd said every day since Cynthia had arrived, bloodied and frightened, on her doorstep.

Cynthia stepped forward to take her hands and clasp them between her own. "I know I shouldn't have asked you to take me in. I'm sorry. It's too much to ask anyone. Did you . . . Did you write to Nick and ask his help?"

"I wrote, but only to inform him of your death." She crossed her arms, only succeeding in making herself look more guilty. "It would've seemed strange otherwise! And he's not Nick, anymore, sweeting. He's Viscount Lancaster."

"Yes," she agreed quickly, and met Mrs. Pell's eyes straight on. "He's not Nick anymore. And we'd do well to remember that. We must get rid of him as quickly as possible, or he'll ruin us both."

"Cynthia, your plan is mad, child. And he doesn't seem so changed. Perhaps he'd—"

"No. Even if he didn't turn me over to my stepfather, there's nothing he can do to help me. I need him gone."

Mrs. Pell didn't nod, but she pressed her lips together and didn't voice whatever objection she had.

"Promise you won't tell him. If he sent me back to my family . . . That man will kill me."

The old housekeeper, more a mother to her than her own mother had been, finally gave a curt nod.

"I'll not tell him. But we will discuss this again, missy. Don't you doubt it."

Cynthia held her tongue, implying consent, but she had no intention of discussing Viscount Lancaster and his imaginary usefulness. If she had anything to do with it, he wouldn't be around long enough to unpack.

She needed a few weeks alone, perhaps only a few days. And then she'd be gone from this place as if she'd never existed. A ghost of a girl that no one truly remembered.

She would be free.

Chapter 3

Lancaster had suffered a bad night. First he'd endured strange dreams of a disheveled woman in white, standing over him.

She'd seemed vaguely familiar and harmless enough. But she'd quickly faded away, only to be replaced by the old familiar nightmares of pain and fear. When he'd awoken, sweating in the cold, he'd regretted ever returning to Yorkshire.

He was regretting it still, as the bouncing carriage reminded him of all the sore spots he'd acquired on the trip from London. The day was still and dreary, a mist-shrouded landscape that seemed cramped and endless at the same time. But he could hear the faint shush of the ocean and smell the salt tang. The reminder that he was, at least, not in London began to wear away his foul mood. Better to be here, even in the cold. Even on his way to pay respects to a dead girl's family.

She was the only Merrithorpe in the house. Her father had died long before, and Lady Merrithorpe had married a stout man named Cambertson who smiled rarely and yelled often. The very reason Cynthia had often fled to Cantry Manor. Mr. Cambertson had not thought much about her as long as she wasn't in sight, and that was the way Cyn had preferred things. Likewise, Lancaster had not thought much about her once she was out of sight, and now guilt was a burr under the skin that covered his breastbone.

But he had too many people to worry about as it was. His mother, totally dependent upon him and unwilling to see the truth of their circumstances. His sister, almost of marriageable age, in need of a Season or two and all the spending that came along with it. And his brother, in his youthful prime and happy to be indulging his oats. The bills for clothing, liquor, and "indulgences" had long since become unmanageable. Like their mother, Timothy couldn't seem to understand the concept of poverty. They had nothing. Nearly all the property was entailed. Lancaster's name and title were virtually the only assets left. His name, his title, and his body.

Heat crawled over his skin, and he pushed the thought away with a physical shift in posture. The carriage window was ice against his fingers when he reached to snap it open, but the freezing air was a welcome distraction. He considered asking the coachman to stop so he could walk the rest of the way, but didn't get the chance. Oak Hall slipped into view and the shell drive crunched beneath turning wheels.

A thump of familiarity resounded in his chest as they approached from the east. He'd probably only been to Oak Hall a dozen times in his youth, but it was one of those strange old memories that lay forgotten and unknown until it was abruptly recalled by a sight or smell. Here, it was the sight of the three ancient trees that twisted taller than the stone building they shaded. And the unusual dusk blue paint that tinted the shutters and gables of the home.

For the first time since he'd heard the news, he felt a wash of true sadness for Cynthia. Gone were his own self-absorption and pity. Cynthia was dead, and she'd never scramble up the tree under her room again, never watch him with frustration edging her jaw into obstinance, never roll her eyes as her stepfather blathered on about some controversial topic.

Once the carriage had rolled to a stop, he stepped heavily onto the drive and trudged up the stairs. Strangely, no servants arrived to assist, but perhaps a pall had fallen over the household. Still, it had been weeks now. Odd. Lancaster was forced to knock on the door.

And wait.

He knocked again. Apparently the title of viscount no longer counted for much in this part of Yorkshire. This was twice in twenty-four hours he'd been caught knocking fruitlessly at a front door. And he was quite sure he'd just felt a raindrop.

Lancaster was glaring up at the sky when the door opened on a whoosh of air.

"Wot?"

Good Lord. The servant—if he was, in fact, a servant and not an invading peddler—stood all of five feet tall. His grizzled gray hair grew in a strange pattern. A peninsula descended over his forehead and a ring grew 'round the sides, but there was nothing else. Unless one counted his ear canals.

"Wot is it?"

Lancaster blinked from his fascination. "Are you addressing me?"

The old man glared up at him, blood in his eyes. Literally. Lancaster could see the blood vessels quite clearly. He'd bet a sovereign the man was a drinker.

And a belligerent one at that.

Lancaster sighed. "Very well. I am Viscount Lancaster, here to pay my respects to Mr. and Mrs. Cambertson."

"Milord," the man wheezed as he bowed, though his expression didn't change. He still seemed put out by the effort. "If ye'll follow me, I'll see if the master is receiving."

So he followed the hunched figure, promising himself he'd never again lament the youth of his own butler. So fascinated was he by the strange wraithlike servant, he almost didn't see the startling changes in Oak Hall. They'd already crossed the threshold of the morning room before he noticed what was missing.

Well . . . everything. Everything was missing. Light squares against the wallpaper marked where paintings had once hung. Tables stood empty, clearly lacking vases or some other small art form. Even the wood floors echoed their bareness, missing the lush, deep rugs that had once softened steps. Lancaster spun in a slow circle as the butler shuffled back into the hallway.

Unbelievable. It looked as if the house were being slowly dismantled. Sold off piecemeal. Foreshadowing of his own future, perhaps.

He was scowling at the thought when the butler returned. "Mr. Cambertson will see you," he intoned, as if there was some question of whether Mr. Cambertson would receive a viscount.

Still, Lancaster said, "Excellent!" and followed again, noticing the way the halls echoed as dust motes danced with each footstep. There wasn't a maid in sight, and no evidence that there had been one for quite some time.

"The Right Honorable Viscount Lancaster," the butler muttered before they'd even reached the doorway to the study. A grunt sounded from inside the room, followed by the squeak of an ancient chair. Mr. Cambertson was pushing to his feet when they entered.

Lancaster struggled not to flinch at the odor of cheap cigars and cheaper gin that filled the room. The curtains were drawn, steeping the room in a brown shade that perfectly matched the stench. And Mr. Cambertson looked right at home too, jacketless, stubbled, and bleary-eyed.

"Milord," Cambertson rasped. "What an honor it is to receive you."

"The honor is mine," Lancaster replied in absolute falsehood. Though Cambertson's curly hair was still black, it had thinned, and the rest of him had aged considerably. Deep pouches drooped beneath his eyes and his wide, stocky shoulders were hunched as if a great weight hung from them. Still, Lancaster walked swiftly forward to shake the man's hand, all jovial good humor as always.

Cambertson's fingers gripped too tight, reminding Lancaster of a drowning man grasping at safety, or perhaps it was the desperation in his eyes that gave that impression.

"Please, sit. *Ewing!*" he suddenly roared. "*Tea!*" The words echoed away, leaving them in dim silence.

Lancaster glanced around, wondering if he'd fallen into some strange midday dream, but his surroundings appeared real enough. "Mr. Cambertson," he said, "I want to offer my sincere condolences to you and to Mrs. Cambertson. I was shocked at the news about Miss Merrithorpe. I can't imagine how difficult this time must be for both of you."

"Mm. The missus has run off to her sister's home. Not sure when she'll be back."

"I see."

He drew a hand over his face, scraping over the black stubble. "Difficult," he said, as if he were pondering a question. "Yes, it's been difficult."

"I'm truly sorry. She was a lovely girl. She's remembered fondly in my household and will be earnestly missed." Poor Mrs. Pell had been so distraught this morning she'd barely spoken a word.

But Cambertson was shaking his head. "Lovely," he repeated. "Lovely enough, I suppose. But in the end, it seems Cynthia was a selfish girl with no concern but her own silly desires. Do you know what she's done to this family?"

"I . . ." Lancaster couldn't begin to think of an appropriate response. He could only stare in shock as Cambertson's face turned from gray to pink and then fully-enraged red.

"She has ruined us. She had the chance to pull her family back from the brink of disaster and instead she indulged her stupid girlish fears and threw herself from a cliff!"

"She . . . *What?*" Lancaster surged forward in his seat, banging a knee against Cambertson's desk. "She . . . She threw herself from a cliff?"

"Yes! As if she were the heroine of some maudlin novel. One of your cliffs, as a matter of fact. What a waste."

"But I thought . . ." He'd thought she'd died from a

fever, or perhaps an accident, but to take her own life? What the hell had happened to the stubborn young girl he'd once known? The room wavered around him. Lancaster blinked hard. "Why?" he finally managed to force out.

Cambertson gave a curt shake of his head. "She had some missish fears about the man she was meant to marry."

"But . . ." He couldn't think what to say, didn't even know what to think.

The old butler shuffled in, offering a reprieve from the conversation, but Cambertson continued on.

"This family is in dire straits, and well she knew it. But still she carried on as if she were the toast of London. 'I won't marry him and you cannot force me,'" he mimicked in a crude parody of a girl's voice. "We have nothing, Lord Lancaster. Nothing but Ewing here, who could drop dead at any moment—" The butler grunted an agreement. "And a deaf and dumb chambermaid whom no one else will employ. I could not even afford to keep my horses. Do you know what it's like to ride to church in a mule cart? And yet she thinks she should be allowed to moon about, waiting to fall in love with some young man whose family likely wouldn't have her anyway. The infuriating folly of youth."

"I don't understand," Lancaster managed to say. Nothing intelligent but at least it was a full sentence. *I don't understand.* Except that he *was* beginning to understand. His gut was telling him that he understood quite well. He met her stepfather's eyes. "You were selling her off for money."

Cambertson leaned forward, planting his elbows on the desk. "I arranged an advantageous marriage to a titled gentleman of considerable means. She had no reason to object. She certainly had no reason to become hysterical. The truth is simple. Cynthia did not like being told what to do, and so she deliberately ruined everything."

"By ending her own life."

"Yes."

Lancaster couldn't look at him anymore, so he glanced away, taking in the darkened room littered with papers and empty glasses, everything covered with dust. "And I thought you were in mourning," he muttered in disgust.

"I *am* in mourning. We are ruined. And of course I did not wish her dead. Of course not."

Unable to stop himself, Lancaster shot him a look of utter scorn.

"Ha!" The man's laugh didn't hold a hint of amusement. "Perhaps you've forgotten what it's like to be a simple 'mister,' Lord Lancaster. Life is not so easy for men who aren't born into such important status. She had a duty to her family and she refused to uphold it. So I am unhappy that she is dead, but I cannot find it in my heart to rend my garments and gnash my teeth. I am too occupied trying to find some other way to devise an income. Our sheep were hit hard with foot rot last year."

A duty to her family. Yes, Lancaster understood quite clearly. But one detail nagged at his mind, and he finally pinned down the problem. "What kind of a titled gentleman can offer an 'advantageous marriage' but finds himself paying for the privilege?"

The man leaned back and crossed his arms. "There were certain circumstances . . ."

Lancaster narrowed his eyes and watched Cambertson's chin jut out in defiance.

"Nothing more than rumors. Enough to make his marriage prospects a bit dim. Richmond assured me there was no truth to them."

Richmond. Lancaster heard nothing beyond "Richmond." His eardrums chimed like a bell. "No," he managed to say, even as the air fell from the space around him and pooled like cool water around his feet. A vacuum formed, pulling the breath from his lungs and drawing all the blood in his body to the surface so that his skin heated all at once. A flash fire that burned away his nerves so he felt nothing.

Cambertson was still talking, saying words that thankfully seemed to need no answer, because Lancaster could neither hear nor respond.

Richmond. She had been meant to marry Richmond.

No wonder she'd killed herself. The man was a monster. A cold sweat broke out over Lancaster's skin.

He'd thought Richmond under control. He'd thought the man incapacitated and impotent. And he'd clearly been disastrously wrong.

"She was being forced to marry Richmond," he heard a voice say, hardly recognizing it as his own.

"Forced!" her stepfather scoffed. "Forced to marry an earl! Hell, the man would have been dead in ten years, I don't doubt, and left her a countess free to do as she pleased. Forced, indeed!"

He could not meet Cambertson's eyes. If he met his eyes, he would lunge at him, slap the arrogance off that hangdog face. "Those were not rumors. The man belonged in Bedlam."

Cambertson sighed. "Of course I would not have granted permission if I believed the tales, but true or not, a little rough bed-sport never killed anyone."

"Pardon me," Lancaster bit out, pushing up to stand on stiff legs. "Please convey my respects to your wife."

Cambertson was muttering something as Lancaster walked out, but he did not try to catch the words. He felt close to snapping, close to turning and throwing his fists against that man's skull.

Rough bed-sport. How dare he. How dare he even think of sending a young girl into that man's bed for the sake of anything, much less *duty*.

Duty. Family. Fear. And death. Death, or at least the desire for it. Lancaster was familiar with it all.

He slammed out of the study doors and rushed down the hall, wondering if every damned family in the empire was the same.

He hadn't remembered making a turn as the butler had led him toward the study, but he was at the end of this hall and had to stop and look from left to right and back again. He couldn't see much in this damned mausoleum, but he thought the entry lay to his left. As he turned in that direction, though, a flash of color caught his eye, a discordant scrap of beauty caught on an otherwise empty wall. Lancaster paused and turned, paying closer attention.

There. He touched a half-open door and the hinges gave way enough to reveal a painting on the far wall of a cozy room. A portrait, actually, of a young woman. It was small but vibrant, and the painter, whomever he was, had captured her likeness perfectly. Lancaster knew this because though he hadn't returned once in the past ten years, he recognized the slightly mysterious smile and wise brown eyes, the stubborn jaw and wide-set cheekbones. He had suspected she'd grow up to be pretty, but Cynthia Merrithorpe had grown into a woman who wasn't *exactly* pretty just . . . inexplicably compelling.

And he'd seen her last night.

The fury that had been working through his body stopped its coursing and then fell away, scattered like dust in the wake of his shock.

He had seen *her* last night. In his dreams. First in the library, and then again in his chambers, in the moonlight, standing over his bed. But how could he have dreamed her like this? Just like this? Perhaps . . .

Shaking his head, he swallowed hard. Ridiculous. She'd grown into an adult, but her features hadn't changed. Of course he'd dreamed her like this. What else could she have looked like?

Lancaster stepped back into the hall, but not before he took one long look at that portrait. Her eyes were sadder than he remembered, it seemed.

With a soft curse, he turned and walked away, relieved he'd never have to set foot in this godforsaken house again. But there were memories awaiting him in his own home, and he dreaded the night to come.

"What did you do?" Mrs. Pell demanded.

Cynthia kept her face very straight. "Nothing."

"Don't tell me 'nothing.' You think I don't recognize that gleam in your eyes? The viscount looked exhausted this morning."

Well, she hadn't done much, honestly. Perhaps he had a weak constitution. Too many years of soft living would do that to a man, or so she heard.

"Cynthia!" the housekeeper growled, then looked around to be sure that young Adam hadn't returned with the new maids. But her gaze fell soon enough back on Cyn.

She squirmed, plucking at her too-large nightdress. "Nothing, I just . . ."

"What?"

"I must persuade him to leave, don't you see? Even if he doesn't catch on, look how many more people will be underfoot. Two girls coming to help already. I'll have to stay locked in that attic for days on end.

"It's harmless," she continued, defensive already. "I just thought I'd . . ." Her hesitation didn't seem to improve the housekeeper's mood.

"Cynthia."

"All right! I thought I'd become a ghost. That's all. I had no idea a harmless female ghost would keep him up all night. He was not so thin-skinned in his youth."

Mrs. Pell gasped so loudly that Cynthia's last words were drowned out. "You were in his chambers?"

"For a moment. He sleeps too lightly. It made me nervous."

"Nervous? I'd say you're quite mad, young lady!"

She shrugged, perturbed that her excellent idea was being dismissed. "It worked, didn't it? If he can't sleep, he's not likely to hang about, is he? And why *is* he here? Did he tell you?"

"It's not my place to ask, just as it's not your place to be in a man's bedroom in the middle of the night. It's not proper and it's certainly not wise. Unless you are hoping to get caught?"

Scowling at the bright encouragement on Mrs. Pell's face, Cynthia said, "No," very firmly. "I have devised a plan."

"Another plan?"

She knew very well what Mrs. Pell thought of her

plans, but there was no other way to escape and ensure her little sister was safe as well. She needed money, and she needed it now. Luckily for her, she had her great-uncle's diaries. *And* a plan.

"I have no other choice," she murmured. "How am I to search the cliffs if *he* is here?"

Mrs. Pell muttered something about danger and bad ideas, and Cynthia cursed Nicholas again. She had only just convinced the housekeeper that the plan would work, and his arrival was undoing days of persuasion. Something had to be done.

Cynthia turned to the kitchen table and busied herself with cutting a slice of brown bread. "What is it you think he could possibly do for me?" she asked quietly. When she received no answer, she pulled the crock of butter closer and shook her head. "It's well known he has no money. Even here in the wilds of Yorkshire we've heard he must marry an heiress, so you can have no fairy-tale dreams that he will scoop me up and carry me away to a life of luxury. Why, he couldn't even afford to set me up as his mistress."

"Young lady . . ." Mrs. Pell started, ready to launch into a lecture, but the words faded away as if she didn't have the heart for it.

Cynthia turned back to her, swallowing a bite of the sweet, dark bread. She shrugged. "I'm hardly mistress material at any rate, so I honestly have no idea how you think the good viscount could assist me."

Mouth opening as if she would speak, Mrs. Pell twisted her apron between two strong hands, but then she only shook her head.

Cynthia looked down at the thick flannel night-dress that Mrs. Pell had loaned her. Aside from the filthy gray gown she'd arrived in, it was all she had.

One could not pack for a suicide, after all. Bound to arouse suspicion.

"Where has he gone?" she asked.

"Off to see Mr. Cambertson. He'll be back soon with more questions than I'd care to answer, I expect." She'd hardly finished speaking when the sound of a carriage snuck past the closed kitchen door. "Go!" Mrs. Pell cried, but Cynthia was already leaving. "And you must keep hidden! No more wandering about!"

Cyn slipped the last bit of bread into her mouth and eased open the panel hidden in the kitchen hall, but she didn't quite close it all the way. Instead she stopped there, just inside the old servants' passage, and waited until Nicholas arrived. When she heard his step, she put her eye to the opening she'd left.

His dark blond hair was disheveled; the uneven swirls of gold curved over and around each other and made Cynthia's fingers itch to smooth them. Or muss them further.

He looked so familiar and precious that her heart stuttered over every beat. Yes, she'd seen him twice already, but both times he'd been sleeping. Awake, he was just as she remembered, and yet there were so many things she'd forgotten. The way he ducked his head when he was thinking. The exact rose shade of his mouth. The line of his nose where a little bump revealed a childhood break. And the deep frown lines between his brows.

Except those had never been there before.

She'd been so absorbed in his face that she hadn't noticed the conversation he was having with Mrs. Pell. The housekeeper was pale and nodding as Nicholas whispered, "I had no idea."

Cynthia hadn't worried overmuch about her family's

response to her supposed death, but seeing the sorrow and concern on Nicholas's face made her realize how self-centered she'd been. She wasn't particularly close to her mother or sister—and certainly not to her stepfather—but she realized now that her mother must be heartbroken and her sister frightened and sad. But the outcome would've been no different if Cynthia had been given over to Lord Richmond: her family would never have seen her again and she'd likely have turned up dead soon enough. She certainly would've wished for it.

Selfish she might be, but she was alive and relatively unscathed.

As Nicholas stared at the floor and listened to something Mrs. Pell was saying, Cynthia began to realize that perhaps the frown lines weren't the only change in him. He was certainly larger than he had been ten years before. Taller and wider and altogether more *male.* And his voice was far deeper and touched with a certain roughness it hadn't had before.

His hair was far shorter than he'd ever kept it, cut close along his nape where once there had been careless curls.

And he looked . . . weary. But perhaps that was only the travel.

Cynthia eased the panel fully closed and made her way blindly toward the narrow staircase along the back wall. She touched her tongue against the ridge of the scar that marred her bottom lip, remembering the feel of a wet mouth sucking at her, of sharp teeth breaking through the skin when she tried to pull free. That monster had liked that, *really* liked it, giving Cynthia her final glimpse of the madness lurking beneath her fiancé's distinguished façade.

The tiny bit of guilt that had started blooming inside of her withered. She couldn't feel bad over a viscount's sleepless nights. She couldn't feel bad over her mother's grief. Her very life was on the line, and no one had seen fit to worry over that. She was on her own.

Setting aside her guilt, Cynthia put one hand against the wall and raced up the steps as quietly as she could to plan tonight's excursions.

Lancaster's neck wouldn't stop its aching, despite the three glasses of brandy he'd downed in quick succession. He shifted against the kitchen wall, crossed his left boot over his right and stared down at the empty tumbler.

He understood what had happened to Cynthia now, or at least the bare bones of it, but there was so much he didn't know. He needed to know, needed to know everything.

His life was spent gathering information and formulating the correct response. Plucking every bit of knowledge he could glean in order to survive. He'd perfected this technique upon his family's move to London. Not only had he never received an education like most boys of his standing—boarding school and all the fraternal bonding that went along with it— his life had been in complete disarray in those first months. So he'd watched and learned and carved out a place for himself among the *ton,* by analyzing every situation he was thrust into.

But this wasn't a matter of social survival. This was life and death and all the suffering in between.

Running a hand through his hair, Lancaster

glanced up to find one of the new maids standing there. She nodded timidly toward the glass.

Lancaster smiled at her pale face, trying to relax her into a state calmer than terror. "Lizzy, is it?"

"Mary, sir."

"Ah, Mary. I apologize. Lizzy is your sister then?" Two of them had arrived shortly after Lancaster had pasted himself to the kitchen wall.

"Yes, sir." Her voice was only slightly above a whisper, but her knuckles weren't quite so white against her skirt.

"Well, Mary, thank you for coming to Mrs. Pell's aid. Seems it takes a household of women to care for one viscount, but that has ever been the case. Could I trouble you to leave Mrs. Pell and me alone for a moment? I wish to speak with her privately."

"Sir!" she chirped, bobbing a ragged curtsy before she bolted from the room.

Mrs. Pell hurried toward him. "Milord, won't you relax in the drawing room until dinner's prepared? It'll be an hour yet. You'd be so much more comfortable."

"I like it here. It's busy." He gestured toward the table and chairs that had been set near the hearth. "Would you please sit down, Mrs. Pell?"

She gasped, "I would say not, sir!" and stared at him as if he'd just pinched her on the rump.

Lancaster held up his hands. "I'm not attempting to permanently upset the delicate balance between man and his housekeeper, I assure you. It's just that I wish to speak with you about something . . . difficult. I thought you'd prefer to be comfortable."

The blood drained from her face. "Difficult?" she whispered.

"Yes." He grabbed a chair and pulled it closer

before the woman could collapse. She let herself be eased down. "It's about Miss Merrithorpe, of course."

The air left her lungs as she slumped. "I . . . I hoped . . . Oh, sir, I pray you can forgive me!"

Collapsing into his own seat, he shook his head. "Forgive you what?"

"Well, I knew. Of course I knew! And while I was sure she was making a grand mistake, I could not think how else to help her!"

His confusion increased tenfold. "But how could you have stopped Miss Merrithorpe's marriage?"

Mrs. Pell's mouth snapped shut and she frowned at him.

"You knew she planned to take her own life?"

"No!" She shook her head hard, then paused for a moment as if to gather her thoughts. "No, of course not. I'd never have allowed such a thing. But I knew how desperate she was. That man . . ."

"Richmond?" The name tasted of bile on his tongue. "Her fiancé?"

"Yes, though she never agreed to marry him, milord." The housekeeper leaned forward in her chair, healthy color returning to her cheeks on a wave of emotion. "She refused. Said he was a devil. So Mr. Cambertson locked her in her room and fed her only bread and water, and still she would not agree."

"My God."

"I was so worried for her, but there was naught I could do. And then . . . And then Mr. Cambertson decided that if he could not convince her, perhaps her betrothed could! He sent for him, and . . . She'd met him only twice before, but she'd seen that he . . ."

Mrs. Pell leaned slightly away and looked at him

carefully. For once, he had no idea of the expression on his face. Horror or just weariness?

"You must know him, being a viscount and all, but I hope he's no friend of yours."

"No."

"Good. As I said, she had heard he was not *right,* you understand. Cynthia wouldn't have wanted to marry a stranger anyway, lord or not. But once she met him, she was afraid. And then that last time . . ." The housekeeper shook her head and her eyes glinted with moisture. "She managed to escape at least."

Escape. By throwing herself from a cliff. Sad to say, Lancaster understood completely.

And what had happened to her before she ran? "I am sorry," he whispered into the silence. "I had no idea."

"Well, how could you have, sir? You're busy with your obligations in London. I daresay the dramas of our little shire have no bearings on life there."

"No, but . . ." Of course, he could not have known that Cynthia Merrithorpe might be forced into marriage, but he should've been keeping watch on the earl. Lancaster was responsible for that wretched life, surely. And by extension, for Cynthia's death.

"I should like to visit her grave," he said.

Mrs. Pell flushed and shook her head. "There is no grave. A suicide can never . . . and besides that, her body was not found."

He raised his head in a sharp jerk. "No body? Then how can we know she is dead? Perhaps she's only run off. That seems more in keeping with the Cynthia I knew."

"I saw her." The woman's words descended in a hoarse rush. "I saw her jump myself, so there's no doubt she's dead. Milord. I mean to say . . . It's just not possible. If . . . I . . . ."

Despite his own shocked pain, Lancaster saw the stiffness in Mrs. Pell's face and knew that he'd asked too much of her. She was in mourning and suffering more than he'd known. How horrible to watch a loved one throw herself into the ocean.

"I regret the question, Mrs. Pell," he said softly. "I apologize for the pain I caused at broaching the subject so callously."

"Nonsense, sir," she answered, though she stood and shook out her skirts all the same. "No apology necessary. Let me refill your drink."

Lancaster watched the amber slide of the liquid as it slipped from the decanter to the glass. He was still watching the play of rusts and golds as the firelight danced against the glass in his hand when he realized he was alone.

Thank God. He needed privacy right now, needed to calm his shaking thoughts. But despite the solitude, he did not reach up to rub the ache at his throat, the prickling heat that spread in both directions before the ends met at his spine. He'd trained himself long ago never to draw attention to the rough scar that ringed his neck, never to touch it . . . even if it did feel tight as a noose today.

He dreamt of her that night. She stood at the edge of a cliff, winds whipping her skirt to her legs and tangling her hair into writhing Medusa strands. When she turned to look at him, her eyes flooded with dark judgment.

Cynthia knew what he knew, was aware of his absolute failure. But he could save her now, reach out and tug her back from the gaping maw of the gray waters.

But something held him back, something rough and tight and strangling him. Lancaster reached up to claw at the tightness, tried to work his fingers beneath it. His eyes rolled as he looked around for help, but no one arrived. In the end, all he saw was Cynthia, as she took one step back and her body slowly tilted away. The pressure tightened around his neck. . . .

Sheer force of will allowed Lancaster to pull himself from the dream. He'd worked hard at the skill, as there were certain parts of his past that he never wished to know again. But it had been years since he'd suffered that kind of nightmare, and so his mind moved with resistance, rusty with disuse.

He forced his eyelids open, though they sunk closed again before he could focus. Only an impression of something white moving in the moonlight floated to his brain. He breathed, feeling his closed throat expand, and tried again. This time there was only blackness, nothing white at all. Lancaster unwound his clenched muscles and sat up, swinging his legs to the floor. The sweat covering his body cooled to an instant chill, a relief after the feverish fear of the dream.

The crisp air was a relief too, and he breathed deeply to calm his hammering pulse. *Just a dream, just a dream.*

The image of a length of white moving across his room flashed behind his eyes again, clearer this time. The shape of a gown, the blur of a face. But that had been nothing. Just a remnant of terror, nothing else. Lancaster scrubbed his hands through his hair, then reached for the mug of water next to the bed. And froze.

The water was there, and the lamp next to it, but something else was there as well. Something small and pale and giving off a faint sheen in the moon's rays. Whatever it was hadn't been there before.

He glanced around the room, toward the door, and saw nothing. Perhaps Mrs. Pell had entered, bringing him . . . What? Lancaster squinted at the unknown object and reached for the lamp. The wick caught with a crackle and revealed a tiny heap of harmless fabric.

The flame grew brighter as he reached forward, adding pink to the paleness. As he lifted the material, Lancaster saw that it was a ribbon. A silk hair ribbon, stiff and discolored, stained with white . . . just as if it had been plunged into the ocean and left to dry on the sun-swept rocks below.

Chapter 4

Richmond would have to die.

Lancaster stared into the low flames of his bedchamber's hearth and nodded at the sparks that floated up. Richmond must die.

His death wouldn't remove the guilt eating at Lancaster's heart, but it was the only thing he could think to offer the ghost of Cynthia Merrithorpe.

She'd entered his room for three nights now, always after he slept, always leaving some token of her presence. A ribbon. A surf-smoothed stone. And last night, worst of all, a cold, wet strand of seaweed on the floor near his bed, as if it had clung to her dead foot on her journey from the cliffs.

Likely, she wouldn't follow him to London if he left; he'd never heard of ghosts traveling. But he didn't think he could live with the knowledge that she was stranded here, wandering these lonely rooms for all eternity. Mrs. Pell might not appreciate it either.

Wondering if he was going mad, Lancaster folded his clothes and eased wearily beneath the icy sheets of his bed. Tired as he was, he didn't think he'd sleep. His thoughts were tumbling over themselves, getting caught up on wisps of bad dreams and hateful memories.

He'd been just fifteen when his father had sent him on that trip to the Lake District. At the time, his family had only recently become sure that the current viscount, a distant cousin, would not pass his title to his rightful heir. The young boy had begun to suffer fits on his sixth birthday and, according to rumor, had only deteriorated as time passed. There had been speculation that he was close to death for years, but the viscount hadn't wanted to admit, to himself or anyone else, that his son would not live to adulthood.

So despite the fact that Nicholas's father would one day ascend to the title, no one could acknowledge it. The family had no social connections and no means of developing them. They were left poor and waiting on the barren Yorkshire moors, like crows anticipating the death of a young boy.

Isolated from society, his family had been thrilled when an opportunity had presented itself. A tour of the Lake District. A chance for Nick to make connections with good families.

Lancaster felt nauseous at the memory. My God, what country fools they'd been. Fish in a barrel, unaware of danger looming overhead.

But it no longer mattered. None of it. Cynthia was dead, and it was Lancaster's fault as much as it was Richmond's. Even the spirit world recognized that.

So Richmond would die. It was the only solution to this mess that Lancaster could conjure up, and it would serve two purposes. First, Cynthia would hopefully be hastened on to heaven . . . or whatever place avenged ghosts went. Second, it would keep Richmond from ever harming anyone again. Plus there was one added advantage: the thought of shooting that man between the eyes satisfied the dark need that lurked deep inside Lancaster's soul.

That primal thing had shaken with joy at the first thought of murder. Lancaster might end up damned for killing, but he would go to hell with a clearer conscience than he had now. He'd neglected this responsibility for far too long. Cynthia certainly believed so, or she wouldn't bother with haunting his house.

A board creaked somewhere nearby, and he raised his head, wondering if this would be the night he'd see her without the veil of sleep to cloud his eyes. But no wraith lurked at the foot of his bed. Just the spirit of the old manor settling around him, or perhaps the new maids readying for bed.

Weariness tugged at him despite his restlessness. Perhaps he would sleep after all, tossing and turning, fighting ghosts and memory. Lancaster lay his head to the pillow and closed his eyes.

Cynthia eased into the narrow space of the old servants' stairs. Her thick stockings were too slippery on the risers, but they were silent. And warm. The rough wooden walls tugged at her nightdress each time she brushed against them, reminding her how narrow the space was. The smallness helped to guide her in the pitch black though. She could only move straight down until she reached the floor below.

It seemed that Nicholas had forgotten more than just his friends when he'd left. He'd been almost too large to fit into the passageways even in his youth, but Cynthia had loved darting in and out of the hidden panels, careful not to be caught by Mrs. Cantry, who would not have appreciated a neighbor child using her home as a personal labyrinth.

But however little time he'd spent in the mysterious passages, Nicholas should have remembered there was a secret entrance to this bedchamber. But he didn't. He'd left his old life too thoroughly behind when he'd gone to London. Cynthia was in no danger of discovery.

Knowing she was close to the bottom step, she ran her hand carefully along the wall until she felt the corner. She could turn left or right here. Left to go toward the other bedrooms and the stairway down to the main floor, right to go to Nicholas's bedchamber. She turned right, careful not to brush the wall that ran just behind his bed.

Her legs began to weaken with nervousness as she neared the panel, but she ignored her own anxiety and pushed ahead. She'd been subtle in her haunting so far, and was having no effect on Nicholas as far as she could tell. Oh, he believed he was being haunted— he'd said as much to Mrs. Pell—but he didn't seem frightened *or* inclined to leave. Strange man. Perhaps he was one of those mystics who thought it exciting to make contact with the dead. She half expected to stumble upon him wearing a turban and chanting over a brace of candles, eager to chat with her spirit.

More drastic action had to be taken. She couldn't possibly scramble around on his cliffs knowing he could decide to enjoy the sea view at any given moment.

She clutched the stick in her left hand and held her breath to listen. He didn't snore, damn him, and it took all her concentration to pick up the faint rhythm of his breathing. It was slow and steady—no chanting—and the unbroken darkness confirmed that his lamp was out. Cynthia eased open the panel.

The relative warmth of the room swept over her, carrying the faint tang of soap. She thought wistfully of a bath, a steaming tub of clean water she could lower her whole body into . . . but there was naught but hurried, cold washing in her immediate future, no matter how much her body shivered at the thought.

His bed lay to the right of the panel, and she could not see him without moving fully into the room, by far the most nerve-wracking point of her expedition. She eased her head beyond the open panel and peeked around it, confirming that he lay in his bed, asleep.

Even the faint moonlight seemed bright after emerging from absolute darkness, and she could see him. As always, he lay on his back, covers pulled high on his chest, one hand wrapped in the sheets. He seemed always to frown in his sleep, which tugged at Cynthia's curiosity. Why was his sleep so troubled? He'd never had a care in the world during his younger years. Perhaps the haunting was working better than she'd expected.

Other than his frown and the lines of his eyebrows, there wasn't much she could make out, though she'd tried hard over the past few nights. She itched to fire the lamp and truly look him over, but that would've been foolish and unnecessary. Completely uncalled for. Still, she glanced toward the lamp before she turned away and tiptoed toward the wall farthest from his bed.

She raised the charcoal and put the end to the faded wallpaper. The first scratch echoed through the room with startling sharpness, nearly pulling a gasp from her throat. As she bit it back, she whipped toward the bed, muscles tensed for flight.

He hadn't moved. His frown didn't deepen, there was no gleam of opening eyes. If his breath had changed, she couldn't hear it over the crazed thumping of her heart.

Just a scratch against the wall. It couldn't have been as loud as it seemed. She steeled her nerves—or tried to—and turned back to her work. The second line of the "L" seemed even louder, but she kept going with only one glance backward. Cringing, she moved on to the "E," then the "A." She was shaking by the time she finished the last letter and finally let herself breathe.

Leave here. Simple, yet hopefully effective. She'd thought the seaweed would do it, but perhaps he was a dullard and needed blatant prodding to get out the door.

She was sliding toward the open panel when it reached her ears . . . silence. No rhythmic shush of air. Cynthia froze. She should have run, but her body locked itself with a nearly audible snap. The hair on her nape stood on end, then gooseflesh spread down her arms.

Don't look. Don't move and he won't be awake.

"It's you," a hoarse voice whispered, and her heart plummeted a frightening distance. Just like jumping off a cliff.

"It's you," he repeated. "Why are you here?"

Oh, God. Oh, God. She'd been caught, found out. He'd send her back to her family and then she'd go to that man—

You are a ghost, something inside her said, scolding. Cynthia blinked and forced down her panic. A ghost. Of course. He still thought her a spirit.

She turned slowly, replacing her terror with a stern look. No need to talk, really, so Cynthia just glared at him.

The man should have been frightened, terrified, but his head tilted as if he were puzzled. Perhaps he really was a dullard. All those London nights of drinking and whoring had taken their toll.

"I *am* sorry," he said softly. "Truly."

She wished she'd brought a length of chain. A rattle would be the perfect sound to leave him with as she slipped away. Lacking that, there wasn't much she could do, so she pointed toward the words she'd scratched and tried to glide toward the door . . . and promptly slipped on the polished wood.

Though she caught herself, the slight stumble seemed to jolt Nick from his daze. He sat up a little more as tension entered the silhouette of his shoulders. She glided faster.

Her movement must have drawn his eye toward the open panel. His head turned toward it, then back to her. She saw the moment he was about to rise, could feel a wave of awareness as his mind fell free of sleep. Cynthia bolted.

Her fingers managed to catch the edge of the panel when she ran past, but it banged on her heel and bounced back open . . . right into Nicholas if his gasp was any indication.

A burst of triumph flooded her veins as she sprinted toward the stairway. He didn't know these passageways and he couldn't see in the dark. Her escape seemed even more sure when a sharp crack sounded behind her. Nicholas cursed loudly and thoroughly, and she imagined him rubbing his elbow while she slipped away into the black maze.

She was planning her next move, mentally gathering up the few belongings she'd stashed in the attic, thinking where she could go . . . and then her foot slipped. A small scream escaped her as the world tilted. Her legs floated in the air for a moment before they crashed down to the hard steps and pulled her back toward the floor she'd just escaped.

The *man* she'd just escaped was waiting at the bottom. His hands closed over her shoulders in an impossibly strong grip.

"Bloody hell," he growled, not sounding like Nick at all. "Who the hell are you?" Every shred of terror she'd managed to tamp down burst free to course through her body.

She pushed her feet against his legs and tried to pull away. Dull pain throbbed through her shins, but she ignored it and pushed harder. Foolish, apparently, as he simply plucked her up and carried her toward the faint silver rectangle that marked the open panel.

"You must be mad, pretending to be a dead girl," he muttered. His fingers dug into her arm and hip. "Completely insane, not to mention heartless and cruel. I actually thought you a bloody ghost." Bitterness had crept into the anger, and now he really sounded like a stranger. She never could have imagined such coldness in Nicholas's voice. He didn't sound the least bit soft or slow now, and nothing close to charming.

"Please," she gasped, as he ducked through the opening.

"Please, what? Ghosts don't feel fright or pain, do they? I can do with you what I like."

What did he mean? The words pushed Cynthia to struggle in earnest, but it was too late. He only laughed and tossed her on the bed. Before she could catch her breath he had one hand wrapped tight around her ankle. She screamed and twisted, but only succeeded in hurting her own leg. Glass clattered, a match flared, and Nicholas managed to light the lamp with one hand.

Desperate, Cynthia kicked out with her free foot, meaning to knock the lamp to the floor, but she didn't make contact with anything but Nicholas's arm. He grabbed that ankle as well, as Cynthia pressed her face to the blankets and reached out to pull herself toward the other side of the bed.

"Well," he scoffed as the lamplight grew brighter around them. "Your thighs certainly look pink enough. I don't think you're dead at all."

Alarm stiffened her spine when she realized that the coolness against the back of her legs was air. His grip stopped her from snapping her legs together or even shifting her position. A different kind of fear was just sizzling over her nerves when he tugged her closer. He moved her ankles together, offering more modesty, but now he was turning her toward him. What to be most concerned with, her virtue or her identity?

Identity, her brain screamed. She had little to no virtue left anyway.

Cynthia made very sure her face was still hidden in the blankets. When his weight dipped the bed and his hold loosened, she shifted fully to her stomach and scooted down toward him, knowing it would push her nightdress higher. Cool air swept under her skirt and Nicholas froze. Her little distraction was working. Now if she could only reach something heavy . . .

* * *

The thief—what else could she be?—clearly had no idea what was happening with her gown. Every attempt to struggle pushed the skirt higher . . . and higher. In fact, Lancaster was just beginning to get a glimpse of the soft, generous rise of her bottom where it curved up from pale thighs. Jesus.

Anger was already pushing his blood hard, screaming through his nerves. He briefly considered that, whoever she was, she was at least in need of a good spanking. But that was ridiculous, of course. He was no rutting hound, and for all he knew she could be somebody's grandmother. But she didn't look like a grandmama from this vantage point. Not at all.

Irritated with his ridiculous train of thought, Lancaster huffed in anger and pushed completely off the bed. "Madam, you may wish to adjust your skirts. Then if you'll stop this meaningless resistance, we can decide what is to be done with you." He'd gotten his voice back under control, but he still felt swelled with rage. A common thief and she'd actually had him believing in ghosts and vengeance and wandering spirits.

She'd stopped wiggling, but her arse was still teetering on the brink of exposure. He glared very pointedly somewhere else—at the back of her head where a tangled mess of braid snaked down her spine. "Mary or Lizzie? Which of you is it? Come now, there's no point putting this off." Her spine stiffened, drawing his eyes back down. . . .

"Oh, for God's sake," he growled, lunging forward to yank her gown down himself. Before the thick flannel was even covering her knees, she'd twisted beneath his hands. He'd finally see her—

Fist. Holding the small clock from the other bedside table. He got a very close view of it when it landed right between his eyes. He'd ducked his head enough that it didn't catch his nose, but it still hurt like the devil. She jerked beneath him, trying to yank her body out from under his, but Lancaster was done with her games and simply put his forearm to her neck. Even if the pounding in his head suddenly overcame him, his weight would work to his advantage.

The woman soon gave up pushing at him and instead began clawing at his arm. Sympathetic to the horror of suffocation, he relented quickly and eased his arm up until the sound of air rushing into her lungs filled the room.

"Now then—" he started, but the words dissolved to ash in his mouth when his gaze finally focused enough to see.

Her. Cynthia. *Her* face, not waxen with death, not hazy and ethereal, but flushed with life. *Her* eyes, not clouded over, but bright and real and blazing with fury.

"Holy bloody hell," he wheezed.

"You sodding *bastard*," she answered.

Lancaster shook his head, leaned closer to be sure his vision hadn't failed him. *"You're alive."*

"Not for long if you don't get your arm off my neck."

He murmured, "Sorry," and climbed off her to stand and stare in shock. His limbs felt numb and yet the rest of the world seemed sharper, more real. "You're alive. *Cynthia . . .* My God. *You're alive.*"

"Yes, well . . ." She rubbed her neck and her gaze moved to him and then around the room and back to him again.

Strangely, her face was growing redder despite that he'd released her. Perhaps he'd injured her throat or—

"You are, um . . ." Her eyes dipped down his body. "You're very naked, Lord Lancaster."

"Am I?" he was saying just as her words hit him. He looked down. Of course. He'd been sleeping. "Yes, I see that you're right."

"It seems inappropriate now that I am no longer dead."

"Of course." But he couldn't move, could only stare at her, breathing and talking. And blushing. "Sorry," he repeated and looked dazedly around for his robe. The dark blue robe lay tossed over a chair, and as soon as he had it in hand, he turned his eyes back to her to be sure she hadn't disappeared.

It suddenly occurred to him that this might all be a dream. After all, not only was she alive and in his bed, but she was watching him quite immodestly as he shrugged the robe on. Not to mention that he'd just seen a good bit of her naked bottom.

Lancaster rubbed his forehead, then jerked his hand away at the sharp stab of pain. Perhaps he wasn't asleep, but knocked unconscious and tumbling toward death.

"This doesn't make any sense."

She blinked as he tied the robe, then finally pulled her gown down to cover her legs. She folded her knees to her chest, tugged the skirt down to hide even her toes, and glared at him. There were the stubborn jaw and wise eyes. Her cheekbones were high, eyes almost slanted at the corners. An interesting, compelling face, just as he'd thought. Relief bubbled up and mixed with his confusion.

"What the hell is going on?" he asked when she said nothing.

"Well, to begin with, you've ruined *everything*."

"You must know I have no idea what that means, Cyn—Miss Merrithorpe."

She frowned, stubborn mouth turning mutinous. "It's not so hard to puzzle out, surely. I am pretending to be dead. Your estate provided the perfect hiding place. Until *you* returned for reasons I can't quite fathom."

Not a dream. This was definitely the working of a damaged brain. He shook his head, then pressed his palm to the spot above his left eye that shrieked with pain. "You hit me."

Cynthia rolled her eyes. "Of course I hit you, what else could I do?"

"Politely ask for help?"

She snorted, but when he lowered his hand to look at her, her snort turned to a gasp. "You're bleeding!"

"I'm not surprised. Are my brains spilling out? It rather feels as if they are."

She scooted off the bed and drew close. "It's just a small cut. Already healing. I . . . Oh, I *am* sorry, but you shouldn't have tried to stop me! You forced me to hit you!"

He felt a smile tug at his mouth. A real smile. Nothing contrived or meant to charm. Nothing false or prompted. It was just joy. "Cynthia," he whispered, as she pursed her lips and stared at his forehead.

"Hm?"

"Cynthia."

She finally met his gaze and her eyes went wide. Her mouth relaxed and her breath hitched a little as she exhaled. "What?"

Lancaster raised a hand and touched one finger, just one, to her cheek. Her skin was warm, soft and tender, and he thought he felt a tiny shiver work through her muscles. "You're *alive*."

Though she'd been still for a few long seconds, she finally moved, her shoulders rising and falling as she took one deep breath. "I must ask you to tell no one, of course. But yes . . ." She nodded. "Yes, I am alive."

His grin widened. He began to laugh.

And then Cynthia smiled.

Lancaster felt a dull concussion, as if something significant had exploded on the horizon of his life. But perhaps that was only the head wound.

Chapter 5

"I won't turn you in to your father," Lancaster was insisting, his brown eyes dark with sincerity. His hands opened, as if to show that he held no weapon.

"You're a man," Cynthia scoffed. Or meant to scoff. But as the words left her lips, she was reminded of the proof of his manhood she'd glimpsed just a few minutes before. Not as impressive as James had been, but most definitely a man. She cleared her throat. "Worse than that, you're a gentleman."

"Pardon?"

"Gentlemen. They're bound by rules of honor. Would you help me escape my family so that I can make my own way in the world?"

"Make your own way?" he repeated, the earnestness in his eyes sharpening to horror. "Of course not. The world is a dangerous place, Miss Merrithorpe."

She raised an eyebrow. "And so you see why I cannot trust you."

"Because I want to keep you safe?"

"Because I mean to escape this place for good, Viscount. And while I could possibly be in danger out amongst strangers, there is no doubt of the danger if I remain."

His full lips pressed together and his body straightened to a hard line. "Richmond."

The name shocked her, and she realized that she and Mrs. Pell had only referred to him as "that man" for weeks now. "Yes," she said, fighting the urge to touch her lip. "A friend of yours, probably, in London."

"No." His voice hadn't risen, but something in that one word fell with the weight of a boulder. When she glanced up in surprise, Cynthia saw something in Nick's eyes that she'd never seen. Ice.

Impossible.

But then, he was no longer the sweet neighbor boy who held her heart. He was Viscount Lancaster, who'd left this place without a good-bye and not spent a moment thinking of it in the decade since, as far as she could tell. God only knew what kind of life he'd led in London.

Whoring, gambling, boxing, drinking. She'd spent years imagining the kinds of trouble he might find there. Even in the deepest throes of girlish love, she'd understood that he would sow his oats in London. But ten years ago, she hadn't imagined the city would become his whole world. Hadn't imagined that he would shape himself to fit so snugly that he could not be budged.

He was changed. The boy she'd known had never flashed eyes so cruel.

"Tell me what happened," he said while she was still reeling over the difference in him. She blinked, and suddenly that stranger was gone. It was just Nick, watching her with clear worry on his face.

"You heard the story from my stepfather, I assume."

"I heard he was forcing you to marry Richmond. But I also heard that you jumped to your death from one of my cliffs, so pardon if I doubt parts of the tale."

Exhaustion rolled over her like a fog, and Cynthia let her weak knees lower her to the bed. Lancaster must have been waiting for her to take a seat, because he immediately reached for a chair and pulled it closer before collapsing into it.

"Blood loss," he muttered, gesturing toward the small cut on his forehead.

"My word, you are dramatic, Viscount."

"Why do you keep calling me Viscount?"

Cynthia huffed. "I know we've never been formally introduced, but it is your title, is it not?"

"Well, my friends call me Lancaster, but you never called me anything but Nick."

"You are not Nick anymore."

It was only the simple truth, so why did she feel guilty when his face fell? "I suppose I am not," he murmured. She had to fight the urge to call him Nick and take his hand. In appeasement, she answered his original question.

"Yes, I was promised to Lord Richmond."

"But . . . why?"

"My stepfather owed him money. A lot of it. When he could not pay, Richmond proposed a different form of payment."

He closed his eyes. "You."

"Yes, me. I . . . did my best to dissuade him. Both of them, actually. It was not the first time my stepfather had tried to marry me off, but none of my normal arguments were effective this time. It became necessary to take drastic measures."

His eyelids rose. So did his brows. "Why do I feel as

if this version of the story has been scrubbed clean of all but the barest of facts?"

She shrugged.

"Mrs. Pell said your father refused you food."

"What child hasn't been put to bed without dinner?"

"What child," he ground out, "has been locked in their room and starved?"

"Melodrama again. My stepfather was never a kind man. I didn't expect softheartedness from him in the face of ruin."

"What did you expect?"

She shook her head. Her stepfather had behaved in his normal fashion. He wasn't precisely cruel. He simply did not understand her. What kind of girl would not want to be a countess?

No, she hadn't expected anything different from her stepfather. What had surprised her was an entirely different kind of suitor. A kind who took delight in an unwilling bride.

"How did you escape?"

Though her mouth burned, she did not let her fingers drift to her lips. No matter how much she rubbed at that spot, the tingle never left it anyway. "My father let me out to visit with my betrothed. Richmond became distracted and I managed to run."

Lancaster's eyes narrowed at her carefully chosen words. He held her gaze for a long moment, but she did not flinch from it. Still, when his eyes dipped lower, she had to fight the urge to turn away. He focused on her mouth, and she didn't want him looking at the jagged pink scar that marred it even though he couldn't know the cause.

"Mrs. Pell said she saw you jump from the cliff. How can that be?"

Thoughts of her scar and the man who'd caused it disintegrated in a blast of alarm. *Mrs. Pell.* "Ah . . . yes. She . . . I made sure . . . Someone had to see me jump or they'd think I'd only run off."

"But . . ." He crossed his legs and the dressing robe parted, revealing his knee and calf. She tried not to stare at the golden hairs on his skin. "How could you have orchestrated an unplanned flight so perfectly?"

"Pardon?" Half of her brain was taking in his small bit of nudity and half of it was screaming that she needed to *think*.

"Cynthia, does Mrs. Pell know you are here?"

"What?" she gasped. "No! Of course not! How . . . how could she?"

Lancaster put his foot down and leaned forward to meet her eyes. "This is her home. She lives here."

"Well, of course she lives here, but she doesn't go into the attic."

"The *attic*?"

"Yes, the attic. Did you think Mrs. Pell had just invited me in and set me up in one of the guest rooms?"

"Well . . . yes."

"Don't be a ninny. I've been living up in the attic like a mouse. Speaking of which, it's late and I'm exhausted." She started to rise, thinking she could run downstairs and warn Mrs. Pell, but Lancaster was on his feet before she could push off the mattress.

"Where do you think you're going?" His chest was only inches from her face. She could smell his soap, the same faint scent she'd noticed each night when she entered his room.

"I'm going to bed," she managed to say past the sudden, overwhelming tightness in her chest. She could not think with him looming over her.

"There is no bed in the attic. You'll stay here."

"No!" She had to get to Mrs. Pell. The woman would spill the truth and incriminate herself before Lancaster even finished his first question. "I can't sleep in your bed!"

"Well, I promise not to be in it with you. This house belongs to me, Cynthia, and I'll not have you living in the attic."

"Another room then—"

"There are two new maids in residence, plus young Adam. If we are to keep your presence a secret, we must not raise suspicion."

Cynthia rubbed a hand over her eyes. Was he saying that he'd keep her hidden from her family?

Lancaster touched her cheek, and she jumped as if a spark had drifted from the fireplace and landed on her skin. "We will work out a plan in the morning. But for now, you'll stay here. I'll be back in a few moments."

She jumped to her feet when he turned away. "Where are you going?"

"I must inform Mrs. Pell of the situation."

"No! Not like this, not in the middle of the night. She's old. Her heart . . ."

"If I don't tell her this instant, she will likely suffer an apoplexy while she is beating me with a broom in the morning."

"But . . . I don't want her to know! She might . . . tell . . ." Oh, she couldn't even finish her ridiculous claim.

Lancaster, just a foot from the door, turned back to her, frowning. He crossed his arms and Cynthia cringed. If he found out the truth he might very well turn Mrs. Pell out. Not for hiding Cynthia, but for lying to his face. No gentleman would support such insubordination.

If Mrs. Pell lost her position, Cynthia would never, ever forgive herself. "I . . ." she stammered.

Strangely, Lancaster smiled as if he'd just heard an outrageous joke. His brown eyes twinkled as Cyn shook in her stockings. "Really, Cynthia." He chuckled. "You are nearly as poor a liar as Mrs. Pell. It's a wonder you two have managed to pull this off without me."

"Ah . . . Pardon?"

He laughed harder. "You look just like you did that time I caught you spying on the village boys swimming in the buff!"

She immediately forgot her nervousness and snapped straight. "I never did!" she gasped before remembering that she, in fact, had. Worse than that, she'd followed them to the beach in anticipation of catching just such a show.

"Ha! I see it's all coming back to you now. There were five or six very naked young men, if I recall."

The blood beneath her face was coming to a boil. "Nick," she scolded, forgetting she'd meant never to call him that again.

That one word broke the tension in the room. Lancaster shook his head, his smile gentling.

She took a deep breath. "Please do not be angry with Mrs. Pell. She wanted to tell you and I begged her not to. Don't put her out."

"Put her *out*? Are you mad? How could I possibly be angry with her when she may very well have saved your life?"

That pulled her out of her worrying. Her own mother had clucked and dismissed Cynthia's assertions that she would not survive being married to Richmond. But Lancaster seemed to accept it as a point of fact.

"Come now," he said. "We will discuss all this in the morning. Into bed with you. Are you hungry, thirsty?"

"No."

He shooed her toward the bed with his hands.

"But where will you sleep?"

"I'll sneak into the chamber next door."

As Cynthia watched in weary shock, Lancaster locked the door to the hallway and gestured toward the door to the adjoining room.

"I'll be right there. The lock should keep the maids from stumbling upon you."

"This is all unnecessary," she protested, but Lancaster was shaking his head.

"Nonsense. Good night."

"Oh, well then. Good night." And he was gone. Just like that. An echo of his old place in her life. An all-consuming force one moment and then vanished in the blink of an eye.

She could only stand there, staring at the fading green paint of the door, her cheek still tingling faintly from his brief, meaningless touch.

When the door opened again, she blinked.

"Pardon me, but . . ." He peeked in. "You will be here in the morning, won't you, Cyn?"

She thought about it for a moment. Should she run? Really, there was no point in fleeing now that he knew she was alive. "Yes, I'll be here," she said carefully.

His eyes narrowed in suspicion. "Promise?"

"I promise."

The relief in his gaze warmed something deep in her belly. "Good." The latch clicked shut.

A few minutes passed before she lowered herself to the bed. Somehow it seemed disarmingly intimate to be in his bed, and even more so knowing he might reappear through the door at any moment and find her snuggled in. But the clock ticked the minutes away from somewhere on the floor, and the room was cold. When her tension began to melt away, Cynthia wilted.

Her nights had been nearly sleepless since he'd returned to Cantry Manor, and the soft mattress proved irresistible. There was nothing to be done. Her masquerade was over. She could accomplish nothing tonight. Tomorrow she would argue her case, and shape her plans to Nick's response.

She curled into the bed. The pillow surrounded her with his scent when she lay her head on it, and Cynthia fell asleep just as she had so many times as a young girl . . . dreaming of Nicholas Cantry.

How in the world could she *sleep*?

Leaning against the doorway, Lancaster shook his head, never taking his eyes off the slight rise in the covers where Cynthia Merrithorpe slept.

She was alive. Didn't she realize how amazing that was? Though perhaps she'd had time to get used to the idea.

He laughed at the thought, half hoping she might wake up and keep him company. But Cynthia slept on, clearly exhausted. When she woke, perhaps the dark circles under her eyes would have faded.

He pushed off the wall and turned back to his cold, dark chamber. Though he'd found a moth-eaten blanket in a chest, he didn't bother lying down. All his attempts at sleep so far had failed, and dawn was less than an hour off.

Each time he'd closed his eyes the fear that Cynthia would disappear again would rise like a starving beast in his mind. Either she would sneak off while he slept, or her presence would reveal itself to be a bittersweet dream when he woke in the morning. He'd found himself rising every ten minutes to ease open the door and stare at her shadowed form. He'd long since given up and left the door propped open as he paced the hours away.

She wasn't dead, he hadn't caused her death, and he would not have to kill Richmond to avenge her.

"Then again," he muttered to the floor. There was no reason to be rash. Richmond still deserved death.

But thoughts of murder could not keep hold of his mind. He was too filled with joy. Somehow everything, even the thought of returning to London for his marriage, seemed easier to bear knowing that Cynthia Merrithorpe hadn't thrown herself from a cliff and broken her body on the rocks below. His life might be a tattered mess, but he hadn't contributed to the destruction of this young woman.

Nearly shaking with energy, Lancaster stalked to the ancient shutters that covered the window. He had a vague idea that he might throw them open with a dramatic flair, but the damned things were swollen shut. It took him a good minute of prying and tugging to get them open, but when he did he was rewarded with the sight of a long line of deep pink rising above the horizon. Dawn, or near enough. Mrs. Pell was likely up by now.

He'd pulled on trousers and a shirt long before, so

he only had to tiptoe into his bedroom to retrieve his boots before slipping out the door. Cynthia slept on.

Before reaching the kitchen he heard female voices, one of them raised in anger.

"If you leave now, you'll never have a job in his lordship's home again." Mrs. Pell's voice quivered with outrage.

"But I don't plan to work here again," a girl replied, nervousness clear in the shaky words. Lancaster snuck his head around the corner.

The two new maids cowered near the door. "It's haunted! We heard ghosts running through the walls!" Mary cried, and Lancaster jerked back with a smile. Perfect.

"Come now," Mrs. Pell scoffed. "'Twas only a mouse."

He dragged a reckless hand through his hair to muss it, then took a deep breath and lurched around the corner. "Damn big mouse if you ask me." All three women gasped and stepped back before dropping hasty curtsies. "I heard it too," he continued. "Banging and rustling. Even a scream, I daresay."

"Yes!" Lizzie cried. "Screams and horrible moaning."

Moaning? Oh, my. Well, perhaps he'd moaned a bit after she'd bashed him in the head. He raised a hand to touch a careful finger to the lump at the edge of his eyebrow.

"Now, milord, I'm sure you're just not used to the sounds of this old place settling at night—"

"I was attacked." He touched the aching spot with a bit more flair. "Pounced upon in my bed while I slept."

The two maids let out little screams and scrambled for the door, but Mrs. Pell's face paled to a sickly white that even the frightened maids couldn't match.

"Attacked?" she croaked.

The door banged against the wall and the maids were gone, vanished into the dim morning.

"You won't be paid!" she called after them, though the words fell weakly from her mouth.

Lancaster pushed a chair toward her and Mrs. Pell sat down hard.

"I do believe those girls have a fear of restless spirits," he said, his mood inching up to even greater heights. If there were no maids about, Cynthia would be free to live openly in his home. "I say, Mrs. Pell, is there tea this morning? I'm parched."

"Yes, sir." She stared at the open door for a long moment before she blinked back to her wits. "Oh, pardon me, milord!" She jumped to her feet so quickly that her skirts flared around her. Her eyes darted to the wound on his head. "I'm so sorry. The water's ready. I'll have breakfast for you in a moment, if you'd like to relax in the library. You're an early riser today, sir."

"I couldn't sleep."

"Aye . . . Well."

"And I'll take breakfast in my chambers, if you please—"

"Of course."

"Cynthia will likely wake soon and I'm sure she'll be famished."

"Yes, sir. I'll . . ." The whites of her eyes showed all around as his words finally sunk in. "Pardon me?"

He was unkind enough to thoroughly enjoy the stunned disbelief etched across her features. "That vicious ghost who attacked me in my chambers last night? I managed to catch her. She's quite lively for a spirit."

"You . . . You caught the . . . ghost?"

"I did."

They stared at each other for a long moment before Lancaster relented and smiled. "Thank you for helping her, Mrs. Pell. She looks quite healthy for a young woman who's been living in the attic for weeks."

The housekeeper's face didn't move.

"But we shall have to find her a proper chamber now."

Her eyes turned liquid. "Milord?" she whispered, just before the tears overflowed her eyes.

Oh, no. He couldn't bear to see a woman cry. "I'm sorry," he said in a rush. "I shouldn't have teased you like that. Cynthia is well. Everything is fine."

"Sir!" Her face crumpled.

"Ah, Christ." Unable to take it a moment longer, Lancaster jumped forward and pulled her into his arms, hoping she wasn't the kind of woman who'd cry harder when embraced.

She took a deep breath. Lancaster held his. Her shoulders ceased their trembling. "I'm so sorry, milord. I should never have kept it from you."

His deep sigh of relief ruffled the few strands of gray hair that weren't pulled tightly into her braid. "Nonsense. You had no reason to trust me." The truth of his own words stung.

Shaking her head, Mrs. Pell pulled away. "You've always been a kind soul, sir. Always."

Not true. Not anymore. Lancaster glanced away and cleared his throat. "If you'd be so kind as to bring a tray up, we can all share breakfast while we formulate a plan. And celebrate."

"Celebrate," she repeated, finally daring a smile. "Yes, I do think this calls for a celebration. I have one last jar of cherry compote I've set aside. And a half loaf of pound cake left from last night."

Cherry compote. His mouth watered at the memory of his favorite treat. Another vivid piece of his past that he hadn't even dusted off in ten years. How much of his life had he left buried here in a vain attempt to forget that one single week?

"Give me half an hour," Mrs. Pell said, already busying herself with the stove. "A celebration calls for more food than that."

He wandered the ground floor rooms as he waited, opening shutters and curtains to let in light. Though he'd been here for days, the place had been inanimate—silent and unmoved by his presence. But now it came alive. Quiet and slumbering in the dawn, yes, but *alive*.

There was his father's favorite chair, so wide that Nick had been able to squeeze in next to him for the first few years they'd lived here. There was the hearth his mother had always hovered near, chilled by the sea air that swept between stones.

They'd moved to Cantry Manor when Lancaster was eight. He'd believed it a magical place, overlooking the sea and riddled with hidden hallways. And named Cantry Manor just for his family, he'd assumed.

It had been lonely sometimes, especially for a boy like Nicholas who'd grown up the pet of all his mother's friends in Hull. But he'd made friends with the boys in the village. And then there'd been Cynthia. By all accounts, she should have been friends with his younger brother. But Timothy had been disdainful of friendship with girls, and Jane had been far too young to care for anything but rag dolls.

So it had been he and Cynthia who would crowd together in front of the kitchen fire on rainy days to play cards or read books. Or lie on their bellies in the grass to play with his tin soldiers. Or creep through the servant passages to hide and surprise each other.

All these years, she'd remained that girl in his mind, never changing.

"Sir?" Mrs. Pell's voice echoed from the hallway. "Shall we wake her?"

Yes, he thought, like Sleeping Beauty saved from her rest. *But,* he amended hastily, *without the kiss.* Strangely, the thought set loose a cloud of butterflies in his gut.

"Cynthia . . ." The gentle voice crept through her dreams, but the mattress was a soft, sticky bundle pulling her down. She snuggled more thoroughly into the feathers and squeezed her eyes tightly shut. The bedcovers oozed warmth.

"Cynthia," Mrs. Pell called. "It's time to get up, sweeting. We've got a big day."

Were they to make mincemeat pies then?

She snuggled into the pillow, telling herself the linen smelled of Nicholas.

Wait a moment . . . Her heart stopped. The linens *did* smell of Nick.

Cynthia opened one eye and tried to focus on the face angled close to hers. Messy blond hair, sparkling brown eyes, wide grin.

"Good morning, princess," Nicholas cooed.

Cynthia's heart shot straight out of her chest. "Good God!" she screeched, jumping up so fast that her flailing hand connected with his nose.

"Bloody hell, woman! Do you never tire of beating me about the face?"

"Language, milord," Mrs. Pell scolded as if he were still a child in her kitchen. He apologized in the same nostalgic manner as he rubbed his nose.

They'd both gone mad. She looked from Nicholas to Mrs. Pell and blurted out, "I told you he would not sack you."

Nicholas snorted. "You were not so sure of it last night. You seemed only moments from throwing yourself at my feet to beg for mercy."

"I certainly did not!"

"Mm. I'd hoped a good night's sleep would improve your mood."

Mrs. Pell tsked. "She's been a sourpuss for weeks, milord."

Mad. Stark, raving mad. "I was forced to stage my own death! It tends to damage one's mood."

Mrs. Pell reached over to pat Cynthia's hand where it clutched the coverlet. "Your situation has greatly improved, sweeting."

"Hardly. I wasn't actually dead even before Lancaster stumbled upon me."

"Stumbled," he muttered.

"But Cynthia," Mrs. Pell scolded. "Lord Lancaster means to help you. You needn't worry now."

"I needn't *worry*? Surely you jest." She glanced toward Lancaster, feeling a momentary twinge of guilt, but there was no way around it. "I need money. And he's got even less than I do."

His eyebrows rose.

"Are you fleeing creditors? Is that why you're here?"

"Cynthia," the housekeeper gasped, but Lancaster seemed entirely uninsulted.

"Still the same unruly child, I see. Perhaps a sweet will cheer you up." He plopped down on the bed beside her, shaking the whole mattress, and gestured toward the tray.

Stung by his evaluation of her maturity, Cynthia looked away from him to stare at the tray. A few heartbeats passed in quiet. Guilt swelled from a kernel to a full bloom in her chest.

She was frightened and frustrated, so she was being rude. It was one of her faults, lashing out when under pressure. But surely Nick remembered that about her. If he remembered anything at all.

Mrs. Pell, clearing her throat, handed her a piece of compote-covered pound cake. She handed a second plate to Nick. "Regardless," the housekeeper said, "he can help with your plan."

Cynthia's eyes flew to his in time to see them widen. "What plan?" he asked, the words muffled by a mouthful of cake.

She waited for him to swallow, then took a bite of her own cake, letting the tart sweetness melt over her tongue as she tried to think what to say. Her shoulders had bunched painfully at Mrs. Pell's words. But of course, there would be no hiding the plan. Even she wasn't childish enough to think so. She'd have to tell him, but her arms wanted to curl around her waist to hold the secret close.

"What plan?" he asked again.

She tried to swallow the cake, but it wouldn't budge. Unfortunately, her dry mouth only bought her a few more seconds, because Mrs. Pell, whose eyes saw everything, handed her a cup of tea.

But she didn't wait for Cynthia to clear her throat.

Instead, she offered her own explanation. "She means to find buried treasure, milord."

Oh, Mother of God. She'd swallowed the cake, but now the tea jumped into her windpipe. Cynthia began to cough wildly.

Lancaster's hand landed soundly on her back, and he thumped her a few times. "Buried treasure? That's quite a . . . scheme."

She shook her head and knocked his arm away. Wonderful. And he'd thought her childish before. "It's not buried treasure," she croaked.

His doubtful hum conveyed understanding and pity at the same time.

"There's treasure hidden in the cliffs."

He took a sip of tea. "*My* cliffs?"

Damnation. In truth, even if she found the treasure, it should rightfully belong to him. "I can't be sure," she said carefully.

"Well, it's either my cliffs or old Inglebottom's and his start ten miles away." He held her gaze, waiting for an acknowledgment she wouldn't give. Finally, he shrugged. "Why do you think there's buried treasure in my cliffs?"

"Not buried," she repeated. "This isn't a fairy tale." Ignoring Mrs. Pell's snort, Cynthia crumbled a bit of her cake, but didn't dare take another bite. "I found an old journal a few years ago. It was written by my great-uncle when he was a boy. He claimed to have come across a smuggler's stash. Said he found a great chest of gold coin and hid it in a sea cave."

"Stolen pirate's booty?" Lancaster crowed. "That's even better."

"It's not a joke, you insufferable lout."

She watched him try—and fail—to twitch his mouth into a serious line.

"It's real, Lancaster. And I mean to find it."

"Right. And why do you assume the gold is still there?"

This she could answer with certainty. "My great-uncle died very young. Only two years after the journal was written."

He inclined his head in acknowledgment. "All right. What do you mean to do with this gold when you find it? Pay for Richmond to be quietly murdered?"

Strange, but he sounded slightly hopeful at that. "Of course not! I mean to pay off my family's debt and buy passage to America."

"Ah. Why pay off your stepfather's debt?"

"My sister. Mary will be fourteen next year. I don't think Mother would let her be sent to Richmond, but . . . she's never been able to stand up to her husband. I won't see my little sister given in my stead."

All the amusement vanished from his face, leaving a mouth that looked as if it hadn't smiled in years. "I see. So you honestly believe this treasure exists?"

"I do."

"Then I'll help you find it."

That seemed a bit too good to be true. "You'll help me? And then you'll send me off to America with well wishes?"

"Er . . . We'll have to discuss that later."

"No, we will not," she said firmly.

Mrs. Pell, still fiddling with the tray, set the teapot down hard. "The viscount is a traveled man, Cynthia Merrithorpe, and you'd do well to listen to him."

"I reach my majority in two weeks and I'll do whatever I like."

"Spoken like a true adult," Lancaster murmured, and she had to fight the urge to punch him in the ear.

"What do you know about it?" she snapped. "Rumor has it that you'll marry an heiress and your problems will be solved."

"Ha." The smile he offered wasn't as cold as the one she'd seen last night. It was bitter and rueful. Another revelation. "True. I will marry. And she *is* an heiress. And we'll live happily ever after in a castle made of gold, so I may as well help you find your own pleasant ending."

Cynthia had thought it shocking to wake up and find Nicholas leaning over her as she slept. But that was nothing compared to this. "You're engaged? You . . . You'll marry soon? We hadn't heard."

"I'm due back for the wedding in a few weeks. So let's make this quick, shall we? Up for a fine bit of treasure hunting this morning?" His attempt at humor fell flat. He didn't sound truly amused and Cynthia couldn't have laughed if someone had offered her a thousand pounds.

Nick would be a husband soon. And some other woman would be his wife.

Chapter 6

Cynthia's foot looked narrow and delicate before she pulled a woolen sock over it and stuffed it into a thick-soled boot. Lancaster slid his gaze to her other foot, studying the feminine shape before she could hide it. She might be dressed in servants' garb, but her toes looked pale and fine.

She wore no stockings today, as Mrs. Pell had whisked them away for mending.

"Are you listening to me?" Cynthia snapped.

"Yes . . . What?"

"I said you'd best find a sturdier pair of gloves."

He glanced down at the gloves he held in his hands and shrugged. "I'm not entirely sure this is safe for a lady."

She heaved a deep sigh and tugged the second boot on. "I've been climbing the cliffs for weeks now. I daresay it's safer for me than it is for you."

"Still, if you were to fall . . . No, I can't allow it."

Her eyes blazed fire and her lips thinned. Lancaster braced himself for a tirade.

"You . . ." she started.

He waited a few seconds. "Yes?"

"You . . . I can't . . . Fine. I'll split the treasure with you fifty-fifty. It's only fair, I suppose. It's your land."

"Do you think that offering a share of the gold—which we likely will never find anyway—will induce me to risk your life?"

"Oh, for God's sake!" Whatever control she'd had over her temper vanished in an instant. "My life has been at risk for months and what have you ever known or cared about it? Mind your own business, Viscount."

The truth stung, but he shook it off. "I don't think it needs to be said that this has very much become my business." He gestured in a wide circle to encompass both his room and his bed. "Every bit of land and property involved in this fantasy of yours belongs to me. So *bother* your outrage, Miss Merrithorpe."

Her eyes narrowed even further. Frankly, he'd be surprised if she could still see. Lancaster shifted his weight to provide better balance in case she felt inclined to fly at him, fists at the ready, as she'd done often in childhood.

But perhaps Cynthia *had* matured. She merely cocked her head. "You said you would help me, and I will hold you to that. 'Help' implies assistance, not tyranny."

My, she actually had grown up. She'd even managed not to raise her voice. Lancaster felt she deserved a reward for that. "Very well, we'll do this together. *But*," he added when her tense mouth slipped up toward a smile. "I may change my mind if it proves too dangerous."

"We'll see." Clearly dismissing his concerns, Cynthia stood, shook out her salt-stained gray skirts, and smiled.

Just like the night before, the force of that smile traveled through him like a thump of sound. His chest tightened.

"What's wrong?" Cynthia asked.

"Nothing. Are you ready?"

She glanced toward his riding boots and shrugged. "I'm ready. Are you?"

"Of course I am. Why wouldn't I be?"

Despite the puzzled look she gave him, Cynthia headed for the door. He followed.

She drew her hood over her head as they descended the stairs and led the way to the door. Mrs. Pell had sent her last set of helping hands out to work in the stables for the morning. The boy, Adam, had been thrilled with the opportunity to spend some time with Lancaster's honest-to-goodness London driver. Still, Lancaster's stomach tightened as Cynthia slipped out the wide front door and hurried down the steps. But whatever his nervousness was, Cyn clearly didn't share it. She didn't even look over her shoulder as she turned east toward the shore.

The wind gusted beneath his coat as he hurried to catch up. "Aren't you nervous you'll be seen?"

She shrugged. "If you look furtive, people notice."

Ah, yes. He understood that. The key to blending in was looking as if you belonged. But . . . "How can you know that? Did you escape from Newgate earlier this year?"

The naughty look she sent him called to mind all the mischief she'd caused as a young girl. "I wasn't actually supposed to spend every day of my childhood at Cantry Manor, you know. The more time I spent here, the more restrictions my stepfather set down. I learned that if I tried to sneak out, one of the maids would notice and inform my mother. But if I simply walked out as if it were expected . . ." She winked, startling Lancaster into a smile.

By God . . . Cynthia was *pretty*. How could he have thought her *not* pretty?

Her head tilted, and she watched him through her lashes as she stepped onto a well-worn path that sloped gently down. Was she flirting with him? His skin tingled when she licked her lips.

"Lancaster . . ." she started.

"Yes?"

"Where did you get that scar?"

The wind gusted, surely twisting her words. "Pardon me?"

"That scar." She stopped abruptly and turned toward him with an exasperated smile. "Around your neck," she huffed. "I saw it last night."

When he started to shake his head, she reached up to trail a finger down the skin beneath his chin. Before her finger could reach the linen of his cravat, Lancaster snatched her hand away.

Cynthia gasped, and he tried very hard not to squeeze her hand too tightly in spite of the way his fingers spasmed. His skin tingled still, but not with pleasure. This tingling was a bright, hard wash of cold.

"Nick," she gasped, and he let her go, murmuring, "Sorry. Sorry."

"Whatever is the matter?"

"Nothing."

"Well, I apologize. I had no idea it was something I was not to bring up."

Here. Here was an excuse. He forced his mouth into a smile—not a hard task as he'd practiced this ruse so often. "I am self-conscious. A burn, you understand. A disfigurement. I hate for it to be noticed."

"Oh." Her shock twisted into impatience. "I see."

"There is nothing wrong with a little vanity."

Cynthia snorted and his panic began to fade.

"I thank you for reminding me of it, as a matter of fact. I mean to purchase a nightshirt with grand frills about the neck before my wedding."

"Grand frills . . . ?" she started, and then her words collapsed into laughter.

Relief shook his breath from his lungs. He was usually prepared for the question. He was usually on guard against an unexpected, intimate touch. After all, there were very specific circumstances when a woman might drag her finger down a gentleman's neck. He hadn't previously counted treasure hunting among them. He wanted to rub her touch away but smiled instead.

"Really, Lancaster." She laughed. "Your vanity is misguided. If you care for this woman at all, you should skip the nightshirt and sleep in your usual attire."

"Oh?" He shook off the last of his worry. Despite her strange approach, she really was flirting with him. "I'm not sure I should accept your advice. You do have a peculiar affinity for nudity, Cynthia. Some ladies might not share your appreciation for the male physique."

"I . . ." Her cheeks flashed to red. "I don't . . . Oh, shove off!"

True laughter escaped his throat as Cynthia spun around and flounced down the trail. The wind lifted the hood off her hair and twisted her skirts around her legs. She snapped the hood back into place, but her dress lifted higher, exposing the tops of her calves.

Lancaster watched her legs carefully for another peek as he picked his way down the rocky slope.

Miss Cynthia Merrithorpe should not be thinking of him naked. And as a betrothed man, he shouldn't be so damned happy about it. But he most certainly was.

Cynthia couldn't find her footing. Oh, she was steady enough on the trail. She'd scrambled up and down this path for days.

But with Nick . . . She was tripping over her thoughts and feelings, dizzy with confusion.

She'd loved him once. She'd loved him so much that she'd hurt inside whenever he was near. But that ache had been a warm and happy pain.

Without any doubt at all, she'd known that some-day she would blossom into a woman and he'd see her as more than a childhood friend. Someone would hold a ball—she wasn't sure who, as country dances were the rule with her neighbors. And Cynthia would arrive in a beautiful dress of white and silver tulle—paid for by some anonymous benefactor, perhaps?

Aglow with beauty, she'd float down a curving staircase. Nick would look up from chatting with his friends, and he would *see* her. He'd see her as a woman. The world would spin to a halt around them. They'd fall in love and marry too young and move to London, and the whole *ton* would marvel at the strength of their passion.

A great screeching invaded the hazy scene she'd conjured, and Cynthia looked up to see an enraged gull swoop toward her head. Waving it off with the anger she couldn't direct elsewhere, Cyn hurried past the nest, too aware of Nick's footsteps behind her.

She still couldn't quite fathom that he was back. Almost harder than believing he'd gone in the first place.

It had only been meant as a monthlong tour of the Lake District with some lordly man named Mr. Trevington. Trapped in the schoolroom with her sister, Cynthia had missed his send-off on that sunny morning. But she'd reassured herself that he'd return soon enough and this horrid sorrow and separation would end.

A few days later, his family had packed up suddenly and gone to join him. And then . . . nothing. Nothing. A month came and went. No one returned.

For weeks afterward, Mrs. Pell had avoided Cynthia's question until the truth had become unavoidable. The Cantrys' possessions had gradually been sealed into crates and shipped off to London. The servants let go one by one until only Mrs. Pell remained. And Cynthia, of course. Cynthia had been left behind too.

She'd written letters she'd never sent, confessing her love; woven excuses from the cobwebs that formed in the places they'd once played; shed tears for him every night.

Despite all that, she'd healed. And now he was back.

Cynthia kicked a shell out of her path and headed straight for the little four-foot cliff that put an abrupt end to the easy part of the trek.

The wind shaped her skirt into a bell when she jumped, hiding her view of the sand, but she landed steady and paused to watch the waves roll toward her.

"Cynthia!" His voice fell toward her just as Nick landed with a thump at her side. "Are you hurt?"

"What?"

He ducked down and reached for her skirts.

"What are you doing?" she cried as his hands delved

beneath her thread-worn petticoat and stroked from her knees to her boot tops.

"Your ankles. You likely turned one with a fall like that."

"I jumped!"

He tugged off his gloves and patted at her skin as if he might discover a shard of bone sticking out.

"Stop that."

His warm hands continued roaming.

"Nick." His hand touched the back of her knee and she jumped clear of him. "Nick!" Legs burning with the memory of his pressing fingers, Cynthia stepped a safer distance away. "I didn't fall, my ankles are fine, and we've another half-mile in this sand," she said before whirling around to walk quickly away.

Gentlemen did not touch ladies in that way. It wasn't proper. Unless, of course, said gentlemen considered that lady a child.

Unfortunately, regardless of what Nick might think of her maturity, her body was very clear on the matter. She was a woman, and Nick was a fine, handsome man with strong, warm hands that she'd dreamed of for years.

James had been a mistake. But Nick . . . Nick could be something better. Nick had already set her limbs shaking with a few simple touches. It was more than James had done for her.

She imagined kissing Nick, imagined him backing her up against a wall. . . .

A little dip in the sand buckled her knee, and Nick's hand closed around her elbow, startling her. She hadn't known he was so close, but now her skin tingled at his nearness.

"Where are we going?" Nick asked, his deep voice nearly swallowed by the surf.

"Just past the cliffs I canvassed yesterday."

"You've only made it a half-mile up the shore?"

"Yes."

"I see. And . . . what exactly does the diary say about the location of this treasure?"

She glanced at him, then quickly away. The diary was her trump card, her only leverage in this struggle with Nick. If she told him the exact wording, he'd likely take over the search himself. And this was her search, damn it. Some small piece of her mess of a life that she could own.

So she muttered, "It's vague," and picked up her pace. The sand sucked at her feet until her muscles burned.

Nick seemed unimpeded. "Well, my God, Cyn. I've miles of coastline. This could take forever."

"Mm."

"There's nothing more specific?"

"Not really." Much to her relief, a distraction appeared ahead in the form of a thirty-foot wall of rock in her path. Cynthia smiled.

He cleared his throat. "Perhaps I should take a look at this diary and . . . What are you doing?"

As she was very obviously tucking her skirts up into the leather cord around her waist, Cyn ignored the question. Nick stared at her knees. He was still staring when she took off at a run for the jagged wall of rock.

"Cyn? What—?"

She leapt up two piles of rock that made halfway decent steps, then made the final four-foot leap across a crevice filled with roiling sea foam. Her feet skidded on the narrow ledge as she leaned in to hug the rock.

A strangled yell followed her, then wheezed into silence.

"Don't hesitate," she called over her shoulder, "or you'll end up very wet."

"I . . . Holy . . . Don't move."

"It's the only way around. Come on." She scooted along the ledge until her heels hung over the sea. An occasional wave sent flecks of foam straight up the rock to speckle her legs and bunched skirts.

"This is sheer madness!" Nick shouted. "Damn it, Cyn. Stop right there!"

"If you can't keep up, I understand. There's no shame in that. You've been in the city for a long time. Stay here. I'll be back in a few hours." She didn't have to look back to know that his face had gone red. She'd always been good at goading him.

"Mrs. Pell will have my scalp if you break an arm," he'd said each time she'd proposed a race to the top of the great oak tree next to the churchyard. Cynthia would nod and assure him that the village boys would likely not consider his forfeit a genuine loss to a girl. They were too fair-minded for that, surely. And Nick would scowl and kick at dead leaves and refuse her challenge. Until she started up the branches.

Perhaps he hadn't changed as much as she'd thought, because as soon as she'd worked her way around to the far side of the outcropping, the air echoed with the scrape of his shoes against stone. And with muffled cursing.

She hurried along the last few feet to the relative security of a crooked boulder, which provided a ramp down to the beach.

Nick materialized, a dangerous scowl marring his handsome features.

"It's actually quite a challenge during high tide," she called innocently. His face threatened to crack in two.

Making sure to hide her smile, Cyn turned and hurried on before he could catch her. But he'd gotten faster in the past ten years. And her skirts had gotten heavier. By the time she realized the thumps vibrating up the soles of her feet were actually Nick's footsteps, it was too late. She only managed a few lurching steps before he was on her, cursing.

His hands grabbed at her, and Cynthia spun away, her heart exploding into pattering alarm. Fear mixed with something else. A startled laugh bubbled from her breathless lungs as she scrambled away, a nimble cat escaping a wolf. Except that this wolf's claws had caught on something.

One side of her skirt tugged free of the leather cord. His eyes met hers, flashing triumph as he jerked her to a halt.

"Let me go!" she shouted.

"You are completely out of control."

She wound her fingers into the fabric.

"You could be killed out here, climbing around like that."

She tightened her grip.

"I will not allow—"

When she tugged as hard as she could, the gray wool slipped from his grasp. She felt a moment of pure victory. And then she stepped backward, right into a hill of sand that sucked her heel deep into the loose pack. She hovered for a moment, arms flailing, the sky tilting slowly into her view.

Then she was down.

And Nick pounced.

The sudden weight pushed a gasp from her throat

as he settled onto her hips, his knees tight against her ribs, hands trapping her wrists against the sand.

"Get off me."

"Why, so you can hang yourself over a bloody cliff and risk your life?"

"I was five feet off the ground."

"Damn it, Cyn, I should tan your hide."

Those words—those words meant for a child—goaded her hot blood into a full boil of fury. "I am not a child!" she screamed, pushing with all her might at his hands.

His fingers flexed and tightened. "You're childish enough to do something stupidly reckless, so I'd say you're childish enough to be turned over my knee."

Fire fizzed through her veins. "You just *try* it."

His gaze flicked to her straining arms. When he spoke again, he leaned menacingly close, his voice dropping low to stroke over her skin. "You think I wouldn't?"

Did she? Did she think he'd dare to flip her over and raise her skirts? Would he humiliate her and beat her like a child? Cynthia growled and gave one last furious, futile yank of her arms.

Nick's eyes narrowed. He looked at his right hand as it slowly tightened to a vise on her wrist.

"Nick . . ."

His gaze slid to her lips. And then his mouth descended.

For a brief moment she didn't understand what part this played in their argument. And then her body reported to her mind what was really happening. Nick was *kissing* her. Just as she'd hoped. Oh, sweet mercy . . .

Shock loosened the iron band around her lungs, and

she parted her lips to find some air. This was apparently just the right thing to do, as Nick moaned in response and slipped his tongue against hers. Wet, warm surprise shivered through her nerves and made her hum into him.

At some point he'd shifted above her, and his weight was no longer pressing just her hips and hands. Now his legs slid down to embrace her thighs. His hips pinned her. His belly lay flush against hers. As if they were making love. As if he *wanted* her.

His tongue thrust harder, and she arched her neck and opened to him.

She'd imagined this a thousand times and a thousand more. She'd thought Nick's lips would brush softly, a gentle taste, a breath of love across her cheek. She'd never once considered he would kiss as if he were needy. As rough as James, even. But better than those stolen kisses with James Munro. Infinitely better.

Nick shifted his head and pushed her arms higher, his grip as tight as ever. When he planted his knee between hers, Cynthia curled her leg around his thigh to offer encouragement. With half the skirt tucked up, his trousers rubbed against her bare thigh. She jerked at the shock of it, and that brought him snug between her thighs. The clear evidence of his arousal rubbed hard against her sex.

Their simultaneous gasps filled the air around them. Nick's gasp seemed rather tinged with alarm though, as he immediately lifted himself on his elbows and gawked down at her.

A splash of foam landed on her knee.

Nick panted, eyes widening with panic. He'd come to his senses.

Cynthia blinked. "I do believe the tide is coming in,"

she blurted out, as inane conversation seemed all that her brain was capable of.

"Cynthia," he squeaked. And then, strangely, "I mean, Miss Merrithorpe."

"Er . . . Yes?"

"I think . . . I do apologize."

She uncurled her naked leg from around his thigh, the action clearly belying the need for any apology. "It's quite all right." When she lowered her foot to the ground, her body rubbed against his hardness.

Nick's head dropped. He rested his forehead against hers for a long, quiet moment. His fingers flexed, trembling against the bones of her wrists. And then he pushed up and let her go. "I'm sorry. I didn't mean to . . . do that."

He made to tug down her skirts, but one side was still tucked up and didn't budge despite his desperate smoothing.

"Nick, it's fine."

"Of course," he answered, scrambling to his feet. She only had to endure a brief moment of being sprawled awkwardly on the ground before he reached down to pull her up after him. She wished he would've given her a moment more. Her feet felt heavy and graceless as bricks, and her legs as unsteady as stalks of grass.

After occupying himself with brushing the sand from his knees, Nick offered a bright smile that didn't match his troubled eyes. "Well then. It seems that neither of us are children, and we shouldn't play at those sorts of games, wouldn't you say?"

"Yes?" she answered, unable to keep the confusion from her voice. Well and good that he didn't see her as a young girl anymore, but what was she to him?

"I hope I did not scare you. Men are . . . unreliable in their propriety."

Unreliable? Cynthia shook her head as she let her skirt down to cover the leg that had wrapped so shamelessly around him.

His smile grew wider and even less natural. "Shall we hurry on, then?"

Trying, and failing, to find a steady thought, Cynthia could do nothing but nod and turn to lead the way up the narrow beach.

What had he *done*?

My God, what had he done?

The feel of her arms pushing against his hold, her body arching beneath him . . . Something had clicked into place inside him. Or *out* of place. That broken part of his soul had shifted into stark distortion. He knew the feeling well enough, but he hadn't ever figured out if it was peace or pain that overtook him in those moments.

Thank God he'd managed to stop himself. Thank God he hadn't abused her further.

He rubbed a shaking hand over the back of his head and stared at Cyn's back as she reached a new trail and began a gradual ascent. Each step set loose tiny rivulets of sand from the pleats of her skirt, a faint reminder of his transgression revealed with her every movement.

Nick could hardly breathe, even before she glanced back, her cheeks reddened by shame or cold or anger.

"We shouldn't have done that," she said simply, and his heart twisted into a sick knot. Cynthia walked on, calm and steady.

"I know," he answered. A lady could not be treated in that way. He knew that. There were other women . . .

women who did not mind a little roughness if the pay was right. He—

"You're in love with someone else," she scolded over her shoulder.

"Who?" Nick blurted out before remembering that he was engaged. His brain began scrambling for an excuse at the same moment that Cynthia jerked to a halt.

Spinning toward him, she threw her hands in the air. "Your betrothed!"

"Ah, yes. Of course. Her."

"Nick!" she huffed, hands still outstretched, palms open to the sky.

He did not look at her delicate wrists. "Yes?"

"What is *wrong* with you?"

His face heated to an unbearable burn. How was he to answer that question? There were so many things wrong with him.

"Nick, do you not care for her at all?"

He let her question sink in for a moment. "No," he whispered then. "Not at all," and the words loosened the tightness in his chest. Finally, some truth.

"But . . . that's awful."

"Yes."

"You would marry this woman for money and nothing else?"

He considered it for a moment, hoping it wasn't true, but what other reason could he give himself now? "Yes," he answered again.

"Good God, Nick, you are as mercenary as my stepfather." The sharp edge of disgust hardened her words.

Lancaster nodded, but it wasn't really the truth. Not quite. A mercenary was paid to use his body to fight. That wasn't what Lancaster would be paid for. He was an entirely different thing altogether.

He must have grown used to the idea. It hardly seemed to hurt anymore. Or perhaps it was distance that made the prospect less real.

When he looked up, Cynthia was yards away, growing smaller as she walked. Nick tugged his coat collar up against the wind, shoved his hands in his pockets, and followed.

Chapter 7

What a horrid day.

Cynthia dropped the stick of charcoal and watched it roll across the desktop as she planted her chin in her hand.

Hours of uncomfortable silence as she and Nick worked together, climbing cliffs and poking their heads into every narrow crevice.

He'd said nothing more about her recklessness or safety. He'd said hardly anything else at all, and she hadn't been in a talkative mood either. But despite their concentration on the task at hand, they'd found nothing. Nothing except the genuine distance that had grown between them over the years.

For a short time that morning he'd seemed so familiar. Funny and handsome and carefree. But then he'd become that *other* creature. That London gentleman whose natural charm had been hammered into a brutal tool. He still had charisma, there was no denying that, but now it was polished to a shine. Like jewelry. Or a weapon. Or armor.

But if he was protecting something, it certainly

wasn't the soft heart he'd worn on his sleeve as a boy. That boy hadn't been able to walk past an injured frog without helping. But this man cared nothing for a woman he'd pledged himself to. He'd said it so callously. With no emotion at all.

Did his fiancée love *him*?

Cynthia snorted at her own question. Of course the woman loved him. Everyone loved Nick. His mother had always said he'd been born with a gift, a way of putting people at ease and infusing every room with joy.

Was it possible he'd used it all up in London? Had it run out?

She sighed so deeply that the sketching paper ruffled and danced. A faint dusting of charcoal floated away, as if sand were blowing off the very cliffs she'd tried to capture.

She picked up the charcoal and darkened a shadow on the rocks.

Her work was not precisely art. Oh, it wasn't anything like art, in truth. Cynthia understood that. The crashing waves looked a bit like tangled hair wound around the rocks. The cliffs resembled sides of beef. But she was improving. And it soothed her, the soft scratch of charcoal against parchment, the sense that she'd accomplished a small task.

But she couldn't think beyond Nick tonight, so she packed the charcoal into the tiny writing desk and pulled out the old journal. The pages were burned into her memory already. She'd read it a dozen times over and found nothing new in the last ten passes. But maybe it would act as a talisman, willing to reveal secrets if only she showed her faith.

When a tap sounded at the door, Cyn rubbed her

eyes. Lord, but she was tired. Perhaps she would skip dinner entirely tonight.

"Come in," she called to Mrs. Pell, but the hall door didn't open. The connecting door did.

"Good evening," Nick said, offering her a cheery smile and a covered white bowl. "Mrs. Pell says that Adam is late finishing up his chores, so we'll have to eat *en privé* if we hope to avoid seeing him."

The smell of leek soup swelled into the room, bringing Cyn's mouth to instant attention. "Thank you for delivering the message. And the soup."

He stepped farther into the room, looking around and making no move to give up the bowl. "Are you settled?"

Mrs. Pell had cleaned while they were out, and the extra chamber was now polished and dusted and smelled of fresh herbs. "All is well."

"Mm." He tilted his head. "Is that the diary?"

Her hands clenched with the instinct to snatch it up. "Yes."

"It's so small." He took another step and stopped only six inches from her shoulder. "And is that a drawing of the site?"

Her heart froze. Her drawings weren't meant for anyone but her. "Mm."

"I'd suggest we study it for clues, but I daresay it's hopeless. How old was your uncle at the time? Eight or nine?"

She snapped her head around to look at the sketch. An *eight*-year-old? Why, the rudeness of—

Nick reached for the paper and she snatched up the journal and sketch and shoved them into the drawer. "He was eleven."

"Not much of an artist."

"Yes, well . . . You can set the soup here, thank you."

He tucked the white crock closer to his chest when she reached for it. "I've bread in my room. Will you join me?"

"I'm very tired." She looked up to find Nick watching her, his eyes all warm pleading.

"Please join me." His mouth quirked up. "I've wine as well." He'd apparently shaken off whatever mood had come over him on the shore. Or perhaps he'd already indulged in a drink. Whatever the cause, the old Nick was back, and resistance was futile. Or she assumed it was. She'd never tried to deny him.

"All right. I want wine, and you have it. So I suppose I've no choice."

She followed him into his room—the room where she'd lain last night—and looked around as if his belongings might be a message left for her to study.

A basin still steaming faintly in the cool air. A cloth that had washed his face, his neck. The bed, now neatly made and absent any evidence of her body. Two wine glasses on a table pulled close to the fire, one empty and one stained with the dregs of his recent consumption.

Nick waved her toward the table. "Sit. You must be tired."

She glanced at the corners of his eyes, reddened as if he'd rubbed them hard. "You must be as well."

As if to confirm her words, he collapsed as soon as she took her own seat. "I admit to a bit of trouble sleeping last night. Unearthly revelations, you know."

My word, he already had her smiling. "I suppose."

After he filled the glasses, they both set into their soup. Heat worked its way from her belly to her limbs. Quiet as they were, this was a hundred times more comfortable than their earlier hours had been. When Nick reached for the bread, his fingers caught her eye.

Long and blunt, they were not as elegant as the rest of him. They tore into the bread, ripping the crust, breaking the thin loaf in half. The firelight glinted off the golden hairs that dusted his skin. The muscles of his forearm flexed as he stretched across the table to deliver half the bread to her plate.

Those big fingers had been on her today. Stroking. Holding. "Thank you," she managed to say.

"My pleasure," he answered, the words soft.

Her gaze flew to meet his. Could he read her thoughts? Did he share them? But his smile was pure and free of flirtation.

Guilt turned the warm soup in her stomach into a hot coal. He belonged to someone else.

"How is your family?" she asked too loudly.

"Well." He did not add more.

"I was sorry to hear about your father. He was so kind. A good man."

A smile flashed over his face. A smile or a grimace. "Yes. A wonderful man." Nick picked up his wine and pushed the half-eaten soup away. A few seconds later, he'd downed the glass of wine and refilled it to the brim. "Kind," he added with another strained smile.

"You must miss him."

"I suppose. It's been a very long time."

A long time? His father had only died two years before. She took a bite of bread to hide her shock. He'd always been so close to his father, a man nearly as warm and friendly as Nick himself. Perhaps his grief made two years seem an eternity.

But his eyes were distant, removed. More like

an ancient wound than a fresh one. *It's been a very long time.*

Another glass of wine disappeared. Her confusion deepened. "Are you not hungry?"

He set down the glass and leaned forward. "I want to apologize again. For earlier. For everything."

"It's all right," she said reflexively.

"No . . . I should explain. Or try to. It's just that . . . The women in London, they're not like you, Cyn."

Her spoon clanked hard against the bowl. She set it down. Did he think she did not know that?

"They're more . . . worldly."

"I'm sure they must be," she ground out.

"You're protected here in the country."

"I'd hardly say that, Lancaster," she snapped.

He blinked. "I'm sorry. Of course. I'm not explaining this well. And there are plenty of women like you in London. I'm speaking in generalizations instead of saying what I mean."

"Which is?" She tried not to remember the phrase "women like you," but had no doubt she'd turn it over in her mind for weeks.

"I'm trying to tell you that the woman I am to marry, Imogene, cares as little for me as I do for her. Less even."

"Perhaps she is only shy."

"No." He smiled again, and this time it reached his eyes. "No, that's not it, I'm afraid."

Cyn reached for her wine. She did not like this conversation, yet she was starved for the information. "I don't understand. Everyone likes you, Nick. And you like everyone."

"Cyn," he started, then began to laugh.

Lord, she wanted to melt at that sound. She'd

missed it. Not only him, but that *sound*. His laugh was deeper now, of course, but just as decadent.

"I was a malleable child," he finally said. "An easy child. I'll give you that." The laughter faded to a sad smile. "But easy is a dangerous thing."

"How?" His words didn't make sense, but perhaps she was distracted by the hand he'd lain idly over hers. His thumb stroked her knuckles.

"Being easy . . . If you were easy, Cyn, if you were recommended by that one trait, you would not have fought against this marriage."

"I suppose—"

"Richmond would have come for you, and you'd have gone with him. And you would be *broken* now, instead of easy." His thumb dipped between two of her fingers and traced their lines.

"Are you admiring my mulishness?"

The corner of his mouth quirked up. "I am admiring your strength. And I am saying that if you liked everyone, and everyone liked you . . . Cynthia, your life would be a misery right now."

She tried to catch his eye. They'd been talking about him, so what did he mean? She wanted to ask, but he stared hard at her fingers and did not look up.

And then he raised his eyebrows and plastered a smile on his face. "As Lady Richmond, I mean. As miserable as one could be, I'd imagine."

The moment was past. And if he'd meant anything else by his words, she had no doubt he'd deny it. So she matched his smile. "I wouldn't be Lady Richmond actually. I'd have married the first man my father promised me to."

That sparked bright curiosity on his face. "Who?"

Was he surprised someone else had wanted her? If

only she could shock him with the glory of the match. Unfortunately, there'd been nothing glorious about it. "Well, the first man was Sir Reginald Baylor."

"Sir Reggie?" he yelped, and she could do nothing but laugh.

"Yes, Sir Reggie, all six skeletal feet of him. He had some very nice grazing land to offer."

"Good Lord, you're kidding me."

"I wish I was. I played the complete harridan until he finally let me be. But then he sent his son around to try his chances."

Nick choked on a sip of wine. "Not Harry?"

"Yes. Harry Baylor. Who, despite his given name, lost most of his hair before he reached his majority. He was much easier to chase off than his father though. Not much spine to that one, despite all the bones."

"Well, you've been a busy bee while I've been gone."

She bit her lip. "Ten years is a long time."

"It is. And I'll have to leave again soon."

Silence settled over them for a few moments and filled her with that old pain. He wasn't back. Not really.

"So," he murmured, "we'd best talk about your plans."

"What plans?"

"You said you would sail to America. I can only pray you mean you have family there."

"I do. My father's sister. She will take me in. My stepfather never found favor in her eyes."

"No wonder. But you would need a companion for the journey. Perhaps Mrs. Pell?"

"No, she won't go. I'll hire a woman. I've thought it out."

"It seems you have."

"I cannot wait to see New York. My aunt's letters . . . It seems a very different place than England."

His hand was still on hers. Did he realize it, or was she as inconsequential as a blade of grass one knotted and then tossed away? She couldn't bear that, not when his touch was sending coils of tension winding up her arm. She eased her hand away and placed it carefully in her lap so that the feelings would not slip away too quickly.

When he curled his hand into a fist, Cynthia pretended that Nick was doing the same thing.

Exhaustion lay over him like a sticky film, invading every pore. A long day of climbing and hiking after a sleepless night . . . and still Nick couldn't sleep.

The day had fit together with all the cohesion of an irrational dream. First, the resurrection of Cynthia. Then the story of smugglers and buried treasure and sailing to America. He could've handled that. He could even have seen his way through the adventure of searching sea cliffs for hidden gold. But what had happened on that damp, windswept beach with Cynthia . . . That he couldn't reconcile.

He loved women. He'd always loved women. Old or young, beautiful or homely. It wasn't necessarily a question of sex. He loved the way they smiled and chatted and laughed. Loved to watch the wheels turn in their mind as they puzzled over a problem. He liked the smell and sound of them. The smoothness of their skin and the sharpness of a witty tongue.

For Lancaster, there was nothing more excruciating than an evening at his club, surrounded by whiskered, loud, bulky gentlemen filling the room with cigar smoke and clumsy gestures.

Yes, he loved women. And that was the great tragedy of his life. The dull, constant ache that he could never forgive or forget. The unavoidable feeling that the axis of his world was broken, and he was being pulled ever so slightly out of balance.

If he were still normal, still whole, Lancaster knew what his life would have been. He could see it clearly, a bright and raucous scene painted in yellows and reds.

He would already have fallen in love a dozen times, sure that each woman was the one, whether she was a shy virgin or the jaded wife of a boorish lord. He would have loved them all, cheerfully and completely. And when it proved time to take a wife, he would have loved that woman too, marriage of convenience or not.

And his nights . . . his nights would have been so different. Hours of pleasure and companionship. Laughter and warmth. Tangles of limbs and stroking hands and kisses.

He'd give anything—*anything*—to simply lie with a woman and *feel*. Be kissed and caressed. Stroked. Held.

Lancaster closed his eyes and tried to ignore the tight band squeezing his chest. It didn't matter what might have been. He was not a caring and careful lover. He was a man who needed something darker than that.

He'd thought he could control it with Imogene. Grit his teeth and ignore his needs. But with Cynthia . . . My God, with Cynthia he'd lost control over a simple kiss.

He couldn't want her like that. He couldn't. And yet his body was hardening at the very thought of her beneath him, her arms stretched high above her head. He wanted her like that again, skirts rucked up, arms pinned down. He wanted to have her there in the sand, like a doxy.

But she was his Cyn, and even if he weren't betrothed, he couldn't do that.

Hating himself, Lancaster slid his hand slowly down his body and took his arousal in hand. The thought of what he wanted made him ill, but that did not stop the wanting. It never did.

Chapter 8

Face pressed to the cliff, Lancaster flinched and tried to tug his fingers out of their rocky vise. "Pardon me, but would you mind removing your foot from my hand?"

"What?" Cynthia shouted down.

"Your foot!" he yelled.

She frowned past her shoulder as if she didn't understand, but her boot finally lifted. Lancaster could only hope that the howling wind stole his groan away.

"Come along. We're almost there."

"I don't like this," he muttered with a glance down to the sand ten feet below him. He didn't like this, but his guilt overrode all his objections. Guilt and Cynthia's ornery nature. So now here they were, perched far too high on this blasted cliff while the wind tried its best to set them flying.

"Cyn!" he called. "Stop! This is far higher than we thought."

"I've reached it!" she screamed back, hoisting herself up and disappearing into the rock.

"Damn it." Lancaster very carefully placed his foot

on the next niche and pushed higher. If she was going
to kill him, very well. His blasted brother could marry
Imogene Brandiss and save the family. The surge of
anger helped carry him up the last few feet. Pebbles
slid and bounced to their doom as he boosted himself
onto the ledge.

The cave wasn't as big as it had seemed from the
imperfect vantage point below. Cynthia couldn't
stand up straight, and it would be a tight squeeze for
both of them to crouch in there together. He briefly
considered the benefits of joining her, but Cyn interrupted his unwise thoughts.

"There's something here!"

"Really?" Despite that they were hunting for
treasure, he'd be damned surprised if they actually
found it.

"Just a moment," she breathed. "I think . . . it's . . ."

He was twisting toward her when she screamed.
Lancaster lurched to his feet while his stomach tumbled right off the edge of the cliff. "Cynthia!"

He'd almost reached her when she backed into
him with a strangled squeal.

"What's wrong?"

"I'm sorry, I just . . . I pulled that out of a hole . . ."
Her whole body shuddered as she pointed at a dull
white object about the size of his fist.

Lancaster leaned closer. "What is that? A cat's
skull?"

She edged past him. "I don't know what it is, but
there's still little bits of . . . *stuffing* inside it."

"Stuffing, hm?"

She rubbed her hand furiously against her skirt.

"Why don't you wait out in the sun while I check
the rest of this cave."

It didn't take long. A few more bones lay scattered about. An ancient bird's nest and some mouse droppings.

"There's nothing here, I'm afraid."

She nodded, but he could see the disappointment in her eyes. "Best to move on then. Maybe we should split up. We'd make better time."

"Not a chance." When he joined her and dared to look toward the ground, Lancaster regretted it. Somehow it hadn't occurred to him that the trip down would be more harrowing than the journey up. And the rope wound around his waist proved a complete waste without a tree to anchor it to. None of the rocks here looked sturdy enough to support a child, much less two adults.

"I'll go first," he said. "You follow."

When she nodded, he took a deep breath, turned his back to the ocean, and eased down to his knees. Four feet later, he finally exhaled. It couldn't be more than another three yards, after all. "All right, Cyn. Slow and careful now."

She dropped a leg over the edge, far too casually in his opinion, then searched around for a toehold for a good thirty seconds. His arms ached with the urge to reach up and help, but there was nothing he could do but hope that if she fell, he would cushion her landing.

Finally, she found a steady perch and eased her body out into open air.

Her hiked skirts dragged even higher. The tops of her mended stockings showed now, then her bare thighs, trembling with strain. Thank God Mrs. Pell had come through with the stockings. Those naked legs had played a significant role in his fantasy last night. Of course, he could see beyond the stockings now.

Perched on the side of a cliff, hanging by his fingertips, Lancaster forgot to dwell on the height and began to dwell on Cynthia's thighs. One of her boots pointed as she lowered a leg. The other knee bent.

The hem of her chemise tightened to a band at an awkward angle, then gave up and inched higher.

Lancaster narrowed his eyes, studying the sunlight glow off the silk of her inner thighs. The muscles flexed, pointing a line upward. His eyes followed. . . .

"All right!" Cynthia called, startling him from his disrespectful reverie. "You can move lower now."

In the end, his guilt proved his undoing. Mind swirling, he stepped blindly down and found nothing but air beneath. His other foot slipped. His hands, sweat-slick for some reason, lost their grip on the rock. He was falling.

The sound of the wind rushing by his ears diminished Cyn's scream to the cry of a startled bird. Her face grew smaller. The waves roared louder.

And then everything stopped.

The world stopped, and he went on, still alive despite the complete cessation of sound and light and air.

Air. He couldn't breathe.

His mind exploded in a melee of fear. He couldn't *breathe.*

Suddenly he could feel it, the rope tightening around his neck. He wanted to claw at it, but there was no air left to power his arms. His lungs burned until the ache rose up to meet the fire at his neck. He was dying. Again.

"*Nick.*" The ringing bell sounded strangely like his name.

"Nick!" Now a chorus of voices shouted, each one barely overlapping the other, drawing his name out for miles.

Something landed hard on his chest. Light flared back to existence. Cold air rushed into his lungs.

"Nick. Oh, God, Nick."

The dark blob hovering over him sharpened into the shadowed oval of Cynthia's worried face.

"Are you hurt?"

He thought of nodding, and her head wobbled, so perhaps he managed it.

"Where?" She moved, looking over his torso. She was touching him. He could see that she was touching him, but since he couldn't feel much of anything, he could let it happen. Just to know that her hands rested on his chest, slid down his arms, measured his legs.

Lancaster smiled at the sky.

"Where are you hurt?" Cyn cried.

"Just . . . Just knocked the wind out," he managed.

"Oh, Lord above, are you sure?"

"Aye." Either that or his spine had cracked like kindling, but they'd find out soon enough.

She hovered for a moment, quiet and calm, then collapsed right onto him, as if she were a puppet whose strings had broken. Her head rested on his chest, her hands held his shoulders. He waited for the panic, but long seconds passed and none came. Lancaster willed his arms to curl around her and they did.

"Thank God," she breathed into his shirt.

Yes. *Thank God.* He held her to his chest and let her weight soak into him, shocked to realize he could feel her now. His hand cupped her head. Her hair slid against his fingers. Then her hands shifted, sliding over his shoulders in a tender caress.

Lancaster closed his eyes against the tears.

"You were right," she murmured. "We shouldn't have dared that. I'm so sorry."

"You managed just fine."

"But we are a team," she answered simply, drawing a smile to his face.

Until she jerked up. "I'm sorry, I shouldn't be squashing you like that!" She pushed off him.

"No," he gasped. "Please don't." But she was already twisting away to lie on the sand beside him.

"Is that better?"

No. No, it was as lonely and cold as it ever was. His fingers gripped the beach instead of Cynthia. And a great glob of sand seemed to have settled in his throat as well. He could neither speak nor swallow it away.

Minutes passed in silence. Real life seeped back into his body, but he didn't move.

"You keep your hair so short now," Cynthia murmured.

The ghost of a cruel grip twisted in his hair. "One must keep up with fashion, of course," he lied, forcing a jaunty smile.

"Of course." Her voice shimmered with amusement. It swelled over him and washed away the last of his inertia.

"All right." Muscles screamed when he pushed to his elbows, but his body seemed in working order. "Back to the hunt."

Cyn sprang up beside him. "Don't be an idiot. We're going home."

Lancaster opened his mouth to protest. He was a man after all, and eager to show off his amazing fortitude. Nothing short of death could stop an animal as virile as he.

But then she said it again. "Let's go home, Nick."

And that sounded like a fantasy. Like an invitation to go *back* where he wanted to be. "Yes, then," he agreed. "Yes, let's go home." When he pushed to his feet, he was glad he'd agreed. Virility aside, his legs hadn't appreciated those moments without air. But he could make them work if it meant going home with Cyn.

The warmth of the kitchen was such a change to her chilled body that Cynthia felt as if she were cocooned in wool blankets. Or as if Nick had teased her into joining him in a glass of whisky.

Their hike home had coincided with the rising tide, and a sudden wave had slapped right into her skirts. It had receded before she'd even had time to shriek at the cold, but the damage had been done.

When she shivered at the memory, Nick poured another serving and pushed the glass toward her, his movement drawing her eyes to his bare forearms. The formality of a coat was hardly called for in the midst of what could only be described as a bathing party.

"I insist you go first," Nick said, tilting his glass in her direction.

"Nonsense. You need to soothe your back."

"My back is good as ever, thank you very much. And I shan't soak at all if you don't go first. I am nothing if not chivalrous. You're cold. And your hair needs washing."

Her hand flew to her hair only to find the braid stiff with dried salt spray. Her face flared to a blush. "Chivalry, my arse."

"Cynthia Merrithorpe!" Mrs. Pell appeared like

a genie from the hall, her arms filled with linens. "Could you please cease shouting out every improper word that jumps into your head?"

Nick nodded solemnly. "Quite shocking."

She kicked his shin and was disappointed when he only smiled angelically at his housekeeper. "Mrs. Pell, won't you take a turn as well? No point wasting all this hot water."

She glanced scornfully at the steaming tub. "I prefer a brace of cold water myself. Toughens the hide."

"Mm, well. We London gentlemen prefer skin with the sheen and texture of a baby's bottom."

Cyn raised an eyebrow. "I would've guessed a horse's arse."

Playing to the singular audience of Mrs. Pell, Nick clapped a hand over his heart and pretended to succumb to an agonizing death.

"You're both impossible," Mrs. Pell complained as she leaned over the fire to check the temperature of the pot of water. When she reached for the hook, Nick jumped up and took it from her, snagging the rag that hung from her apron as well.

"I think that should be enough," he murmured as he poured the water out in a great cloud of steam. His neckcloth gave up any pretense of stiffness in the dampness. Nick tugged impatiently at the knot, then used the cloth to wipe his brow. Sweat and steam dampened his shirt, pressing it to his skin and turning the scene into an exposition of male beauty.

My, oh my.

Cyn glanced toward Mrs. Pell and found that she was staring too, though her eyes looked shocked instead of satisfied. Had she forgotten he'd grown into a man? Cynthia certainly hadn't.

He worked the pump to refill the giant black pot, and the shirt revealed his back to be just as lovely as his front. From the dip of his spine, the muscles of his back curved out to strong shoulders. His arms tightened under the weight of the water.

"Well then." He hung the pot back over the fire and dusted his hands. "I suppose Mrs. Pell won't allow me to stay even if I promise to do no more than peek."

"Cheeky." Cynthia laughed. And he had a right to be. She'd have been happy to let him wash her back.

"But Mrs. Pell," he continued, "I beg you. Keep an eye on her for me. I seem to recall a panel hidden in that wall, and Miss Merrithorpe is not above a peek herself."

Cynthia snorted. "I prefer a strapping country lad myself."

He raised a knowing eyebrow. "Yes, I know that about you."

Though she looked about for a stale roll to toss at his back, there were none at hand, and Nick escaped the room unscathed.

"The nerve." Cynthia stood and shook out her sodden skirts, then started to turn her back to Mrs. Pell, but the woman still stood near the hearth, forehead crumpled in thought.

"Mrs. Pell?"

She startled and shook her head, muttering, "Yes, of course," before starting on the hooks of Cynthia's dress.

Cyn lost herself in thoughts of how lovely whisky was until Mrs. Pell cleared her throat.

"I think you should be a bit gentler with him," Mrs. Pell said softly as she pulled the dress down and started on the corset.

"Who?"

"Lord Lancaster. He's not the boy he once was."

"Clearly. He's a London gentleman now. I'd say he needs a bit of shaking up."

Stripped of her corset, Cynthia shrugged off her chemise and rushed to the tub. "Do you know how long it's been since I had a proper bath?" She slipped one foot into the water and groaned. "Sweet mercy."

The water rose up in heavenly inches as she lowered her body. The heat seemed to soak right through her skin and deep into her bones, releasing so much of the anxiety she'd carried for weeks and months. But when she looked up to Mrs. Pell, her smile froze in place.

She leaned forward so fast that a little wave sloshed over the end of the tub. "What's the matter?"

"Nothing."

Cyn shook her head. "Don't tell me nothing. You look as if you may cry."

"Don't be ridiculous."

"What is wrong?"

The housekeeper dipped a cloth into the water and worked the ball of soap into it. "London must have been hard on him. That's all."

"What in God's name are you talking about?"

"The viscount. London isn't a place for a man like him."

"Apparently it is just the place. He went happily enough."

She began to wash Cyn's back with too much force.

Cynthia frowned. "He was hardly homesick. He never once even scrawled a note to me."

"It wasn't what you thought." The quiet words swelled with such warning that Cynthia put her hands on the edge of the tub to brace herself. The scrubbing stopped. A pitcher appeared in front of her as Mrs. Pell scooped up water. She had only a moment to catch her breath before heat cascaded over her hair. But it was still in its braid.

"Oh, mercy me," Mrs. Pell sighed. "I didn't even take down your hair." She reached for the braid, but Cyn stopped her hand.

"Mrs. Pell." She wrapped her fingers around the woman's small wrist. "You're not saying something. What is it?" The only answer she got was a shake of Mrs. Pell's head. "Please tell me."

A great sigh shuddered through her as her blue eyes filled with tears. "I didn't think it was true."

"What?"

After a quick glance at the closed door, she looked at the floor. "What they said about Master Nicholas."

The water had only held her tension as a passing courtesy, it seemed. All the anxiety was leaching back into her flesh now. "What did they say, Mrs. Pell?"

"After he left here . . ." She looked into Cynthia's eyes. "Something happened. Some scandal. I don't know what. And Nicholas meant to kill himself."

The words evoked no response from her gut, they were so ridiculous. "That's absurd."

Mrs. Pell nodded, but not in agreement. "They said he hung himself. And the rope . . ." Her right hand touched her neck, and Cynthia suddenly understood.

A burn, he'd said. A burn that had scarred his whole neck.

"That's absurd," she repeated, because it must be.

"I thought so too." The tears finally spilled over her eyes and Mrs. Pell brushed a wrist across her cheek. "The old coachman . . . he told me that a family friend found Master Nicholas hanging and cut him down. They thought he was dead already."

"No."

"His parents took him to London to recover where no one knew him. That's why he left. But I didn't believe it. I told that coachman if I ever heard him repeat those lies again, I'd have him turned out." Mrs. Pell finally collapsed into a chair and let the tears flow. "I didn't believe it."

Cynthia stared at the fire and told herself it couldn't be true. Life had always meant joy to Nick. He had left here *happy*.

Her stomach sunk in on itself and cramped in pain. It didn't make sense. What could possibly have befallen him to change him so completely?

What had he said to her? Something about how being easy could be dangerous. But that meant *nothing*. Nothing when compared to the laughing, joyful young man he'd been.

It couldn't be true.

She didn't know how long she stared at the fire, but by the time Mrs. Pell touched her shoulder and drew her out of her own mind, the new pot of water was steaming away.

"Best to finish here," the woman murmured, her fingers working through the braid. Shivers began to course through Cynthia. The bath had cooled. When Mrs. Pell poured lukewarm water over Cyn's loosened hair, she shivered harder.

"It might not be true," Mrs. Pell said softly.

"It isn't true," she insisted. "It isn't true and I will never believe that. He burned himself. That's all."

"Of course," Mrs. Pell answered, her voice holding all the worry that was breaking Cynthia's heart in two.

Chapter 9

Did she know?

Lancaster watched Cynthia brush a few breakfast crumbs off the kitchen table, avoiding his eyes as she had all morning. She touched the end of her braid as if to be sure it was still secure, then filled a pail of water and set it near the hearth.

Did she know that he'd pleasured himself again last night? Did she know that he'd thought of *her*?

After his bath, he'd found her before the fire in his room, bundled up in nightdress and robe and brushing out her hair. He hadn't seen her hair down before, and the sight had been startlingly intimate. As if she were getting ready to lie down. With him.

But then she'd noticed him and hurried out, babbling that there was no hearth in her room and she'd needed the heat and she wouldn't bother him again and good night. By the time he'd raised a hand to stop her, she'd been gone, the door to her room closing firmly against him. But the thought of her straight brown hair gleaming in the dim light had remained.

Lancaster had wrapped an imaginary fist around it.

He'd pulled her close and kissed her hard and told her exactly what she would do to please him. Then he'd tied her hands above her head and secured her to a bedpost. She hadn't tried to resist at all. Her body had writhed in pleasure, not fear. And he'd climaxed to the thought of pounding into her until she screamed for mercy.

She couldn't know that. And yet she behaved as if she did.

Self-disgust roiled through him. He swallowed the last of his tea, amazed that his throat could be so dry even when filled with liquid.

"Ready?" he rasped, and she nodded without looking up. Perhaps she could sense the perversion in him, like prey scenting a predator.

Lancaster shoved his arms into his coat and led the way toward the front door as Cynthia pulled her hood over her head.

A gorgeous day greeted his scowling face when he threw open the door. Birds calling, sun shining, the breeze tinted with warmth instead of damp. He narrowed his eyes against the beauty and focused on the figure approaching through the tall grass just past the road. A man, neither tall nor short. He approached from the west, but his hat kept his face in shadows.

It wasn't until Cyn started to slip past him that Lancaster realized he should be very alarmed.

He shot out an arm and shoved her back through the door.

"Say! What—"

"Someone's coming."

"Who?"

He pushed her farther in and slammed the door.

"Does it matter? I'm the only one who knows you're alive. Now hide, damn it!"

Her mouth formed an "O" that would have been comical if Lancaster's heart hadn't been doing its best imitation of a diving hawk.

"Oh. Right. Sorry. I'll just . . ."

She darted away while he wondered if the man had seen them. If the visitor's face had been in shadow, his head had probably been lowered, picking a safe path through the rocky meadow. Lancaster had been so absorbed in his own dark thoughts that the image wasn't clear.

Damn.

A quick glance around didn't reveal any obvious signs of Cynthia's presence. Lancaster was wiping his damp palms against the wool of his coat when the knock came.

After a deep breath that helped to open the tight knot in his throat, Lancaster pasted a smile on his face and threw open the door. "Good day!" he boomed before realizing there was no one there. But then a man popped into view and Lancaster nearly swallowed his tongue.

Cynthia's stepfather. He rose from a crouch and held something out to Lancaster. "Here."

Lancaster blinked down at his gloves. "Ah. So sorry. Did I leave them in your study?"

"What?" Cambertson's bulbous nose crinkled. "No, I found them here on your step. Right strange, if you ask me."

"Yes, of course. On the step. I just had them. Thank you." He was babbling now. "So sorry," he added in case there was any doubt that his mouth was working independently of his mind.

Cambertson eyed him cautiously, his chin tucking in. "Right then. Might I come in?"

"Um . . ." No good excuse presented itself, so Lancaster offered a weak, "Yes."

As soon as Cambertson stepped in and closed the door behind him, Lancaster realized he should have just muttered something about the stables and taken the man for a walk. By God, he'd always lied quite well in London. The fresh country air must be interfering, infusing his character with wholesomeness. Though it hadn't reached too deeply, it seemed.

The thought of unwholesomeness made him think of Cynthia and what was at stake, and Lancaster managed to draw up his spine. He'd lived a charade his whole life. Fooling Cambertson shouldn't be hard.

"So! What can I do for you, Mr. Cambertson?"

"I wondered . . ." the man started, then stopped to look around as if he might be invited to have a seat. When no invitation presented itself, Cambertson shrugged. "I heard a story." His eyes flickered from Lancaster to the hallway and back.

"A story?"

"I heard . . ." He took off his hat, revealing matted hair and a pale forehead. "I heard you had a ghost."

Lancaster's throat clicked shut in shock and he made a strange sound that might have been "Gahn?"

Cambertson nodded. "It hardly bears asking about, but . . ." He met Lancaster's eyes for a heartbeat of time before looking back to the floor. "Is it true?"

Lancaster watched the top of the man's head for a long moment. The pale skin of his scalp gleamed beneath curls of thin hair. This man had given Cynthia over to a madman. He'd declared her selfish and ungrateful. Lancaster felt calm return to his heart. "Are you asking if my home is haunted, Mr. Cambertson?"

His scalp turned pink. "I know it sounds foolish, but the villagers are talking. They say there's a woman here, roaming your hallways."

"A woman?"

He looked up, but his gaze didn't hold the suspicion Lancaster had expected. Instead his bloodshot eyes were brimming with resignation. "Some say they've seen her pacing the cliffs. Where she died."

Lancaster didn't quite know what to say. If Cynthia had been seen, the legend of her ghost could only be a good thing. "The new maids did indeed get spooked. They ran off. And I admit to hearing a few strange noises here myself."

"So it's true? It's Cynthia?"

"Uh . . . I suppose it must be."

"Aye. She took her own life. She's damned for eternity." Cambertson crumpled his hat in his hand and began to pace. "She blames me, I'm sure."

Lancaster glanced uneasily around. He wouldn't put it past Cynthia to pat some flour onto her skin, pull the hood low over her face, and make a ghostly appearance just to torment her stepfather.

"Mrs. Cambertson won't come home," Cambertson muttered. "She blames me too, I don't doubt. But I didn't know. I'd heard the rumors, of course, but . . . that's neither here nor there. And now Richmond's man is hanging about again—"

"His man?" Lancaster blinked to attention. "Who do you mean?"

Cambertson waved an impatient hand. "Bram. Richmond calls him a secretary, but he don't seem like any secretary I've ever seen. Always just looming about, quiet as you please, watching. He looks just like Richmond, only twenty years younger, if you take my meaning."

No, he didn't take the meaning at all. "This man has been here? Recently?"

"He came by Oak Hall last evening. Said Richmond wanted to know when my lovely young daughter would return home."

Fear shocked his heart like lightning. "But she's dead."

"Not that daughter." Cambertson shook his head. "My little Mary. That heartless wretch hasn't even let us grieve a month!"

Oh, of course. Little Mary. "Did this Bram ever meet Cynthia?"

Cambertson shot him an exasperated look. "Course he did."

Well, damnation. If he got a look at Cynthia, things would come quickly to a head.

"I heard she fell upon you while you slept."

"Um . . . pardon?"

"The ghost. I heard she assaulted you bodily. Was it the witching hour?"

"Well . . . I'm sure it was. It must have been."

Cambertson grunted in thought, then darted his gaze around, touching on each corner of the room before he began to back toward the door. "Perhaps you could let her know that I've forgiven her. I wouldn't like her to stop by Oak Hall."

"You've forgiven her, hm? Well, I'll pass the message along the next time she visits my bed."

"Aye. Well." Cambertson slapped his hat against his palm a few times before shoving it onto his head. "You're a braver man than I. Good day then."

When the front door closed, a panel in the hall jumped open as if pulled by the vacuum. Cynthia emerged, face flushed with anger. "He's *forgiven* me?"

Lancaster rubbed his chin. "Who is this Bram fellow?"

Cynthia stopped her angry pacing and hugged her arms to her chest. "You heard my stepfather. He's Richmond's man."

"What does he do for Richmond?" Lancaster couldn't say he'd exactly kept a close eye on Lord Richmond over the years, but he'd never heard any whispers of an accomplice.

"I don't know."

"Your stepfather implied that he might have been Richmond's son."

"He could be. They certainly look related."

Cynthia's frown distracted him from his puzzlement. He didn't like the way she rubbed her hands over her arms. "Why does it make you nervous to speak of him?"

"I don't like to speak of either of them!"

Well, he could certainly understand that. Especially when Cynthia's hand went to her mouth. He'd noticed the scar before. Still pale pink, the jagged line bisected her perfect bottom lip like a reminder of fresh pain.

Lancaster crossed the room and touched his fingers to hers. The distance vanished from her eyes as she snapped her hand away from her mouth and backed away. He followed.

When her back touched the wall, he put his fingers to her cheek and feathered his thumb over the scar. "He did this to you, didn't he?"

She made no pretense of answering. Her eyes blazed a bright combination of sorrow and frustration.

"Richmond or his man?"

Her lips parted, and the heat of her breath on his skin shocked him. "Richmond," she whispered. "Bram never touched me."

"But Richmond did?" Fury sprang loose in his chest, the perfect complement to the new lust she was inspiring. "I'm sorry," he breathed.

She shook her head and the moistness of her mouth dragged over his thumb. Something inside him broke. He didn't want to know, but he asked the question all the same. "What did he do, Cyn?"

"He just . . . I made him angry. And he wanted me to be scared, I think, and I wasn't, and that made it worse."

Every word touched his skin and burned him. Yes, Richmond liked to inspire fear above all else.

"He was on top of me, and he . . ." She shook her head. "It doesn't matter. But when I spat on him, he snapped. I thought . . . I thought he was kissing me too hard. I tried to shove him off and his teeth . . . they tore my lip. And I screamed that he was *biting* me. I screamed for help and Bram . . . he just stood there."

"Bram was *there*?"

"He was always there, but . . . I don't know. He was there, but he looked right through me, and I was bleeding everywhere and crying—"

"Oh, Cyn."

"And my mother came in, thank God. I ran past her, and then I was free."

"You ran here?"

One tear touched his knuckle, scalding hot before it cooled on his skin.

"I ran here," she breathed.

"I'm so sorry," he murmured, as her wide eyes drew

him in. "I'm sorry he hurt you, and I'm so glad you came here." She went still. So still, and Lancaster leaned closer, as slowly as he could bear, and brushed her lips with his own.

He'd meant never to touch her again, but he needed to kiss this pain away. He couldn't resist her and didn't want to.

Cynthia didn't seem interested in resisting either. She parted her lips and rubbed her tongue into his mouth. Her hands fisted in his shirt, and he was relieved he wouldn't have to hold her wrists and disappointed he'd miss the chance.

Whatever hesitance he might have retained disappeared when she pulled him closer. Lancaster went gladly. He pressed her into the wall and kissed her too hard, just the way he wanted. Long seconds passed as he plunged into her mouth the way he wished he could plunge between her thighs. But when Cyn groaned, his conscience flared to life.

He tried to pull away, but her hands wound tighter into his coat.

"I'm sorry," he moaned, but Cynthia shook her head.

"No, don't. I want this. I want it. Please."

Oh, God, why was she saying that? *Please,* she'd begged him in his fantasies the night before. *Please.* His cock swelled to sudden, painful need. "I can't," he groaned, but she surged up on her tiptoes and kissed him again.

His mind tumbled over itself until he was dizzy. Wrapping his fingers around her arms, he clung to the taste of her mouth and the slick slide of her tongue on his. Her hands pulled at his coat as if they were struggling. And she was so hot inside. So hot. He wanted deeper and more.

When he dragged his mouth over to her jaw, she moaned. When he sucked at the softest spot on her neck, her pulse beat against his tongue.

"Please, Nick," she groaned and everything inside him swelled to an ache.

Sometimes a man simply couldn't walk away from what he wanted. Sometimes he had to stay and face it.

This was wrong.

It was wrong for so many reasons, and Cynthia didn't care. There was no future for them, and it didn't matter. There was now.

All night she'd thought about Nick. About his un-happiness and her own. How had they both come to such disastrous paths? How had they both lost their hope for joy along the way?

But now, as his mouth tasted her neck, all her worries fell away. This was joy, and they could have it for a moment.

As long as they weren't interrupted.

"Here," she muttered. "Come." Reaching blindly to her right, she pulled open the panel in the wall and revealed the narrow passage within. Nick didn't seem to notice, but he followed where she led. She shut the door, and they were plunged into darkness.

He looked up for a moment as if startled, but she put her mouth on his and brought him back to her.

In the dark she could feel everything. In the dark it was just Nick and his taste and smell and touch. In the dark there was no fiancée and no scar around his neck and no ship to America.

He devoured her, consuming all her strength, and she let the wall support her weakening body.

Her skirts rustled when he lowered his hand to slide them up. *Yes,* she prayed. *Yes, yes.* He tucked them up in one heavy bunch, and then his hand spread over her thigh, each finger an individual brand on her skin. *This is Nicholas,* she reminded herself, smiling as they kissed. *This is Nick sliding his hand up my bare skin.*

His palm traveled higher, and he pushed her harder to the wall as if to brace her. Cynthia gasped for breath and let her head fall back, pressing her skull to the solid wood behind her.

When his fingers brushed the hair that covered her sex, a whimper slipped free of her throat. Then he touched her fully. His hand cupped her, and his fingers slipped along the seam of her body with shocking ease.

"Ah, God," he groaned as she gasped in surprise. The pads of his fingers slipped deeper as he caressed her with short strokes. "My God, Cyn, you're so damn wet."

She was. Her face blazed with humiliation. That had never happened before. "I'm sorry."

Nick nuzzled the skin beneath her ear. "Mm?"

"I'm sorry. I don't know . . . why."

"Why what?"

He didn't stop stroking her, and Cynthia found that his fingers were somehow stealing her breath. "Why I'm so . . ." she gasped, "so damp."

His fingers froze, much to her disappointment. He raised his head as if he might look at her despite the dark. "I'm sorry," he whispered. "Of course, you wouldn't . . ." Nick was frozen, the pressure of his hand decreasing as the seconds ticked by. He was going to stop, because of her.

"No," she whispered. "Please don't stop." Tears sprang to her eyes. She only wanted this. Just this, and it didn't seem too much to wish for. "Just touch me. Please."

His breath quickened on her cheek. His fingers shook against her sex. He pressed in, and one finger slipped deeper.

"Yes. Oh, Nick, yes," she begged.

He was panting now, despite that she wasn't touching him. But as his finger rubbed tiny circles against her, he shuddered. "You're wet," he breathed, "because you're excited."

There was a tight pressure, and she felt him slip suddenly deep inside her body. "Oh!" she cried out as Nick groaned her name.

"You're wet because your body wants to take me in."

He was stroking her now, pushing inside her before pulling out to rub those same small circles over her wet flesh.

"It wants to ease my way," he panted, "against the . . . *tightness.*"

Yes, that was exactly right. She wanted to be filled with him. Stretched by his body. Taken. Her whole world became that place inside her where his finger thrust. The pressure increased. She could feel her flesh squeezing him.

"Cynthia," he breathed. His teeth touched her neck, his tongue pressed against her.

She needed . . . something. Needed him closer.

She let go of his coat and slipped her hands higher to pull him tighter to her body. When she felt the cool softness of his hair, she curled her fingers into the strands and tightened her grip, holding on as her body rose.

* * *

He'd never been afraid of the dark, but he should have been. Out of the darkness, a nightmare grabbed him. A hand in his hair, forcing him down.

On your knees, boy.

He tried to pull away.

Don't worry. You'll learn to like it.

The hand curled harder.

Lancaster jerked back too quickly. The top of his head cracked against the low ceiling.

"Nick?" Cynthia gasped.

"Don't. Please." He let her go and stumbled back until he touched the far wall. The crown of his head sang with startled pain.

"What's wrong?"

"We can't . . ." He tried to shake off the shame that clung to him like a net. He tasted musk and sweat and something more. Bile rose in his throat, as his body tried to expel the memory.

Her fingers touched his chest, but in the dark, the hand could have belonged to anyone. "I'm sorry," he blurted out. "We shouldn't be doing this." He reached blindly to the right and pushed. The passageway filled with merciful light that seemed to blind Cynthia. She blinked rapidly, her eyelids like the fluttering of butterfly wings.

"What happened?"

"This is wrong." He slid past her and gulped in the cool air of the entry. "We can't do this." He dragged a forearm over his brow to wipe away the sweat.

"My heavens!" a voice gasped.

Lancaster looked up to see Mrs. Pell standing frozen in the hall.

"What in the world are you two doing?"

"Uh . . ." He couldn't think. This was too much all

at once. Half his mind was still struggling with the past. The other half wanted to step back into the wall, close the door, and finish making love to Cynthia Merrithorpe.

Speaking of which . . . He looked over his shoulder to see her still standing in the black rectangle of the opening, her forehead creased with utter confusion. Her gaze bruised. At least her skirts had fallen into place. But her mouth was a swollen clue to why they'd been hidden away in the passageway.

"Mr. Cambertson was here," he blurted out, swinging his head back to Mrs. Pell. She didn't seem to have heard him. Her eyes were locked on Cynthia.

She finally glanced to Lancaster. "He what?"

"He was here. Cyn and I almost walked right into him. I thought we'd better hide in case he'd spotted us and decided to come right in."

"Well, did he?"

"No. He knocked a few times and then left."

She looked back and forth between them again, eyes narrowed. "I didn't hear a thing."

"Were you upstairs, perhaps?"

She swept a suspicious glance down his body. But he wasn't giving anything away. Not anymore, at least.

"I was upstairs. I suppose I might have missed it."

"Right-o. Well, we'd better be going. God knows when he might return."

Feeling Mrs. Pell's eyes burning straight into his back, he walked calmly to Cynthia, took her hand and tugged her out of the passageway. "Let's find some treasure, shall we?"

Though she stared at him as if he might have lost his mind, her feet moved her forward when he pulled.

"Pull your hood up," he suggested, and she did. "Perhaps we'd better go out the back."

Mrs. Pell followed closely, as if she suspected Lancaster might whisk Cynthia upstairs to a bed if they were left alone.

He took care opening the back door. "Where's Adam?"

"Gone to buy fish," the housekeeper answered.

"We should leave before dawn tomorrow."

Cynthia didn't answer. When he glanced back to her it looked as though her shock was wearing off to reveal a welling anger beneath. A fully understandable anger.

She pulled the hood down further when he met her eyes.

"Right then. Let's go."

They probably should have stayed inside to be safe, but the prospect of quiet hours together felt anything but safe to Lancaster. Locked in that house for the day with a woman who would want an answer to one simple question . . . *What is wrong with you?*

Once he was out in the sun, once the wind filled his lungs with fresh air, the last cobwebs of memory swept away. He took Cynthia's hand and strode faster toward the path.

If she hadn't touched him, perhaps they'd still be hidden behind that door. She'd been so close to her peak. He would've swallowed her scream with a kiss. Perhaps brought her to climax again, with his tongue this time. With the taste of her filling his mouth.

But no. Falling to his knees . . . that simply wasn't an option.

Swallowing hard, Lancaster made sure to look carefully around as they drew closer to the shore. He watched the horizon carefully for the silhouette of a spy, but the bright sun revealed nothing. They were alone.

As soon as the path came into sight, Cynthia drew away and ran toward it. Fearful that she'd spotted someone or heard something, he chased after her, following her down until their heads were below the level of the grass.

Then she rounded on him. "Why did you stop?" she shouted, throwing her fists against his chest.

"Ow!" He pushed her hands off him, but they just descended again, striking him harder this time.

"Bastard!"

"Stop." Christ, she was stronger than she'd been ten years ago. He finally managed to snag her fists and keep hold of them.

"You," she gasped. "You just *stopped*."

"I know. I'm sorry. I swear to you that I'm sorry."

She threw off his hands and backed away. "But *why*?"

The truth simply wasn't an option, or not the whole of it anyway. So Lancaster grasped at a lesser truth. "I shouldn't have done that, and you know it."

"Well, you *were* doing it. That's not an explanation." The last word broke, and the speaking of it seemed to set free her tears. Cynthia began to cry, and Lancaster shook his head hard.

"No, don't cry. Cynthia, I'm sorry. Don't cry."

She growled in frustrated anger and tried to wipe the tears away, but they were coming too fast.

When he approached, she tried to hit him again, but Lancaster wrapped her in his arms and pulled her close. "I'm sorry. I shouldn't have done that, and I shouldn't have left you so close."

She shook her head, then paused. After a hard sniff, she asked sullenly, "Close to what?"

Lancaster squeezed his eyes shut and took a deep breath. He was not going to answer that question. "Cynthia, we're not married. We're not even engaged to be married. I shouldn't be touching you, even right now."

Her snort was something shy of delicate. "Don't patronize me, Nick. I'm fully aware that everything that can be done inside a marriage can be done outside it as well."

"That doesn't make it right, Cyn."

"It doesn't make it wrong either."

"Of course it does!"

"Oh, really? And I suppose I'm the first woman you've ever touched?"

"I . . ." Nick sputtered. "I don't—"

"Oh, let me go already."

He let her go.

"Nick," she started, and then seemed to stop herself. Her shoulders slumped as she took a deep breath and let it drain from her body in an audible sigh. "Don't you want to be happy?"

Lancaster frowned down at her. *That* was her question? What kind of nonsense was that? "Of course I want to be happy. Doesn't everyone?"

Cynthia very deliberately put her hands on her hips and met his gaze. "If that's true, then why would you marry a woman who doesn't even like you?"

"I need money. Badly."

"Don't try to tell me you couldn't find an heiress who'd at least enjoy your company. For God's sake, Nick, you're charming and handsome and . . ." She waved a hand in disgust.

He could tell her. He wanted to tell someone. Here was a woman, a *friend*, asking him for the truth, and the story burned in his gut like a coal.

When he spied a flat boulder not two feet from Cynthia's skirts, Lancaster headed for it and dropped to the hard surface. The sea was calm today, nearly as smooth as glass. A flat, dark span of a hidden world.

"You want to know the truth?" he asked and saw Cyn nod out of the corner of his eye. "When I inherited the title of viscount from my father, it came with a cruel revelation. My family was hovering on the brink of ruin. My father had never said a word, never curbed our spending. It was shocking to say the least. And there was no doubt of what my duty was. It only took a few months for the whole *ton* to realize that I needed an heiress. But I was only twenty-three, and I resisted for almost a whole year." He laughed quietly.

"But resistance was futile. I met Imogene last year. She was lovely. Smart and beautiful. Independent and witty. And her father wanted a connection to a title. I'm not . . ." He rubbed the back of his neck and tried to think how to phrase this. *I'm not choosy.* Not quite the thing to say to a woman you'd almost made love with.

Cynthia turned toward the water and waited.

"I like people, as you said yourself. I thought Imogene and I would get on just fine. I thought—Ha! I thought we could be friends. As you and I are friends."

She darted a glance in his direction before looking back to the sea.

"I spoke to her father. I proposed, and she accepted. But then the threads of our connection slowly unraveled. I thought the idea of marriage made her shy. I thought it was charming. But in the end, she wanted me to know the truth, I think."

"What truth?" Arms wrapped around herself, Cynthia finally faced him.

"That she's in love with someone else."

Her expression of obvious disbelief soothed his painfully wounded pride. "Who?"

Lancaster stretched his legs out and leaned back against the rough face of the cliff. "A man she can't have. Her father's man of affairs. He seems a decent enough fellow."

"She told you this?"

"Ah, no. I walked in on the two of them in a rather intimate embrace."

"Oh!" Cynthia's eyes widened in horror. "That's terrible."

"I admit to an acute case of bruised pride."

A sudden gust of wind blew Cynthia's skirts up in a bell, and she angrily slapped them down. "Well, you can't marry her now, Nick. No one would expect you to."

A pleasant kernel of warmth bloomed inside his chest. The truth was that everyone would expect him to marry Imogene regardless. Everyone except Cynthia. "I'm afraid that's not true. This isn't about love or even affection. It's about money and power."

"So find a *nice* heiress to marry! Don't marry her."

He closed his eyes and breathed in the green salt smell of the ocean. The waves only lapped today, instead of crashing, and suddenly it was summer and he was fourteen and the world was so damned simple. The gulls screamed and the sun shone and Cyn stood over him with her fists on her hips, outraged about something. As usual, he could only smile at her. She was always so cute when she stomped her little foot and growled.

"Nick!" she grouched, and he opened his eyes.

No, he wasn't fourteen, and Cynthia wasn't a child.

And the world might be simple, but it wasn't the least bit kind. "It doesn't matter, Cyn."

"Of course it matters. You're not happy. I want you to be happy."

That kernel grew into a flame that singed his heart. No one had tried to protect him from anything in so many years. In the end, not even his own father had looked out for him. "I am happy."

"You most certainly are not."

"On the contrary, I'm well known as one of the happiest gentlemen in the *ton*."

She tucked her chin in. "By people who scarcely know you at all, I take it?"

"I . . ." Lancaster didn't know what to say. How could she see what others could not? How could she know that he was profoundly empty inside? He watched the sun reach out across the dark blue water. "Cease, every joy, to glimmer on my mind," he murmured to the sea, some maudlin bit of Scottish poetry that had stuck in his head.

"What?" The clipped word radiated Cynthia's impatience.

He snapped from his reverie and met her eyes. "Who is ever happy? You're not happy. How could you be, with the specter of Lord Richmond hanging over you?"

She stared at him for a long moment, her gaze clear and steady. "That's true. But I will be happy someday. And Nick . . . I'm happy now, when I'm with you. I always was."

His heart swelled. He blinked hard several times as the truth of her words hit him. Since the moment he'd discovered she was alive, he'd felt peaceful. Happy. As if he'd come home.

Perhaps it would've been better if his parents

hadn't trundled him off to London to recover. He should've come home to Cantry Manor so that he could recall who he was.

Cynthia slowly lowered herself to sit beside him on the wide boulder. She twitched her skirts a few times and then grew quiet, joining him in his study of the sea.

"Why did you stop? In the passageway?" she whispered.

The cold of the stone had begun to seep into his thighs, but she felt warm next to him. He wanted to drag her back to that passageway and finish what he'd started. He wanted to take her upstairs and bind her wrists and show her why he'd stopped. But more than that, he wanted to go back in time and be what she deserved.

"I was free here," he said. "You and I, we were free. But I am the viscount now. The head of a family drowning in debt. What I want no longer signifies and it never will."

"Nick—"

He shook his head. "But you will have what you want someday. You'll sail to America and meet a young American man and be charmed by his industriousness and drive. You'll fall in love. And when you marry him, you'll regret me."

"That's nonsense. To speak of unknown people in some future time."

"It's not nonsense, and I won't ruin you." When she started to interrupt again, Lancaster held up a hand to stop her. Miraculously, she closed her mouth. "Cynthia, your virtue is like a jewel."

"A jewel?" she sputtered while he nodded.

"Yes, a precious jewel. Or a flower. Yes, it's a flower.

A fragile and priceless gift to be given only to your husband. A flower can only be plucked once, after all." He'd finally managed to penetrate her stubbornness. Cynthia fell silent, her brow furrowed in thought.

"You would not hand a flower to a . . . Actually, perhaps it is more of a jewel. Because you would not place a priceless jewel in the hand of a passing friend. You'd keep that jewel safe and hidden until your marriage."

"Because my husband must like jewels?"

"Precisely." Lancaster nodded again and slapped his hands against his thighs. "Right then." He pushed to his feet and rolled his shoulders. "Keep that hood up, just in case. Now let's find your treasure."

Chapter 10

A jewel? Her virtue was a jewel?

Cynthia watched Nick's back as he descended the trail in front of her. She hadn't known what to say to that ridiculousness, and she still didn't. He'd seemed quite pleased with his platitudes.

But his words were in vain. That flower had been plucked long before.

Or, if it was a *jewel,* she'd snuck it carelessly into the pocket of a man who certainly hadn't considered it precious. Perhaps her jewel had been made of shoddy paste.

A laugh snuck up on her and escaped loudly enough to draw Nick's attention. Coughing into her hand, Cyn waved him on, determined not to hurt his feelings. If he thought his less-than-poetic speech had been profound, there was no point in setting him aright.

He was a sweet, thoughtful man. It was no wonder she'd once loved him.

Oddly though, his sweetness did not seem to extend to his lovemaking. He might be thoughtful, but he was certainly not gentle.

Cynthia ran a hand across her forehead and wondered why this didn't disturb her. Her first lover hadn't been gentle either, but for some reason Nick's rough hands excited her into a strange bundle of shaking nerves.

Well, she didn't know much about it. Likely, they were all the same. But Nick wasn't as large as James had been, and the difference in size could only recommend him. With Nick it would be easier. *Better.*

"Nick," she called as he reached the sand of the beach and paused.

He held up a hand and knelt down.

Puzzled, she hurried to catch up. "What is it?"

"Hoof prints."

She skidded to a halt, her heart turning over in alarm. "Are you sure?" But she could see them herself now, clear in the dry sand, and even clearer at the water's edge.

"These are fresh, Cyn." He stood and stepped farther out onto the sand to peer down the beach. "Stay there."

She backed up until her shoulders touched rock and watched as Nick strode straight out into the water to get a better view. Before the water could reach the top of his boots, he turned and surveyed the coast.

"I don't see anything, but there's only one set of prints here. Whoever he is, I don't think he's come back yet. We'd better go."

"He might have only ridden to the next trail."

Nick stared down the beach, eyes narrowed. "It's not worth taking the chance."

"But we're going the other way, and a rider couldn't make it past that outcropping. We'll be fine."

He turned his narrowed eyes on her. "I don't like it."

"As usual." She set off toward the north, confident he'd follow. Unsure as he was about this search, she could tell he was enjoying the adventure of it. He'd taken to whistling as they walked. But there was no whistling behind her today. They both ran.

Sand sprayed up her legs with each step. The faster they ran, the more likely it seemed that someone chased after them. Fear spread through her.

With her heart beating so hard, it seemed to take only seconds to get to the outcropping, and her legs lifted her easily up the rocks. Nick was right behind her. As soon as she made it to the far side, Cynthia dropped to her knees in the sand and gulped for air.

"Good God," Nick gasped. "I believe you're faster than I."

"It's that . . . civilized . . . London lifestyle."

"Mm. Too many biscuits with my tea."

"I was thinking more of . . . brandy and whores."

Nick smiled. "I was too."

It took her a moment. "Biscuits," she murmured and then collapsed in laughter.

He grinned so widely she could see his back teeth.

"You're doing a terrible job of preserving my delicate sensibilities, milord."

"Well, if you're saucy enough to speak of whores, there's not much I can do for you."

"True." She was still laughing as he helped her to her feet, but she noticed the way he glanced at her mouth, as if all his earlier words had been futile protests against his true desires. His smile wavered for only a brief moment before springing back to full life.

When they began to stroll, Nick kept hold of her hand, centering Cynthia's whole world on their clasped fingers. It felt like spring today, and she imagined she and Nick were out for a romantic stroll.

If she were bold, she might slip off her boots and stockings and cool her feet in a shallow wave. Viscount Lancaster would try to hide the way he stared at her feet, waiting impatiently for glimpses of her ankles. His admiration would make her bold, and she might occasionally lift her skirts high enough to show off the curve of her calves. He'd be overcome with passion and stop her right in the wake of a wave to declare his love.

"Bollocks," Nick said, startling her so much that she stumbled over her own feet. "Sorry," he muttered. "Boots are full of water."

He might not have been mocking her daydream, but somebody should. What utter bollocks to descend back into the self-same fantasies she'd had as a child. Delusions that Nick would love her and they'd ride off into the sunset together.

Well, Nick wasn't free to love her. And she couldn't ride a damned horse at any rate. But she would take what she could and be satisfied with that.

"Do you want to stop?" she asked him.

"No, we're almost there. And I fear if I take them off they might not go on again." He squeezed her hand briefly and then let go, leaving her skin tingling with grief.

"Ah, here's the infamous spot of my early demise."

"Don't even joke about that," she scolded, smacking his arm as hard as she could. "I really thought you might have been dead."

He winked, but that didn't stop the horrible flutter in her stomach. He'd hit the sand so hard, she still couldn't believe that he was fine. She hurried past the spot, and they rounded a short outcropping that didn't quite reach the water.

"Oh, look at this," Nick said.

Cynthia stopped to stare. The land curved in here, creating a small horseshoe-shaped cove. But instead of being filled with water, it was flat sand broken up by piles of boulders.

"I remember this place," Nick said, turning in a slow circle. "Close to the full moon, it fills with water at high tide. Do you remember?"

"I do," she answered. Of course she remembered. She'd been here the whole time.

While he looked around, she began a careful study of the cliffs around them. An hour later, she collapsed into a defeated lump on the sand and threw an arm over her eyes. "There's nothing here."

"I know. We should head home soon or you'll be burned."

"I don't care."

"I know that too." He chuckled. "But considering your foul tongue and awful temperament, you've only your fine skin to recommend you. Best to protect it."

"Scoundrel," she muttered. The pleasant weather and Nick's good mood had begun to annoy her. Was gloominess too much to ask?

"I should have brought . . ."

When his silence drew out, Cynthia lifted her arm to find him staring off into the distance, head cocked at a slight angle. "What is it?"

"I thought I heard something."

She held her breath, straining to hear. And then it came again. The clink of metal on metal. Nick's head jerked up, his gaze locking on the tops of the cliffs on the far side of the little cove.

"A rider."

When the wind brought the sound of a horse's snort, she jumped to her feet and looked frantically around. The largest boulders were too far away to reach quickly. There was nowhere to hide.

"Over there," Nick bit out, pushing her toward the pile of rocks closest to them. "Pull the cloak over you and curl up as tightly as possible."

The largest of the rocks was perhaps two feet wide. She knelt beside it, though she nearly tripped over her skirt when she saw that Nick had removed his coat and started unbuttoning his shirt.

"What are you doing?"

"Going for a swim. Now get down."

She did as he instructed, tucking the gray cloak under her knees and pulling the hood fully over her head. She curled into a ball, and barely squeaked when something landed on her back.

"I'm going to pile my clothes on you. Do not move."

She felt a lighter thump of weight on her back. And then another and another. A few moments passed, and then the sound of churning water filled the tiny woolen cave she'd made. She thought there might have been a horrified curse mixed in with the splashes as well.

Spring day or not, the water was undoubtedly cold.

Though she held as still as possible, her heart thudded so hard that she was sure her whole body must be jumping in time with her pulse. Her neck began to ache almost immediately, but she kept her forehead pressed tight to her knees. The sound of his splashing grew more distant. All she could hear now was her own breath blasting against the sand.

Time ticked by. Sweat trickled down her temple. She thought she heard that clink of metal again, closer this time, but it could have been her imagination, weaving danger from threads of fear.

Her thighs began to shake. Sand dug into her fists, scraping her skin until she thought she might risk everything just to shift an inch.

It seemed half the day had passed before she heard the swish of Nick returning. "He's gone," he called in a hushed tone.

She popped her head up and gasped for breath. But the divinely fresh air froze in her throat.

Nick was still two feet deep in water. And he was totally naked. The skin of his chest was paler than his arms. And his scar stood out a dull pink against his neck. Her eyes skipped over the damaged flesh and followed the dusting of golden hair over his wide chest. His body narrowed at his waist and hips, and his muscled thighs were rough with hair.

As was the area around his sex.

She stared, taking him in.

"I couldn't see him clearly," Nick muttered, gaze still locked on the cliffs above. When his eyes fell to her, he cursed and his hands flew to cover his private bits.

"Christ, Cyn. Don't look at me."

"I've already seen you naked," she said, easing up to a sitting position as her back screamed its outrage.

"But not like this! I'm not . . . I'm not at my best. The cold water . . . You don't understand."

No, he certainly *wasn't* at his best. He was even smaller than he'd been that first night. She just shrugged.

"Close your eyes, damn it, and let me get dressed. It's damned cold in there."

His lips did look a bit blue. Cynthia turned and faced the rocks.

"Thank you," he snapped. She heard the sound of fabric being shaken and his grumbling as well. "Remind me to bring along a fishing pole next time."

"That was a good idea," Cynthia offered. "Going for a swim."

"I figured if it was Bram, he'd be suspicious of me just wandering the beach on foot."

Her eyes flickered up. "Do you think it was Bram?"

"Maybe." He sat on the rock behind her. His back brushed her shoulder. "All I could make out was a man on horseback. He was neither slim nor portly. Didn't seem old. But he did stand in his stirrups and watch me for a long time."

"Perhaps he only liked the view."

Nick shot her a dark look. "We need to get home. Now." His teeth chattered over the words.

"Why don't we wait for you to warm first?"

He tugged his boots on with shaking hands. "I'll warm faster if I'm moving. And we'll need the day to come up with a new plan. Your days of wandering the beach are over."

"I won't be brushed aside like a child," she complained for the fourth time. Nick just kept walking, head down. He'd stopped shaking anyway, though it had taken a while. They were only yards from the front door of Cantry Manor.

"Hurry," he urged, and she did, but her legs were starting to ache from the fast pace he set.

"You can't dictate to me."

"I most certainly can." He rushed up the steps and

tugged open the door to wave her through. Once they were safely inside, he slammed the big wooden door and kept moving, brushing past her to head toward the kitchen. "We'll discuss this after a dram of whisky. My b—, er, my guts are still frozen."

She wanted to push him and scream and argue, but instead she bit her tongue. She could wait till he'd had a glass of whisky. Hell, she could use one herself.

So Cynthia pushed back the hood of her cloak and rushed after Nick. And almost immediately came to a rocking halt beside him in the door of the kitchen.

"Oh, no," she whispered at the sight of Mrs. Pell. Standing next to Adam.

He was backing out the narrow door, the housekeeper's hand on his chest providing the momentum. Mrs. Pell's knuckles turned white with the pressure, but Adam had ceased to move.

His eyes locked on Cynthia. His mouth opened in an "O" of shock, transforming him from a young man of twelve to the five-year-old he'd once been. "Miss Merrithorpe?" he squeaked.

They all stood there, silent. A frozen quartet of pale, stunned faces. The fire crackled. The wind blew the door open another inch. And still they didn't move.

Cynthia decided there was only one thing to do. "Ooo," she moaned, undulating her voice in a spooky vibration. She tugged the hood up and moaned again. "Oooooo!"

Though she elbowed Nick, he only gawked at her and edged away. Following him, she wailed in his direction and nudged him again, raising her eyebrows meaningfully toward Adam. Nick frowned and shook his head. She jerked her chin in Adam's direction and glared at Nick until he finally rolled his eyes and dropped his crossed arms.

"Oh, Lord help us!" he cried out with half-hearted enthusiasm. "It's the ghost of Cynthia Merrithorpe!"

"Wooo-o-o," she answered, waving her arms in a slow swimming motion, expanding the cloak around her.

"Her spirit has followed me from the sea!" Nick flung one arm over his forehead and stumbled back.

Cynthia glanced toward Adam to find him still frozen in the same spot, though his brow had fallen from shock to confusion.

"Leave now," she howled. "Or I'll drag you to my watery grave!"

Adam shook his head. "Miss Merrithorpe, is it really you?"

"Yes, 'tis I! The ghost of Cynthia Merrithooorpe."

The boy frowned and cocked his head.

Nick dropped his arms. "Oh, for God's sake, Cyn. Stop making a fool of yourself. He can see you're not dead."

Disgusted, she planted her fists on her hips and spun toward Nick. "Damn you, I almost had him convinced."

"You're delusional," he snorted.

"*You* weren't even trying!"

"You're alive!" a broken voice squeaked, and they both turned to face Adam and his amazed smile.

She crossed the room to put her hands on his shoulders. "Adam, you can't tell a soul." Whatever else she'd been about to say was cut off by the sudden vise of his arms squeezing her ribs. Skinny he might be, but his arms were already strengthened from years of hard work. She hugged him back briefly before trying to extricate herself.

"Don't break her back, boy," Nick called. "She's only just risen from an untimely death."

He finally let her go, then stood beaming up at her. "You look right good."

"Thank you. But you can't tell anyone, understand?"

"Sure I do!" he answered, then began to chatter at a nearly impossible speed. Cynthia heard the word "ghost" and "spirit" several times, along with the names Tommy and Simon and something about old Mr. Doddy.

She met Nick's eyes and watched them cloud with worry. Finally, Nick smiled and walked over to clap a hand on the boy's shoulder.

"Well, Adam, we could use more help around here. We had to let the maids go for obvious reasons. Do you think your mam would allow you to move in here with us for a week or two? Now that you know our secret, I'm sure Mrs. Pell could make room somewhere."

Adam brightened even more. "There's a second room over the stables!"

"Wonderful idea. Perhaps my coachman might even teach you a few basics of caring for horses while you're here." Nick glanced out the door. "He is still here, is he not?"

"Oh, sure he is," Adam said. "Though he's spent a few afternoons at the alehouse."

"Excellent. Best to keep him occupied as well, then. A splendid solution all around."

"I'll run home and tell my mam!"

Nick's grip stopped his lunge for the door. "Not a word, Adam. Is that clear?"

"Yes, sir." And then the boy was gone, sprinting out the door and down the path before Cynthia could so much as blink.

"She won't like it," Mrs. Pell murmured. "Adam's her youngest. She's a mite protective."

Nick glanced toward the fire that roared in the hearth, his shoulders slumping. "Right then. I'd better speak to her myself. I don't think that boy could keep his mouth shut for more than one full day."

"Nick, you don't have to—" Cyn started, but he just waved a farewell and set off for the village. His boots squished faintly as he walked.

Cynthia watched him go and wondered if this grand plan of hers was about to come to a spectacular end.

Chapter 11

The brush eased gently through Cynthia's hair as Mrs. Pell searched for tangles. Once she'd worked through all the knots the wind had tied in the strands, she brushed more firmly.

"Ah, that feels like heaven," Cynthia sighed.

"I've finished the dress. Would you like to wear it for dinner?"

Her heart jumped with excitement. "Are you kidding? Do you know how sick and tired I am of that old gown?" She clapped her hands at the thought of the new dress. Not that it was new. It was simply a second-hand frock Mrs. Pell had bought to alter for Cynthia. It had been far too large as Mrs. Pell had been forced to purchase something that might have been altered to fit her, but Cynthia didn't care about a perfect fit. She simply wanted something else to wear.

"Can I see it now?"

"Just a moment." Her quick fingers pulled Cynthia's hair into a braid high on her head, then coiled and pinned it neatly on her crown. Strangely, she then paused to work a few tendrils loose at Cyn's temples.

"What are you doing?"

"Making you look pretty," she murmured, stepping back a foot to look over the work she'd done.

"Why?"

"Well, you've a new dress, haven't you?"

Cynthia couldn't argue with that logic, so she only touched a careful hand to her hair and wondered if she really did look pretty.

When Mrs. Pell strolled to the wardrobe and pulled out the dress, Cynthia ceased to care about her hair.

The dress was beautiful. Oh, it was no tulle ball gown. In fact, it wasn't anything she would have considered beautiful a year ago. No frills or lace or decorative lines. But the pine color glowed with depth. And the curve of the neckline promised to show off her collarbone at least, if not any hint of cleavage.

"It's beautiful," she breathed.

"Oh, hush. 'Tis naught more than any simple woman would wear to church."

"It's so . . . green."

"And you've been wearing gray for too long, it seems. Out of that rag, now. Though there's no hope but that you'll have to wear it again tomorrow. The new one won't do for crawling through sand. Now turn 'round."

Cynthia stared at the fine wool draped over the bedstead as Mrs. Pell worked at the hooks of the old dress.

"What happened between you and Lord Lancaster this morning?"

"What do you mean?"

"In the servants' hall."

Her blood skidded to a halt in her veins. "Oh, that? We were hiding. Together. Nothing more. Just hiding."

"Nothing more, eh? Well, you must've had an awful time of it in the dark then."

Cynthia hesitated. "How so?"

"Why, your mouth was all pink and swollen. I daresay you banged into the wall two or three times. Awkward place to hit your face though. Poor thing."

Trying her best to think as Mrs. Pell tugged the dress down her arms, Cynthia held herself still. She breathed in and breathed out and told herself not to worry.

Mrs. Pell cleared her throat. "You know, if his lordship takes your virtue, he'd likely marry you."

"Pardon?" The word nearly choked her, it leapt so quickly from her mouth.

"He's an honorable man. He always has been."

"What, *exactly,* are you suggesting?"

"That you follow the natural course of events and lie with him."

"Mrs. Pell!"

The housekeeper shook out the gray dress with a snap. "Oh, don't 'Mrs. Pell' me. You think I don't know what you two were doing in the dark?"

"We were kissing!"

"And you both clearly enjoyed it."

"I . . ." She watched as the woman casually gathered up the new dress and brought it over. Even as flummoxed as she was, Cynthia still couldn't keep from sliding a hungry gaze over the soft waves of green fabric. "I hate to disabuse you of your ridiculous imaginings, but perhaps you didn't see the way he bolted out of there like a man chased by an angry boar."

Mrs. Pell eased the dress over Cyn's head. "If he's afraid of his feelings for you, it only goes to show how strong they are."

"You're mad." The dress began to tighten around her as Mrs. Pell fastened the hooks. "He couldn't marry me regardless." Her stomach flinched at her own words.

"Men have done stranger things."

"As if I'd want to ruin his whole family by tricking him into matrimony."

The housekeeper sniffed. "Fine then. 'Twas only an idea."

"A fairly shocking one, I'd say."

Mrs. Pell seemed unmoved by her outrage. "I was a young woman once too, you know. I've been tempted to the occasional roll in the hay. Some of them even when I wasn't so young."

That distracted Cyn. "With who?"

"There was once a rather handsome stable master employed at Cantry Manor."

"Took him for a ride, did you?" Cyn giggled before it occurred to her just who the stable master had been. "Old Mister Thurgood?" she squeaked, trying to imagine the appeal of the gruff man with the gray beard.

"His name was John. And he wasn't so old. No, he wasn't old at all, missy. Now then. Let's sneak into his lordship's room so you can see yourself."

Swimming through new images of Mr. Thurgood that she didn't care for, Cynthia let herself be pulled into Nick's room.

Nick.

In the space of a few hours' time, both he and Mrs. Pell had spoken of her virginity as it related to marriage. Was that the only obstacle to this seduction? Her nonexistent maidenhead?

If she told him the truth, perhaps he'd indulge her curiosity. Or perhaps he'd recoil in horror at her slatternly nature and demand she cease to disgrace his good home with her soiled presence.

It seemed unlikely, but stranger things had happened in her life. One couldn't expect too much from gentlemen, she'd found.

"There," Mrs. Pell said, brushing fussily at Cyn's shoulder. "The fit seems good."

Turning her mind from her thoughts, Cynthia raised her gaze, caught sight of herself in the mirror, and gasped. "It's perfect!"

Mrs. Pell beamed over her shoulder.

The deep green set off Cyn's pale skin, transforming it from plain white to soft pearl. Her dark hair looked darker. Her lips more red. And the neckline showed off her shoulders as well as her collarbone.

A boot fall alerted her to a new presence just before Nick's voice filled the room. "Oh," he said. "I apologize. I didn't know you were in my chambers."

Well, it wasn't quite silver tulle floating down a staircase, but Cynthia smiled, took a deep breath, and turned to face Nicholas Cantry.

Nick tripped over the threshold of the door, despite that there was no discernible difference in the height of the floorboards. Cynthia, or some strangely mature version of Cynthia, lost her smile and frowned at him.

"Well, hullo," he babbled. "Got a new dress?"

"Yes," she answered.

They stared at each other. It wasn't just the dress, somehow. Her hair looked different. Softer and more sensual. Her neck seemed longer and her shoulders more . . . bare.

Mrs. Pell broke the silence. "I've got a pudding to check," she called as she bustled out of the room.

Nick nodded. A few moments later he found that he was still standing there, nodding blankly at Cynthia. He smiled brightly to cover his confusion. "You must be relieved to have a new frock."

"I am, yes." She twined her fingers together in front of her hips, drawing Nick's eye. "I'm sorry we took over your room. It was the mirror we were after."

"I understand."

Strangely, Cynthia seemed to have grown a pair of hips. Or was it her waist that had been missing in that oversized dress? A puzzle worth pondering for interesting amounts of time.

"All right," she murmured. "I'll leave you be."

"No! Wait."

She jumped a little at his sharp tone, so Lancaster forced his smile wider.

"I wanted to speak with you. About the treasure hunt. Our treasure hunt." She arched a doubtful eyebrow, so he hurried on before she could interrupt. "I think I should take a look at the journal. Give it a fresh eye."

"That's not necessary."

"I didn't say it was necessary, but I think it will help."

Cynthia folded her arms and set her jaw.

"Cyn, let me help. You said we were a team, didn't you? Yet I'm feeling strangely like a pack mule."

"You're more than a pack mule."

He gave her a disappointed frown. Cynthia tapped her foot. Her bare foot. Tipped with lovely pink toes.

"You must promise you won't take the journal and go off on your own. This is *my* treasure hunt, Nick."

Nodding, Lancaster studied the arch of the bones of her foot.

"Oh, fine," she huffed. "Just read it."

"Hm?" He watched her walk to her room, bare feet padding, new hips swaying.

"Come on."

"Right." He followed the view of her hips into the smaller room.

Cynthia slumped into a chair and opened a drawer in her desk. "Here it is."

"Thank you." The cover of the diary lay rough against his palm when he grasped it. He didn't know what to say now. Their conversation was over, but he didn't want to leave.

Just as she was closing the drawer, Lancaster spotted what had lain beneath the journal. "Say, what's that? Another drawing?" He reached toward it and Cynthia nearly slammed the drawer shut on his fingers. "Hey!"

"It's nothing," she snapped. And she was right, of course. Just another crude drawing by a young boy. But it was something to speak of, all the same.

"Looks like that habit of spying on nude bathers runs in your family."

"Pardon me?" she barked.

"Your great-uncle. It looked like a drawing of a nude woman in the sea. Or a nude man. I couldn't quite tell because the waves come up to her, or his, waist. And the rest of it was, well . . . indistinguishable." Nipples came in both kinds, after all. And the figure's hair had been rather *seaweedy* in appearance. A mermaid, perhaps.

"I think it was a man," she grumbled.

"I'm not sure. The shoulders were rather wide, but

that's likely just a problem with the proportions. I remember what I thought about at age eleven and it had a lot to do with unclothed females."

"You can leave now."

Well, perhaps that hadn't been the right topic of conversation. Nick very slowly and reluctantly turned and plodded out of the room. But he left the door open just in case she got the urge to follow.

He had the journal anyway. That was what he'd come for, but strangely, his hands felt empty as he dropped into a seat next to the fire and stared balefully at the cover. A faint trace of the name "Edward" ghosted across the upper corner, though it seemed to fade the harder he looked.

He ran a finger over the name before carefully turning back the cover. "Edward Merrithorpe," the first page read. "Spring, 1797." Strange to think that members of Cyn's family had been canvassing these cliffs, searching out nudity for decades. Centuries, perhaps.

The first few pages seemed to be solely devoted to the lambing of 1797, followed quickly by the excitement of shearing season. Edward Merrithorpe, as the son of a conscientious landowner, had been expected to learn all there was to know about owning and breeding sheep, and he thoroughly enjoyed the education. The boy was a gifted storyteller, painting a picture that Lancaster recognized from his own childhood. Despite that the boy hadn't yet mentioned the cliffs thirty pages into the journal, Lancaster found himself spellbound by the descriptions of Edward's world.

"Nick?" Cynthia's voice shocked him so much that he dropped the book in his lap. She stood only five feet from him, one hand clasped around the opposite wrist.

"I haven't found anything yet, I'm afraid. Though your great-uncle was a far better writer than he was an artist. A natural storyteller."

She shifted her feet against the wood, and he saw with some disappointment that she'd slipped on thick stockings.

"Would you like to keep me company until dinner?" When he gestured toward the chair opposite his, Cyn nodded and sat down, tucking her feet beneath her. Lancaster picked up the book and tried his best to get back to the narrative, but he found himself sneaking constant glances at her face to see if she watched him or the fire. So far, she'd only looked at the fire.

He crossed his legs and tried to look serious as he read the same line for the third time.

> *Rain has flooded the north field. One ewe drowned and now her lamb has been killed. I found an excuse to avoid the butchering, though father didn't notice He was—*

"There is something I wished to tell you," Cynthia murmured, relieving him of his pretence of reading.

He closed the book quickly and set it on the narrow table to his left. "What is it?"

"Our earlier discussion . . ." She paused to brush a stray thread from the skirt of her new dress. "I wanted to make something clear."

A blush touched her cheeks. Or perhaps the fire was too warm. He dipped his gaze down to her chest to see how low the pink extended.

"As far as the garden goes," she murmured, "my jewel was already plucked."

Yes, the flush spread down her neck, all the way to

her chest. "Pardon?" He cleared his throat. "A garden? I believe you're mixing metaphors."

"I thought you preferred them thoroughly stirred," she snapped, her voice crackling with annoyance.

Lancaster rolled his shoulders and tried to take his mind off her pinkening skin. "I'm sorry. What are you saying?"

"Nick, my flower has already been plucked. So it's not something you need concern yourself over."

"Your flower . . . ?" The metaphors were trying hard to explain themselves, but Cynthia couldn't mean what he thought she meant.

She took a long, deep breath. "I'm not a maiden anymore, Nick."

"You . . ." Her words were vague for a few precious seconds before the meaning hit him squarely between the eyes. Cynthia wasn't a virgin. Her skin wasn't the only thing that looked red to him now. The whole room had gone scarlet.

He jerked to his feet. "I'll kill him."

"Who?" She watched him with round eyes.

"Richmond. I'll shoot him through the gut as I should've done years ago."

"It wasn't Richmond."

"That bastard doesn't deserve a bullet through the head."

"Nick, it wasn't him!"

He paused in the act of pulling his fist back to give the wall a good beating, then swung back to look at Cynthia. "Of course it was him."

"No, I'm quite sure it wasn't."

"Bram then. Is that it, Cyn?" He dropped to his knees to meet her eyes. "Did Bram . . . did he hurt you?"

"I told you he never touched me." She waved her

hand dismissively. "It was someone you don't know. That's not the point."

"You're right. It doesn't matter. Whoever it was, I'll kill him. No man who'd take a woman against her will deserves to live. Just—"

"Oh, for God's sake, Nick. I didn't say I was forced. I was quite willing, if you must know the truth."

"But . . ." Perhaps the event had shocked her so much that she couldn't recall the details anymore. Because her words didn't make any sense. Cynthia Merrithorpe was a good girl who lived out in the fresh, clean air of the country. She didn't go to balls and flirt with London rogues who might tempt her into ruin. She wasn't the type to accept one man's hand while clasping another to her bosom.

The clock ticked louder in his ears. His knees began to hurt. "I'm sorry but . . . what do you mean?"

Cynthia sighed. "To use your turn of phrase, I placed a priceless jewel in the hand of a passing friend. Now the important thing is—"

"Who?" he shouted.

Cynthia pulled her chin in and shut her mouth.

"I apologize," he said. "But would you please tell me who it was?"

"Why?"

Why? Because it was only the most important question he'd ever asked her. Cynthia Merrithorpe had made love with some man. With some *other* man. Could she not see how horrifying that was? "Please?" he pleaded.

"He's no one you know," she sighed, slumping in the chair.

"How? I know all the gentlemen in this county. Oh, God, it was Harry Baylor, wasn't it?"

"No! Good Lord, Nick, you're missing the entire point."

"I don't think I am. You gave away your virginity and I'd like to know *why*. And also *who*."

Cynthia stared at him, her eyes unflinching. If he'd expected shame on her part, it seemed he'd be waiting a long time. She looked more irritated than regretful.

"Why?" she repeated. "There were two reasons, I suppose. First, I thought my lack of a maidenhead might deter any unwanted suitors my stepfather foisted on me. Second, if he managed to find a man who would take me, unwilling as I was, at least I would've had my way in one thing. I chose who my first lover was. No one else. Small as that is, it might have been my last free choice."

Her explanation was logical, he supposed, but rather emotionless. "So you were in love with this man?"

"With *James*? No, definitely not."

James, she'd said. *James*. Lancaster felt his nails dig into his palms. His knees screamed in protest, so he finally backed up to his chair and collapsed.

"It was years ago and—"

"It was?" He heard his own voice rise on a note of hope. Not that it should matter when it had happened. But he was very glad it hadn't been last year. Or last month.

"Oh, bollocks. I shouldn't have told you at all. You're as insufferable as the rest of them." Cynthia pushed up from her chair, clearly meaning to flounce from the room, but Lancaster leaned quickly forward and snagged her hand.

"Don't go. I'm sorry. It's just so . . . shocking."

"Well, it's not exactly easy for me to speak of."

"Of course. I mean . . . I'm honored, I suppose,

that you chose me to tell. I'm sure it's been a burden all these years."

"A burden?" she snorted, looking down on him as if he were a simpleton. "You're hardly a priest, Nick. I didn't come to confess. I just wanted to make clear that I'm not a virgin, so there's no good reason we shouldn't be lovers. It's as simple as that."

"What?" He dropped her hand. As simple as that? Was she mad?

"Yes. I have neither a delicate flower nor a priceless jewel to offer the imaginary husband of my future. Your conscience is absolved."

"But . . . so this *James* just caught your fancy and you offered yourself to him? A few years ago you were nothing but a child, Cynthia."

Growling, she threw her hands up in the air. "Why are you so focused on that? Do you even understand what I'm saying?"

"How old is this James?" he demanded, wondering why his voice sounded so loud in his ears.

The skirt of her dress twirled out in a pretty circle when Cynthia spun around. He reached out for her hand again, but it was gone along with the rest of her. Her door slammed before he could even rise to his feet.

What was wrong with her? Wasn't he the one who should be upset?

Outraged now, Nick lunged to his feet and stalked across the room. He jerked open her door and stepped into her chambers. And spied the heel end of Cynthia's boot flying straight for his chest.

Nick squawked and swept an arm out to knock the boot aside. Luckily she had two. She belted the other in his direction, but it flew wide and struck the wall beside him. "What the hell's wrong with you?" he shouted.

"Go away!" she yelled, but he just came closer.

"Not until you tell me why you're throwing boots at me."

She turned her back on him to look for other items to throw. A warming brick sat tucked beneath the foot of the bed, but that seemed excessive.

"Did you expect that I wouldn't be upset by your . . . youthful escapades?"

"Are you a complete imbecile? I just told you we could be lovers, and all you can talk about is that other man!"

Nick stopped in the middle of the room. His arms, upraised to defend himself, fell to his sides. "Oh," he said, eyebrows flying high. "I think I see."

"I didn't tell you just so you could yell at me." She wasn't going to cry. She might be mortified and hurt, but she wouldn't cry.

Nick cleared his throat. "Was I yelling? I apologize." As she watched, his face slowly turned red. "Cynthia," he said, "we can't be lovers."

Her throat tightened. Her heart tripped. "I suppose not. I'm soiled goods now."

His horror wasn't feigned. She watched it fill his eyes before it took over the rest of his face. "That's not what I meant. Not at all."

"Then what?"

"I . . ." His flush deepened, almost as if he were embarrassed. "You're my friend, Cyn. I can't do that with you. You're my *friend*."

She nodded. That was true. It *felt* true. But she

wanted more. "I know. I just wanted to ask more for us. Just for a little while. Just until we both have to go."

Pain flashed over his face like a quick flutter of dark wings. "I'd like more too," he whispered. "But I can't. Not with you."

The pain was hers this time, a flutter of wings, only there seemed to be thousands of those tiny dark birds circling her chest, flying faster and faster. "Not me," she murmured, nodding.

She was not one of those women. Those London women who knew how to dance and flirt and seduce handsome men. She was the kind of woman a man could befriend. She always had been, hadn't she?

She'd fought him 'til now, because she'd been angry and frustrated and a little afraid. But this was something worse, and she couldn't make herself pretend to fight him.

They're not like you, he'd said. She glanced down at her simple country dress and thought of lace and perfume and powder and delicate slippers that would prove useless weapons if thrown at a man's head. Though it nearly killed her, Cynthia tried to smile. "I understand."

Nick lifted his eyes from the floor and shook his head. "No, you couldn't possibly understand, Cyn. And I wouldn't want you to."

As if he were bidding her farewell, Nick lifted his hand and left her alone.

She forced her feet to carry her to the hall door.

Mrs. Pell would need help with dinner and she was good for that, at least.

Chapter 12

"I have it," a deep voice barked, inserting itself into her dream. A nude Nicholas stood in the lapping waves of the sea and smiled at a beautiful woman clothed in silver tulle. The blond lady giggled and fluttered a lace fan against her bosom. When the sunlight caught the iridescent spark of pearl on the handle of the fan, the reflection jumped against Nick's chest.

The lady reached out to trail a polished fingernail over his skin, tracing the dancing lights.

Didn't she know her dress was being ruined in the salt water?

"Cynthia," Nick said, turning back to her. He caught the lady's hand and pulled it up to his mouth to kiss her fingers. "Wake up."

He wanted Cyn to leave them alone, apparently. But she'd be damned if she'd let this woman have him.

"Get up, woman!" A hand grabbed her and yanked her off the beach.

Cynthia sat up and opened her eyes to find Nick jerking his chin out of the way of her forehead.

"I have it." He waved the journal in front of her face.

"I know," she grumbled. "I gave it to you." She pushed his hand away and collapsed back into the bed. She'd tossed and turned for hours last night and wasn't prepared to face the man who'd caused her turmoil.

"You've been searching in the wrong place, Cyn."

She burrowed her head beneath the heavy weight of the pillow.

"Are you even listening?" Though she wrapped her hands around the edges of the pillow in anticipation, Nick still pulled it from her grasp and tossed it to the floor. "You're searching in the wrong place."

"What time is it?"

"Just before dawn. Now look at this."

She heard the rustle of paper and smelled the ancient mildew scent of the journal. When she opened her eyes, she found a blur of faded ink and white paper only an inch from her nose.

"Fine," she groaned. "Just let me sit up." She pushed her arms against the mattress and twisted around. Nick helpfully propped the pillow behind her back and put the book on her lap so that his hands were free to light the lamp.

"See this?" He pointed to a line about halfway down the page.

"'Down the bridle path,'" she read. "I know. I've read it a hundred times."

"Right, but this journal was written in 1797, Cyn."

"And?"

"He must mean the *old* bridle path, not the one we're using now."

Her heart finally stuttered to a waking state. "What old bridle path?"

"The one on the other side of the village. You can

follow it all the way to the old breakwater, remember?
I forgot you never rode as a child, but Timothy and I
used to take it at least once a week."

"The one past the town," she murmured. A surge
of anticipation swelled through her belly. "Nick . . .
Nick! Oh, mercy, you might be right!"

"I know." He beamed at her like a little boy proud
of his ciphering skills.

Despite her exhaustion, despite the pain she felt at
being near him, Cynthia grinned. He was as adorable
as a puppy. And just as messy. Still wearing the clothes
he'd worn to dinner, he looked either to have slept
in them or planted himself in a chair to read all night.
She had her suspicions. He smelled a bit strongly
of wine.

"We'll start today," she said, clapping her hands in
excitement.

Nick cringed. "I'd like to forbid you from coming."

"But—"

"It's not safe. That Bram fellow might be hanging
about."

"You don't even know that it was him!"

He tilted his head toward her. "True. That's why
I'm going into the village this afternoon. But what I
was going to say before you interrupted is if you insist
on going to the cliffs with me, we'll need to go now,
before the sun rises. We'll take the carriage to the
head of the trail, and try to make the most of one or
two hours' work. Does that sound reasonable?"

"Reasonable?" Not quite able to hold back a squeal,
Cynthia vaulted up and threw her arms around Nick's
neck. "Thank you."

"My." His hands folded around her for a brief

moment. Too brief. "Get dressed now. I'll send Mrs. Pell to help after I wake my coachman."

"All right." Well, he'd effectively taken her mind off her mortification, at any rate. All her heavy lethargy was gone, replaced by the excitement of the hunt. And it didn't hurt that she could still feel the warm imprint of Nick's hands on her back even as the door closed behind him.

The sun had disappeared behind rain clouds in the first hour of their search. They should have returned then, but Cynthia had insisted on continuing. Not that Lancaster could blame her. This old path offered a whole new landscape, one riddled with holes and caves.

Cynthia was giddy. She was giddy even now, soaking wet from an hour spent hunting for treasure in the rain. Now she formed her own puddle on the carriage seat as they slowly rolled back toward Cantry Manor.

Lancaster watched a shiver work its way up her body as she pulled the carriage robe closer around her and beamed at him.

"It's got to be there, Nick."

He smiled at the reckless hope in her voice. "Never count your chickens before they've hatched."

"It's there. All those caves . . . You're so very, very clever."

"Really? You're the only one who's ever recognized that."

"I'm exceptionally perceptive then."

"Obviously."

Cynthia giggled, reminding him of how sweet and feminine she'd looked the night before. Then he remembered that stricken look when he'd rejected her, and Nicholas turned to watch the gray damp through the window.

"What will you do with your half?" she asked.

He threw her a questioning look.

"Your half of the gold."

"We'd better see how much it is first."

Cynthia shrugged her wet shoulders. "You are all doom and gloom today."

"Yes, it's strange to be the serious one. I'm not sure I like it."

"I'm certain I'll be in a foul mood again soon enough. Enjoy the novelty."

Her eyes sparkled with amusement, and Lancaster wanted to draw closer. To be part of her joy. Thankfully the carriage lurched to a halt before he could do anything stupid.

"Your cloak," he murmured, as he shoved open the door before Jackson could descend.

Cynthia pulled her sodden hood back over her head and tugged it low to cover her face.

"Take the blanket too." He handed her down and watched her scurry toward the kitchen door, her identity safely concealed. His coachman was under the impression that he'd been carrying Mrs. Pell around, and he'd been helped along by a very generous gift of whisky from his employer.

The man dropped heavily to the ground and closed the carriage door.

"Thank you for waiting so patiently in the rain, Jackson. I'll be heading to the village after lunch. You are free until then."

"Thank ye, milord." Jackson touched his hat and glanced toward the door. "Mrs. Pell, eh?"

"I'm sorry?"

The coachman listed slightly to the left before over-correcting himself right into the side of the carriage. "A bit long in the tooth," Jackson explained. "But a man likes a bit of soft flesh in his hands, don't 'e? Nothing wrong with that."

"Er . . ." Lancaster didn't want to impugn Mrs. Pell's reputation, but what other explanation could he offer for a few secluded hours on the beach with his housekeeper?

"Nothing wrong with that at all," Jackson boomed, punctuating his statement with a firm pat on his master's back. After providing the lubricant to loosen him up, Lancaster really couldn't fault the man for his insubordination.

"See to the horses, Jackson. Better ask Adam to help. He needs the training."

"Right-o, yer lordship."

Lancaster rolled his eyes and headed for shelter. He needed to dry off and warm up—again—and get some food in his belly before heading to the village. Unless the residents had changed greatly in the past decade, Lancaster was certain they'd be happy to speak of a new visitor and his traveling habits, though they might expect a friendly pint of ale in return.

"Mrs. Pell," he called as he stepped into the warm kitchen. "May I get—"

"She's gone out."

He looked up to find Cynthia filling a teapot with steaming water. She'd formed a new puddle on the floor next to the hearth.

"Gone where?"

Cynthia tilted her head toward the long kitchen table. A tiny scrap of paper lay bright against the golden wood. "Off to buy beef. Though I doubt she'll walk back in this rain. If I had to guess, I'd say she and Mrs. Painter are holed up in the Painter cottage, gossiping about their friends and sharing a dose of medicinal sherry."

"Oh."

"But I've made tea. Thankfully, she left a pot boiling."

"Wonderful." Strange, but somehow this felt very odd, knowing they were here alone together. What a completely illogical thought. They'd been alone together all day on the beach. They'd been alone on her *bed* this morning.

Still, the intimacy of this new situation pressed on him with the weight of an approaching storm.

Cynthia didn't seem affected. She moved cheerfully through the motions of making tea. The dress clung heavily to her hips.

"I should change," he announced and broke for the hall. She didn't stop him, and he breathed a sigh of relief at the top of the stairs.

His intentions were good. Honorable, even. No matter how much he wanted to make love to Cynthia Merrithorpe, he couldn't do it.

But Cynthia was wreaking havoc with his resolve.

I want more for us, she'd offered so simply. The honesty of that would have touched him even if his heart hadn't already been shaking with need. He wanted more too. More for himself and more for Cynthia, and more for them *together*. He could see it now, the promise of what might have been. A friendship suddenly sparked with lust. A happy kind of love that would take them quickly and last forever.

He pulled loose the cloth that had grown too tight around his neck, then shrugged out of his coat.

Maybe she was right about Imogene. Maybe he didn't have to marry her. But there was no way in the word he could marry Cynthia. If he did, he would change his family's course in history.

They'd become members of the gently impoverished. His brother and sister would be forced into the very choice Lancaster was trying to avoid. Marry for fortune or live a life of shabbiness. He couldn't shirk that duty only to see it placed on his siblings' backs. Besides, he was the only one who could marry up and pull them all along behind.

Marrying Cynthia wasn't an option.

But if given the chance, would he? Would he subject her to a lifetime of nights in his bed?

He jerked his wet shirt over his head and glanced at the mattress on the other side of his chambers.

She wasn't a virgin. Perhaps a lifetime was too much to ask, but what about one night? He could picture her there, arching herself into his touch, just as she'd done the day before. She'd liked that, and she would like it again. And when he—

A staccato knock dropped into his fantasy and freed a surge of anger for his own thoughts. "Cracked bastard," he muttered. The knock came again.

"I've brought your tea!" Cynthia called.

Lancaster slipped into his dressing robe and moved warily to open the door. He felt exposed, both by his state of undress and the tenor of his thoughts. But Cynthia's smile was wide and cheerful, and he had no excuse to keep her out.

She hurried past him to set the tray on the table. He could do nothing but accept the cup she offered and murmur his thanks. Cynthia stood in front of the fire and sipped her tea, and his fear began to retreat like the receding tide. It was probably helped along by the strong bite of brandy that stung his nose.

"How many cups of *tea* have you had?" he asked.

Cynthia winked. "Only one. This gown is freezing."

He froze, the cup only two inches from his mouth. He looked at her wet dress, wondering why it seemed a suddenly ominous prop in this strange drama.

"I'll need help getting out of it," she said.

Ah. There it was. The tide hadn't retreated at all, it had only drawn up its strength in anticipation of crashing over his head. Again, Cynthia didn't seem to notice his turmoil. She smiled at him, and he felt his mouth smile back. He appeared perfectly normal, it seemed, as his mind spun 'round and 'round the prospect of helping Cynthia undress.

His willpower was a brittle plank, riddled with cracks and holes, and creaking beneath the weight of his desire. Now Cyn had decided to leap onto it, full speed.

"Are you quite sure Mrs. Pell isn't back yet? It'll be time to fix luncheon soon."

Cynthia scoffed at his question. "She likely thinks we can handle slicing bread and sausage on our own."

"Mm. Quite."

She held up the teapot and Lancaster looked into his cup and found it empty. She refilled it with a steady hand, and Lancaster politely drank every drop she'd poured.

Heat seeped into his muscles.

"May I change in front of the fire? I don't think I can bear to walk away from it."

"Of course." Of course, she should have the chance to feel the flames glow against her bare skin. To watch the fire lick warm color into her cool flesh. He couldn't deny her that.

"All right, I think I'm warm enough to dare it." She set down her cup, gave him one last smile, and turned her back.

Lancaster stared at her dress, at the long seam that hid the hooks of her gown. He curled his fingers tighter around the cup. Cynthia dipped her head impatiently to the side.

"Right then," he murmured. As he placed the cup carefully on the table, it was as if he watched someone else. Some other man reached forward and eased his fingers beneath the back of her gown. Some dispassionate gentleman unfastened the first hook and felt his knuckles rub her skin.

Cynthia tilted her head forward to give him more access. Soft tendrils of her hair dragged over the back of his hand. He undid the second hook and the third. The material began to part.

When the top of her corset was exposed, Lancaster became part of his body again in a terrifying rush of sensation. His cock was already swelling. The scent of her hair filled his throat. Her skin slid against his fingers, and her spine pressed into his hand every time she drew a breath.

His hands worked their way down the hooks without his permission. When the dress began to gape, Cynthia twisted and wiggled until she freed her arms from the clinging wool. Suddenly there was a whole landscape of skin before him. Her flat shoulder blades. The arch of her neck. Her shoulders curving down to bare arms. Gooseflesh dotted her skin, then spread to every exposed inch.

Lancaster worked faster. Within seconds, the dress fell to the floor in a sodden heap.

Cynthia rolled her shoulders, then twisted her one thin petticoat around to untie it. The damp petticoat was nearly transparent, and once it slipped to the floor, he saw that her chemise was damp as well.

The skin of her bottom showed pale pink past the thin white fabric. Her legs were bare beneath it. She must have left her stockings to dry by the hearth downstairs.

"Nick," she said, turning half toward him with an exasperated eye. "The corset now?"

"Yes," he said, "Of course." Did she not notice the strained rasp in his voice? Apparently not, as she bounced a little on the balls of her feet and rolled her eyes.

That tiny bounce drew his attention back to her corset. Not the fashion of the thing, which was plain and clearly well-used. But the fit.

Perhaps it had been made for someone else. Or perhaps purchased years before. Regardless, it no longer fit. Her breasts spilled above the top, nearly flattened to her chest by the tight edge.

"Turn around then," he murmured, and reached for the ties.

His fingers shook against the ivory ribbons. When he tugged one free, he thought perhaps the whole contraption would part on her next breath, but it stayed tight. He had no choice but to slide his thick fingers along her spine and work the laces loose.

A small groan vibrated from her ribs to his hand. "That feels good."

Yes, it felt good. Her skin was hot here. He slid one slow hand up to her shoulder to hold her steady while he tugged, and then he closed his eyes and imagined holding her steady for another reason.

Eventually, the corset was loose enough, he supposed, because Cyn began to twist and wiggle, working it down over her hips. He let his hand linger on her shoulder as long as he could, then slid it down her arm, a marvel of cool silk flesh.

She shivered and stepped out of the corset. "Thank you so much."

"You're welcome." His words came out a whisper.

"May I borrow a blanket?"

Cynthia shook out her dress as he opened the chest at the foot of his bed and retrieved a blanket of fine red wool. He was sorry to be done with his task, and thankful as hell that she was about to wrap herself up and leave.

He needed her so badly, and it was wrong to want her.

"Here—" he started as he turned to offer the blanket. But the sight of Cynthia stopped him cold.

The nightdress she wore to bed was sturdy and far too large to reveal even a hint of the body beneath. But her shift . . . her shift was a thin veil. Worn to a sheen, damp from the rain, it clung to her breasts and floated down to flirt with her hips. Her nipples were tight pink buds pressed against the sheer fabric, her breasts shockingly full and round.

Cynthia Merrithorpe was a sensual dream.

As if she realized the strength of his thoughts, Cyn crossed her arms over her chest. "Can I have it or did you decide to keep it for yourself?"

"What?" He'd give her anything she wanted.

"The blanket."

"Of course." Aware that he was tempting the beast

inside him and no longer sane enough to care, he crossed the yard of space between them. He let the blanket fall open and settled it over her shoulders. He was too close now. Far too close.

His conscience tumbled over the edge of reason and disappeared from sight.

Lancaster cupped her jaw and looked into her happy eyes. "You are so beautiful."

Those eyes went wide and the happiness blanked to shock. "What?"

"You're beautiful, Cyn." He trailed his fingers along her jaw, all the way to the tender skin just below her ear, watching the contrast of his hand against her fine texture. His body swelled to an ache. So did his heart.

She covered his hand with her own. "Nick?"

"I'm sorry," he breathed and pressed his mouth to hers. She still smelled faintly of rain, as if she were the purest thing in the world. Another reminder that he should leave her be.

Lancaster slid his hand down her neck and lower still. Cynthia didn't move. She didn't even seem to breathe. But when he curved his hand under her breast, she gasped. She was a heavy weight against his palm. He dragged his thumb over her nipple, amazed at the contrast of hard against soft.

Cynthia whimpered.

"You like that?"

She nodded, eyes closed, as he pulled back to look at her.

"You're amazing." Greedy for more, he tugged her chemise low enough to expose her nipple. He traced the deep pink areola with his blunt fingertip and watched it tighten even further, drawing itself up.

"Nick," she whispered.

He traced one more circle, then reached for the gathered neckline of her chemise and pulled it the rest of the way off.

Her nude body yanked his breath from his lungs in a brutal theft.

Yes, her breasts were full, and they only looked larger against the contrast of her slim waist. In perfect balance, her hips flared out, rounding down to the soft curve of her thighs.

Lancaster's mouth watered.

As he watched, her hand moved to cover the dark hair between her legs. He followed the movement, slipping his hand over hers to press her fingers tight to her own body.

"Don't hide," he murmured. "You're so beautiful."

Her mouth opened as her breath came harder.

Lancaster tucked his thumb under her fingers and eased her hand away. The sight of her dark curls twisted his heart into a knot.

And suddenly being with Cynthia didn't feel like a mistake at all.

Chapter 13

The way he watched so closely filled Cynthia with the need to cover herself again. No man had ever seen her nude before. Not Richmond and not even James. She had no idea how she *should* look, so she didn't know what Nick might see.

His fingers trailed down her hip, singing along her skin, and Nick lifted his eyes to her and smiled. Not a charming smile or a jaunty grin, but a genuine joy that reached his eyes.

Sweetness swelled into her blood. This was what she wanted. Peace with him, even if it was momentary.

He'd called her beautiful, so maybe she was. Still, her skin was tingling from the intensity of the exposure, so she finally gave up and pulled him along toward the bed.

She yanked back the covers and slipped beneath them. "Now you," she said once she was covered.

Still smiling, he shook his head in question. "Now me?"

"Your clothing." She pulled the sheet up past her chin to hide her blush. "Take it off."

"Are you sure?" he asked, laughing.

"Very." She liked the way he looked naked. Despite the scars that made her think of things she didn't wish to, his body was fascinating.

Nick's smile faded, and he unknotted his dressing robe and let it part. He still wore his breeches beneath, which was a bit of a disappointment. But when he dropped the robe, she took her time looking over his shoulders and wide chest. She wanted to touch him the way he'd touched her, but that would mean emerging from the shield of the bedcovers. She was cozy there and enjoying the show.

He didn't look away as he reached for the buttons of his breeches, didn't seem to hesitate at all. He very calmly unfastened each button and then slipped off his breeches and drawers in one motion.

When he stood straight again, Cynthia shrieked. Just a little.

"What is it?" Nick glanced back toward the door as if someone else had surprised her.

"You were smaller," she whispered in horror.

"Pardon?"

"Nothing."

Nick frowned. "What's wrong, Cyn?"

"Nothing." There was nothing to be done now. She'd just have to smile and nod and bear it. And she wasn't a virgin anymore. It shouldn't be too bad, really. She'd just assumed it would be *easier* with him. "Everything's fine."

"Can I come in then?"

She lifted the covers slowly enough that he could change his mind if he chose to.

She didn't understand. He hadn't seemed particularly soft that first night she'd seen him in the nude, but there must be degrees of . . . *measurement* to the thing.

"As many naked men as you've seen in your life, I didn't expect you'd be shocked," he muttered as he slipped in beside her. He slid across the sheets and pressed against Cynthia.

"Ah," he murmured, but she was too stunned to even breathe. The whole hot length of his body was pressed into her, burning her, as if in the space of one second she'd become part of him. His hand settled on her belly, fingers spread wide.

"Oh, my."

"You're so soft," he breathed, his lips brushing against her cheek.

Hands still clutching the sheet to her chest, Cynthia turned and kissed him. She felt his fingers press tighter to her belly and then gave herself up to the kiss. She drank him in, consumed him, as his hand began a slow journey.

He cupped one breast, then the other, curved his fingers around her ribs, and dipped his thumb into her navel. He *explored* her, as if he'd wondered about her body. As if he'd anticipated these first few touches.

Because they were still kissing, a moment passed before she realized his hand had left her. Nick freed his arm from the covers and took hold of one of her fists. When he eased her hands down, the blanket slid down too.

Her breasts were exposed, and then her belly.

He lay his arm across her, trapping her tight against him. Her hands bunched the sheet against her pelvis.

"Look at you, Cyn," he breathed just before he lowered his head and closed his lips over her nipple.

His mouth drew at her, even as his tongue rubbed circles, urging startling feelings from deep in her belly. Then his lips parted and it was just his tongue, tracing her nipple, teasing her into a tiny whimper.

He teased like that for long minutes, alternating between light touches and heavy demands, until Cynthia had given up whimpering and was moaning with need.

She'd never felt anything like this before. So needful and hungry. She no longer cared about her worries or his sadness. Her body had taken her over and it would have what it wanted.

Cynthia let go of her death grip on the sheet and pulled her arm free of his hold. She curled her fingers around his upper arm, amazed at the strength in his solid muscles. He was so *male*, looming over her, and yet she felt safe and treasured.

His arm flexed, pushing at her hand. These workings of his body were a new discovery for her senses.

Nick lifted his head and looked at her with heavy-lidded eyes.

She dragged her grip higher, up to his shoulder, then down to marvel at the hair that covered his chest. His eyes followed her, then slowly rose to meet her gaze. The wide pupils looked impossibly black, as if they opened to a well of dark water.

His heart rose to a thunder beneath her palm. And though the hair on his chest was crisp and light and nothing like fur, she couldn't help but think of a panicked animal.

Not understanding what could be wrong, she waited for some reaction, but Nick said nothing. Drawing a soft circle against his skin, she asked, "Does that feel good?"

He closed his eyes, cutting off the strange fear that had crept into her. "Yes," he whispered, just before he drew back.

He turned her then, lifting her shoulder so that she faced away from him. A moment of lonely confusion left her cold, but his body made for an excellent distraction from ugly thoughts. He pressed into her back, matching himself to the hollows and curves of her body.

There was no avoiding the largeness of him in this position. His hard length branded her buttocks, a startling heat even against the rest of his warm skin.

But she couldn't think of that, because Nick wrapped his arms around her and pressed his mouth to her neck. "Are you sure, Cyn?" The words trailed down her shoulder.

"Yes," she answered immediately, even if it wasn't quite the truth. This was Nick, and she wanted all of him she could have. She needed to gather him up into her soul and force these memories to stay forever.

"Yes," she said louder as his hand slid to her sex and stroked there. Whatever this was to Nick, for Cynthia it was a *home,* more real than any she'd had before. This would carry her along the road that lay ahead of her. Through a new life in a strange place among people who did not know her. This memory of Nick would be her home there, whatever else happened.

Pulling her more firmly against him, Nick sucked gently at her neck. His fingers slipped over her in a slow rhythm that made her squirm. Cynthia closed her eyes and tried to catch her breath. It proved an impossible task, even before Nick pushed a finger deep inside her.

Her cry echoed through the room.

"Cyn," he groaned, driving deeper into her.

She arched into him, parting her legs in encouragement. This felt good. Unbelievably good. His hard body against her back only made it more wickedly delicious. She gasped his name and pressed her head back.

His teeth scraped her neck and made her moan. When he pulled his finger from her body, she whimpered in need.

"Shh," he whispered, and suddenly there was pressure as he slid two fingers in.

It was almost too much. Cynthia tried to push away and found that she couldn't move. He slid his fingers out, then slowly pushed them deeper. "Oh, God. *Nick.*"

"Is that good, love?"

Was it *good*? It almost hurt, and yet as the pressure reached toward pain it somehow became something else. Every stroke came closer to unbearable pleasure.

Her body grew more slippery, and the resistance to his fingers was suddenly gone. He slid easily in, and then very slowly out. She didn't want him to go.

"No," she whispered, her sex suddenly empty. This was how she'd felt in the hidden passageway, when he'd suddenly stepped back and left her panting. "Don't stop."

"I won't," he said, even as his wet fingers dragged up her belly.

"Don't!" she protested, but he didn't obey.

His hand slid higher and cupped her breast. Nick kissed down her neck to her shoulder, then sucked her flesh between his teeth as he teased her nipple with his thumb. When he pinched her, she cried out and pushed hard against his manhood.

She could feel the cool touch of wetness on her

nipple, and knew it was from her sex. That seemed terribly improper, somehow, which only made her squirm harder.

"Nick!"

He ignored the pleading in her tone and rolled her nipple between his thumb and forefinger. A coil deep inside her body tightened.

"You can't know how good you feel, Cyn," he murmured. "So warm and soft and right. I wish . . ." He let the words fade away.

When he dragged his hand back down to slip it between her legs, Cynthia pressed the heel of her palm into his wrist to urge him on. Perhaps that decided something for him, because instead of teasing her further, he put his hand on her hip and pushed her around, so that her belly touched the bed. He spread her legs with one knee, then knelt between them.

This was it then. He would have her now.

He crouched over her to kiss her shoulders and her back. The hot weight of his arousal dragged over her bottom.

It was Nick above her this time, so she knew it would be different. Not beautiful or magical perhaps, but better than it had been with James. And yet as he gripped her hips and urged her up to her knees, Cynthia cringed. What if it wasn't different at all?

Lonely horror welled up inside her. She didn't want this with him. Didn't want to feel alone as he rutted at her. Didn't want to feel dirty as he grunted and groaned and spent himself inside her. She'd felt like a used handkerchief after James had finished. Why had she not considered that Nick might leave her feeling exactly the same?

His hand smoothed down her buttocks and Cynthia

cringed. She pressed her hands into the mattress and
stared hard at the scrolls of the headboard, and when
the tips of his fingers touched the most secret part of
her, Cyn felt a tear drop from her eyelashes to vanish
into the rumpled sheets below.

He stroked her again, drawing a slow line along the
seam of her body. When his hand slipped forward, he
touched a spot so sensitive that she jerked against
him. His other hand tightened on her hip as he
rubbed more firmly.

"Oh," she sighed, relaxing just a little. Whatever
else might happen, this was quite lovely.

He shifted behind her, and suddenly something
else rubbed her there. His long arousal slid over that
spot as he rocked against her.

"Oh, my." Perhaps the thing wasn't entirely awful.
It felt rather nice and smooth as it rubbed along her.
Cynthia was shocked to find that she had lost the
desire to brace herself and hold her breath. Instead
she pushed back against him and rocked on her
knees to set the pace of his rubbing a little faster. That
coil inside her made itself known again. "Mm."

Then, quite to her surprise, it was actually *happening*. Nick shifted, and when she pushed back, he was
sliding *into* her instead of along her. There was pressure and stretching, and she would have pulled away
but, strangely enough, Nick was already pulling back.

She was so shocked that she simply froze and
blinked down at her hands. It wasn't until he pushed
forward again and sank deep into her body that the
realization hit her. His sex was inside her, pushing in,
and it felt . . . good. Smooth and sliding as it had been
before, but this time it was tightness too. But no pain.
None at all. She didn't need to hold her breath and

bite her lip and beg him to please stop because she'd changed her mind and . . .

Nick thrust a little harder, and Cynthia gasped in pleasure. The muscles inside her tightened at the shock of it.

"Ah," he gasped. "Cynthia, you . . . You're . . ."

Heat washed over her at his broken words. He thrust harder and faster and it felt better and better.

She wasn't lonely. She was *filled* with him.

He thrust hard and deep and then held himself there, snug inside her. His low gasps echoed through the room. Sweat slicked the skin where their thighs pressed together.

When his breath had calmed a bit, Nick leaned over her and curved one arm around her chest to lift her up to her knees. The other arm curled around her belly and he pressed his hand over the curls of her sex. His chest flush against her back, Nick circled his fingers over that little pearl at the top of her sex, and Cynthia cried out.

"That's it, Cyn," he murmured, lowering his hips before he thrust up high and hard.

"Oh, God," she groaned and spread her knees wider.

"Yes." His fingers teased her as he drove deep. "That's it, isn't it, love? That's what you need."

"Oh, yes," she moaned. This was exactly what she needed, and she'd had no idea. But now she needed it so *much*. Her body was tightening up into one great pulsing pleasure that wanted more and more.

"Please," she begged. "Please, Nick."

He thrust faster. "Say it again. My name. Call me by my name, Cyn."

"Nick." Her belly wound itself tighter. "Nick, you feel so good." And then she couldn't make her mouth form words. She could only scream as the pleasure inside her swelled up and devoured her soul. The world went black and bright at the same time.

She heard Nick cry out her name as he pulled free of her body. Heat splashed against her back and dripped down her bottom. His fingers dug bruises into her flesh and she didn't care in the least.

Cynthia exhaled for a very long time and let her chin fall to rest on Nick's arm. Thank God he still clasped her to his chest, or she would have crumpled into a useless pile of limbs.

It seemed ages before his breath returned to normal. "Cyn, are you all right?"

She nodded, too weary to speak. When his arms eased her down to the bed, she nuzzled her face into the cool pillow with a brand new kind of pleasure. A weakness that made her sigh.

He was quiet behind her for a long time, but she couldn't manage to lift her head to see his expression.

"I'll just . . ." he finally said, then cleared his throat. "Don't move."

No chance of that. She thought she'd only just closed her eyes, but suddenly the bed dipped and a cold cloth touched her back.

"Sorry," he said when she gasped out a little shriek. The towel caressed her lower back and then her buttocks and thighs. "I got you a bit, um . . ."

He finally lay down at her back with a deep sigh. When his arm snuck around her waist, she smiled. This was a better kind of happiness than she'd dreamed.

Lancaster was rather worried about the state of his heart. It had pounded like mad when they'd made love, of course. But it still beat so hard and fast that his chest began to ache. It wasn't quite anxiety, though that was part of it. Mostly, it was an excess of pleasure. Physical pleasure, yes, but something emotional as well.

He'd never felt quite so . . . *connected* during sex. He'd never felt treasured or even valued, because he didn't let women that close.

Over the years, he'd learned how to manipulate his sexual encounters. Unless he was paying a woman specifically to indulge his roughest desires, he made sure his partners weren't aware of his need to control. But these machinations kept him distant. Always removed even in the friendliest of encounters.

He'd manipulated Cynthia in the same way, and that made his gut burn with shame, but somehow he'd felt her joy too. Her joy in *him*.

No one had ever felt joy just to have him near. Desire, yes. And lust and satisfaction and maybe amusement if it was a rare encounter that didn't involve coin. But not joy.

Pressing his forehead to Cynthia's shoulder, he breathed in her skin. He felt almost . . . normal. Almost peaceful. Until Cynthia spoke.

"That wasn't at all what I expected," she sighed.

His heart finally slowed. Actually, it stopped entirely. He held his breath, but Cyn seemed happy to leave it at that. "Oh?" he croaked. "How so?"

"It wasn't anything like my first time."

He pressed his forehead a little more firmly to her back and squeezed his eyes shut. She'd realized. She'd known.

Her first lover had probably laid her down in a field of wildflowers. He'd probably kissed her all over and held her to his bosom and whispered of love and moonlight and stardust.

While Lancaster had taken her from behind like an animal. "I'm sorry," he breathed into her skin.

Cyn laughed. "Sorry? You must be mad. My first time was horrid. This was . . . Well, this was rather spectacular."

He opened his eyes and stared hard at the pale peach skin in his vision. "Really?"

She flipped to her back, forcing him to pull away. "Are you fishing for compliments, Nick? Come now. You're the more experienced one here. Shouldn't you be petting me and telling me I was lovely?"

He couldn't quite believe she was smiling at him. His brain hadn't made the transition from horror to relief yet. "You were lovely," he answered stupidly.

"Thank you." When she laughed, his brain finally caught up with the conversation.

"Why was your first time horrid?"

The smile faded a little. "It just was."

He supposed he should feel glad that her first time had been with someone else. He hadn't been the one to cause her pain. But he didn't like the sadness in her eyes. Lancaster stroked a finger down her cheek. "Because it hurt?"

"Yes." Her gaze flickered down to his chin.

"And?"

"And," she sighed, "because it was a mistake. An awful mistake."

When he laid his hand against her cheek, Cynthia closed her eyes and nuzzled closer.

"Well, I can't disagree with that," he said. "First, because you were with another man. And second, because it makes you look sad to speak of it. Will you tell me?"

Though she shook her head, she opened her eyes and began to speak. "He was an artist. While he was working on a commission in Scarborough, he engaged in a bit of gambling. When he lost to my stepfather, they agreed he'd pay his losses in trade. Not that my stepfather was happy about it, mind you, but what could he do?"

She shrugged, her shoulder rubbing against his chest. "So James painted my portrait. And we flirted. He kissed me a few times. It was very exciting. I was seventeen—"

"Seventeen," Lancaster growled, but Cynthia ignored him.

"And he was very handsome and sophisticated. I'd already been offered up to Sir Reginald, and Harry was being discussed, and I decided to make myself unmarketable."

"By losing your virginity."

"Yes."

"You were too young."

"Old enough, I gather. Regardless, he finished the portrait, but there was some argument as he was leaving. The agreement hadn't covered the cost of paint and canvas, only James's commission, but my stepfather refused to pay for the supplies. I saw James storm out and followed him to the stables, knowing it would be my last chance. I asked him to take my virginity, and . . . he did."

Lancaster waited for more, but she offered nothing else. "Well, that's a fine way of saying nothing at all. What do you mean 'he did'?"

"I mean that he did. I thought it would be romantic. He was an artist, after all, and I'd very much enjoyed our kisses. But it wasn't romantic at all, and I'd been stupid to think it would be, I suppose. He kissed me a few times, and I was rather . . . interested. But then he began to chuckle, and he pulled me into a stall, leaned me over a barrel, and—"

"He did *what?*"

Cynthia jumped at his shouted question. "He was still angry, I think. Feeling foolish for being tricked out of his funds. And I'm sure he thought a girl willing to give herself so cheaply didn't deserve kindness."

"Cyn," he gasped in horror. "Don't say that."

"It's true, isn't it? I asked for exactly what I got. I didn't believe myself in love with him. I didn't even try to couch it in feathery language. I simply said, 'Will you have me?' and so I was had. And when he finished, he buttoned his trousers, tucked in his shirt, and said, 'Tell your father we're squared away then.' And he left. That was it."

Lancaster couldn't speak. Cynthia didn't have tears in her eyes, but he felt like weeping for her. He smoothed the hair away from her forehead. "Tell me his name."

"Why?"

"Because I shall hunt him down and beat him half to death."

She laughed. How could she laugh when his heart was breaking? "He was only being a man, Nick. There's no punishment for that."

"Being a man?" he sputtered. "He acted like an animal!"

"He only took what—"

"Do you think *I* would ever do that to you? To *anyone?*"

She met his eyes easily. "No, not you."

"What kind of man would hurt a woman that way? You must have been terrified."

This time her eyes did fill with tears, and Lancaster felt so much rage fill his soul that it frightened him. He could kill this James, easily. "Don't cry, Cyn."

She turned her head into his neck. "I'm sorry," she whispered. "I shouldn't have done it."

"Hush."

"I wish it had been you. You were beautiful, Nick. It was beautiful."

Beautiful? He wrapped her tight in his arms and tried to calm his raging heart. Beautiful. He should kill that bastard just for making her think sex with him was beautiful.

But despite his anger, he wanted to ask her to repeat that over and over again. *You were beautiful. It was beautiful.*

Maybe with Cynthia it was.

"Nick?"

"Yes?"

She tipped her face up to look at him. "Why didn't you want me to touch you?"

All the air in the room drew away from him, eluding his lungs. It belatedly occurred to him that there was a problem with this genuine connection. A friend would notice things a stranger would not.

Why didn't you want me to touch you? What could he say to that? He could only lie to her. Familiar as he was with falsehoods, the words still felt like cotton in his mouth.

"I can't imagine what you mean."

"I wanted to touch you the way you touched me."

Lancaster swallowed hard to clear the truth from his throat. "Men do not care for that kind of attention."

He'd hoped that her inexperience would prove to her disadvantage, but Cynthia pulled her chin in and gave a brief laugh. "Pardon? As far as I can tell, men enjoy every bit of attention they can get. And *you.* You used to sit at your mother's foot and read while she stroked your hair like a cat."

"I was a child," he muttered, and that was the truth at least. "And men are not . . . Men are not conditioned to need that kind of touching."

Her nose scrunched up in doubt. "Are you quite sure?"

"I think I would know."

"Well," she scoffed, "we may have to work on that. I'm keen to pet you a bit."

Lancaster laughed in that way he'd perfected. A laugh that sounded real because he'd trotted it out for nearly ten years of deceit. "I'm flattered. But you'll have to leave the petting to me."

"We'll see," she answered ominously. She hesitated for a moment, and Lancaster braced himself for more poking and prodding, but she managed to surprise him. "So . . . what was your first time like? Very exciting I'd suppose."

"Er . . ." Good God, the woman had some sort of awful gift for uncomfortable topics.

"I've listened to the village boys speak of their conquests for years. It's nothing I haven't heard before."

"I . . . As your first lover was, at best, a miserable failure, I feel it's my duty to explain that the warm glow of pleasure one feels after lovemaking is best sustained by quiet contemplation or perhaps even sleep."

"It's the middle of the day."

"Aren't you sleepy at all?"

"No." But she quieted down, nuzzling her nose into his chest and relaxing with a deep sigh.

He was a fraud. He knew nothing about the proper

way to behave after making love as he always simply pulled on his clothes and left. There had been no sweet whispers or warm embraces after his first time, nor had there been any in the years since. Until now.

Breathing in the scent of her hair, Lancaster let himself feel the way her naked skin pressed his. How hot their bodies were together. She shifted her knee, sliding it a few inches up his thigh.

He could smell her skin and her sex. He could feel her from her toes all the way to the top of her head. Her breath tickled his chest. Her heart beat close enough to hear.

Lancaster closed his eyes.

"It was awkward," he said softly, and she went still beside him. "Exciting and frightening at the same time. And I wish . . . I wish it had been you."

Chapter 14

"'E's a right odd fellow," the old boat maker said. His tongue poked through his teeth as he considered his own words. "Strange."

"Strange how?" Lancaster did his best to hide his frustration. Everyone seemed to agree that Bram was an odd man, but no one could explain why.

"Ain't got a soul, far as I can tell," the man offered with a shrug, as if that were a perfectly normal observation.

"No soul," Lancaster repeated tonelessly.

The boat maker nodded. "Nothing there."

"And you say he's been here?" The tiny inn was cloudy with peat smoke and packed to the rafters with fishing net. It hardly seemed a likely stopping place for an earl's man.

"Every so often, yup. Come in to wet his whistle three days ago."

"What's he looking for?" Lancaster asked, though he already knew the answer would be vague.

"Don't know. Never says a word."

"All right then." Lancaster slapped his hat against his knee. "Thank you for your kind attention."

"Honored, yer lordship."

Lancaster slipped his hat on and glanced around to be sure there were no newcomers in the inn, but the same five men stared back at him. He raised his hand in farewell before stepping out into the rain.

If he remembered correctly, and he wasn't sure he did, Richmond's land started a good five-hour carriage ride to the west. Less than that on horseback then. It was possible Bram made the trip from Richmond's every few days and then returned immediately home. If he was staying somewhere nearby, no one in the village suspected.

Despite the rain, Lancaster ignored the carriage and crossed to the lane where Adam's family lived. The boy's mother had been taken by surprise yesterday, caught between the excitement of a viscount visiting her tiny cottage and the fear of letting her boy go live in a house beset by spirits. She hadn't wanted to say yes but had been unable to say no. Feeling guilty for her worry, Lancaster braved the short walk in the rain to offer a good day and assure the woman her youngest boy was settling in well.

After that, he crossed to the Painter home to check on Mrs. Pell, but she'd set out for home during a brief lull in the storm. Hopefully, she was already home, dry and safe, and working hard at a meaty stew for tonight's dinner.

Lancaster, feeling a bit lost, glanced down the road before stepping up into the carriage. He hadn't accomplished much aside from giving himself time to think about Cynthia.

Her arguments for making love had made perfect

sense in the confines of that small room. It had all been very logical with the sight of her naked skin gleaming in the firelight. Of course they should make love. What a grand idea.

But now he was reeling. What had he done? He couldn't marry her, but he couldn't *not* marry her now. She might be pregnant this very moment, despite his attempt to prevent it.

She'd been so lovely and tempting and warm. And so familiar despite the newness of this physical desire.

Lancaster rubbed his knuckles against his forehead. He shouldn't have made love to her. And yet the thought of taking it back twisted a knife into his gut.

Even more painful was the thought of sending her on her way when this adventure was done.

He couldn't marry her, and he couldn't not marry her.

His head began to throb. They'd roll up to Cantry Manor soon. He should have some idea of what he would say to her. "We can't do that again," seemed like a good opening. And then what?

The knife in his gut turned another revolution.

"Jackson," he called, slamming his fist against the ceiling. A small panel slid open. "Take me to Oak Hall."

Jackson's reply was lost in the wind, but the panel slid closed.

Instead of going home, Lancaster would question Mr. Cambertson. Find out more about this debt and Bram's mysterious appearances. If he stalled long enough he just might have an inkling of what to do with Cynthia Merrithorpe. Right now all he could think to do was help to solve her problems.

Bram was a mystery. His identity, his whereabouts, his intention. Perhaps Lancaster should just kill him and ignore the mystery altogether. Cynthia said he hadn't hurt her, but he'd *allowed* her to be hurt. He'd stood by and watched her attacked by a monster.

Then again, Lancaster already planned to kill Richmond. And then there was that animal, James. Three murders might be beyond the pale. Probably Cynthia wouldn't appreciate his collecting corpses for her like a macabre bouquet.

Perhaps this Bram fellow did not deserve murdering per se. Perhaps just a good thrashing. Well, that took him down to two killings. Was two a reasonable number? The beast deep inside him seemed to think so.

Five minutes later he was about to knock on the door of Oak Hall when it opened quickly enough to create its own breeze.

"You got my message?"

Lancaster stared in shock at Cambertson, whose hand still clutched the door handle. Where in the world was the decrepit old butler? Had he finally keeled over?

"Come on, come on," Cambertson muttered, waving him in.

"What message?"

"I sent a message 'round with the idiot maid. Didn't you get it? Good God, how many trials can one man go through?"

Lancaster didn't like the odd implication that Cynthia's death might somehow be equated with trouble with the help, but he bit his tongue and followed her stepfather down the hall and back to his shabby study. The butler sat, sound asleep, in a chair outside the door.

"Bram paid another visit," Cambertson barked as he rounded his desk and collapsed into his seat.

"Today?"

"No, yesterday noon. Reminded me that Lord

Richmond only wanted to know when my Mary would be back. Nothing more. I told him it didn't matter. The girl is only thirteen!"

"And why are you telling me this?"

"Because you're the only man around who can understand."

"Me?" Lancaster shook his head in disgust. "Understand what?"

"What it's like to live with this pressure. The life of a gentleman and all the debt that goes along with it."

He wanted to spit in this man's face and scream that they were nothing alike. But he only shot his cuffs and stared at a smear in the dust atop the desk.

"I know you think I did wrong by Cynthia, but I meant her to have a good marriage. Her father was a knight, after all. She wasn't meant to marry low. I tried my best to honor his name."

"How much do you owe Richmond?"

"Thirteen hundred," Cambertson muttered.

Thirteen hundred pounds. It wasn't so much. It wasn't worth the life of a young girl. It certainly wasn't worth the life of two. But it was probably five years' income on this land, assuming he hadn't already sold off great swaths of it.

"So what will you do?" Lancaster asked.

"What can I do? He's threatened to see me hauled into court once already. It was either give him Cynthia or sell the land. Without the land, we'd have nothing."

"But without Cynthia, you'd be fine."

"Of course we'd be fine," Cambertson snapped. "She would've married someday regardless. And we will be fine without Mary as well, if only I can make my wife see that."

Amazingly, there appeared to be a sheen of tears in

the man's eyes. But it was just as likely grief for his debt as it was for the fate of his daughters. Lancaster could understand how untenable it would be for the man to sell his land, but if he sold off his whole family, whom would he pass the land to?

On the other hand, if Lancaster simply removed Richmond from the equation, the whole situation might be solved. Except that the debt would then be held by whomever inherited.

"Do you think Bram is Richmond's heir?" he asked.

Cambertson shrugged. "It's possible. Richmond's been married three times."

"And widowed."

The man ignored Lancaster's pointed tone. "I never heard anything about an heir, but it's clear he's related."

"Can you find out?" He didn't want the fate of Cynthia and her sister falling into the hands of a man who supposedly had no soul.

Cambertson shrugged again. "He asked about you, you know."

"Who?"

"Bram."

Well, that was disturbing. Bram had little reason to be looking in the direction of Cantry Manor. "What did he ask?"

"Asked who you were and why you'd returned."

"And what did you tell him?"

"I told him you were the viscount and I expected you could visit your estates anytime you liked. And I figured you were hiding from your creditors."

"Ah. There you have it, then." A perfectly logical reason for him to remain on this lonely coast. Certainly more logical than keeping company with a dead girl who wasn't actually dead.

Cyn's stepfather cleared his throat so loudly that Lancaster jumped in surprise. "So," Cambertson drawled. "Did you tell her?"

"Pardon?"

"Did you tell the ghost what I said?"

Lancaster watched him rub his hands together in nervousness. He felt utterly ridiculous even answering the question, but Cambertson was all serious attention. "I shouted it out at midnight in a darkened room, but I can't confirm the absence or presence of any spirits."

"Hm," he grunted. "She didn't respond?"

"A strange feeling of warmth did come over me."

His eyebrows flew up. "Really?"

"Oh, yes."

"A friendly feeling?"

"Decidedly so."

Cambertson nodded sagely. "A good sign. Perhaps she'll be at peace if she knows I won't hate her."

"She did seem happier." Tired of toying with the man, Lancaster shifted toward the edge of his seat. "Do you know if Bram is still about?"

"He said he would explain my position to Richmond, so I gather he meant to return home."

"Send a note if he shows up again, will you? I'll see myself out." He paused in the doorway to glance down at the old butler. "Is your man quite well? Looks a bit pale."

Cambertson snorted and waved him on, so Lancaster left the old man to his nap, hoping it wasn't a permanent rest.

As he started around the corner of the hall, Lancaster stopped in his tracks and pivoted toward the closed door of the music room. He pushed with the flat of his hand and the door swung in to reveal the bright square of the portrait of Cynthia. He'd thought it would look different now, knowing who the artist was, but it only seemed more beautiful. This time, looking at that stubborn jaw and those slanted eyes, he felt a warm swell of comfort.

He leaned forward to peer at the signature. Munro, it said. James Munro.

Bastard he might have been, but the artist had captured that elusive shimmer of beauty about her. Something that glowed from her eyes. Something not born of perfect features, but of spirit. She was stubborn, yes, but grounded in peace all the same.

Staring at that portrait, Lancaster felt a certainty snap into place inside him. He would marry her, family and fortune be damned. He'd find a way.

Bram was gone, at least temporarily, so they could spend the whole day tomorrow searching the cliffs. They'd find that bloody treasure or he'd die trying. And if it truly was a fortune . . . Well, the gold that would purchase Cyn's freedom could purchase his as well.

"Scoundrel," Cynthia growled as Nick raised a glass of wine triumphantly in her direction. "Beast."

He pursed his lips in mock sympathy. "Poor dear. Taken advantage of by a worldly gentleman."

While Cyn glared, Mrs. Pell shook her head and tapped the tabletop. "You two act as if you're playing for coin instead of beans." She slid one card toward Nick and then laid her hand down, face up. "And it's a good thing you're not or you'd both be beggared. That's in, then."

She and Nick both looked down in time to watch

the housekeeper sweep the last few dried beans into her pile.

"Damn me," Nick muttered, which prompted another warning about language from Mrs. Pell.

"Really, milord. You'd think you'd never been around a decent young woman. I'm off to bed then." She untied her apron and folded it over a chair. "I'm too old to stay up past ten. Sleep well."

When the door to her room closed, Nick arched an eyebrow. "Decent, eh?"

Cynthia blushed at the gleam in his eye and tried to keep her laughter quiet. "You *are* a scoundrel."

"A very happy one."

Happy, he'd said. She grinned down at her last few cards and pushed them around the table. She was happy too.

Worry had overtaken her in the hours he was gone. He'd left solemn and frowning, not the type of man to take such a thing lightly. But he'd returned as the charming Nick he'd been so many years before. Not polished and perfect, but *easy*. Happy.

"We've another early day tomorrow," he said, and Cynthia's heart raced ahead to the night to come. Lust twined around her limbs and tightened.

"Best to retire then," she murmured, stealing a glance at him through her lashes.

Nick's smile gentled. He reached across the table to take her hand. "We can't do that again, love."

Love, he called her, as if she really were his love. That was all she heard for a moment. She sat straighter and gave up looking coy. "Can't do what again?"

"What we so thoroughly did earlier. I can't . . . have you like that again."

She narrowed her eyes at him and leaned closer. "How can you have me then?"

"Cyn . . ." His helpless look offered only apologies.

"I'm sorry, Nick, but you've . . . you've introduced me to the pleasures of the flesh. You can't cry off now."

"I didn't *intend* to introduce anything!"

"Well, you did, and that's that. Perhaps you'd like another glass of wine?"

He pulled his hand from hers and crossed his arms. "Cynthia Merrithorpe, you listen to me. We are not going to make love again. Not until after we're married."

"We—" His words flashed through the room like lightning. *"What did you say?"*

"Marry me, Cyn."

"No!"

He smiled and reached for her, lacing his fingers through hers. "Please do me the honor of becoming my wife."

"I will not!" Sweat sprang up along her hairline and she shivered at the sudden chill. "And you are already engaged, you fool."

"To a woman who hates me,"

She tried to tug her hand away, but he held tight.

"You said you wanted me to be happy, Cynthia. Marrying you would make me happy."

"Don't say that."

"It would."

His thumb stroked the ball of her hand, brushing tingles into the sensitive flesh. How horrid he was, offering her everything she'd ever dreamed.

They'd fall in love. The world would spin to a halt around them. They'd marry too young and move to London, and the whole ton *would marvel at the strength of their passion.*

But no. That wouldn't happen at all. If he married her, they wouldn't be able to afford a fashionable life in town. And the whole *ton* would be too busy marveling at the abject foolishness of the match to even notice their passion.

"We cannot marry. Even if you don't marry that woman, you can't take me as a wife."

"I can and I will."

"Don't I have a say in this?"

That finally dimmed the sparkle in his eyes. "But I thought . . . I love you, Cyn."

Damn him. How could he say that so simply? How could he look at her with those clear brown eyes and make it true? "You love me as a friend."

"I love you as a woman. And I've never told a woman that before. I've never even thought it."

She couldn't believe that. Nick must have fallen in and out of love a dozen times over by now. At heart, he'd always been a romantic. Surely he'd loved many women.

The room spiraled around her. Only Nick stayed still, the calm center of this quietly raging storm.

His warm gaze held her captive. "I told you we couldn't make love unless we planned to marry."

"I thought you'd gotten past that foolishness! Nick, listen. Please. Even if you do love me now, it wouldn't last long once the creditors descended."

"I'm happy here, with you, with nothing but a kitchen table and a pot of stew between us."

My God, he looked like himself again. Young and hopeful. Her foolish Nick. The man she'd always loved. "This isn't real. It's not. What of your family? Your sister and brother depend on you. Your estates must need improvements. Your family would hate me. They would all hate me, and then you'd hate me too."

His smile was patently puzzled. "Where do you get these ideas?"

"I've lived in a home drowning in debt for more than fifteen years. It is all my family thinks about. Money. *Money.* Can we afford new dresses? No. But if a new dress will help me find a better husband, can we afford it then? If we sell the carpets, will the neighbors notice? If they notice, will their sons shy away from marriage? But if we don't sell the carpets, we will lose the horses, and that will be hard to hide."

"Cyn—"

"There is no room for love when you cannot pay the servants, Nick. Or when your mother cries into her tea every evening. Or when your sister is forced to marry a tradesman and ceases to exist in the eyes of the *ton.* I've been the bane of my stepfather's existence for years now. I won't be the bane of yours as well."

He hadn't looked away from her during her whole speech, and he didn't look away now. "I know what it means to sacrifice for my family, Cyn. Believe me, I do. I understand duty and obligation."

"Then you know that we can't marry."

One side of his mouth quirked up. "We shall see."

"We shall *not* see." Tears burned her throat, swelling into a lump too large to swallow.

Nick raised her hand to his lips and brushed his mouth over her fingers.

How could he be such a fool? Such a lovable, awful fool?

Cynthia jerked her hand from his grasp and ran from him and his storybook dreams.

* * *

The cold of the floor soaked through her stockings and numbed her feet, but Cynthia kept pacing. It was late, and they faced another early morning, but she couldn't sleep. She couldn't even sit down.

After fleeing to her room, she'd cried for a good quarter-hour, but once her tears had dried, her imagination had roused itself.

What if they did marry? Perhaps his estates could be economized to provide more income. Perhaps there was jewelry to be sold. Perhaps there was more than enough income and the family was simply living too extravagantly.

These kinds of thoughts had wound through her head for nearly an hour. She'd even sat down at her little desk and sketched a picture of her and Nick, holding hands, walking down a sunny lane.

How utterly ridiculous.

Thank God the wind had picked up and rattled the shutters. When the cold air had snuck past the seams of the wood and ruffled the paper on the desk, Cynthia had looked up in surprise. Her eyes had fallen on the open wardrobe, and the two dresses hanging inside.

Two dresses, one of them more rag than gown at this point.

One pair of boots, scuffed and scarred and leached of whatever color the leather had once held.

One nightdress, one corset, one petticoat, one chemise, one tattered pair of stockings. And one ancient diary upon which she'd pinned all her hopes.

This was what she owned. This was what she would bring to a marriage.

And Nick?

She'd looked slowly around the cold, bare, drafty room.

Nick clearly needed more than what she could offer.

And so, here she was, angry and alone, pacing the perimeter of her tiny chamber, wondering how her plan for a torrid affair had descended to this sad state.

Actually, there was no need to wonder. It was the one thing she'd feared from the start. Gentlemen's honor.

"Blast it," she muttered, hitting her palm with her fist. Men and their stupid honor. By God, it would drive her to her grave.

Honor had turned her into a piece of chattel to be given over to any man owed a gambling debt. Now honor would ruin her plans and lull her into becoming a lifelong burden on Nick's family.

She wouldn't do it. Nick's kind of honor could go to hell. She had honor too. And plans. And dreams and desires. She'd wanted something simple and good before she left the only place she'd ever known. She'd been honest about what she wanted, and Nick couldn't change the rules now.

Crossing her arms, she glared at the door that led to his bedroom. He'd knocked a half-hour before, but she'd ignored him just as he deserved. Was he asleep now? Was he lying there smug in his assumption that she'd fall in line with his honorable plans?

Was he still sleeping in the nude?

Cynthia set her jaw and stripped off her nightdress. She narrowed her eyes and pushed down her stockings.

He could take his honor and stuff it.

Chapter 15

He was just floating into a lovely dream involving Cynthia, a pot of honey, and a set of silk ropes, when a floorboard creaked and snatched him from his fantasy. The sound set off a vibration of fear that traveled through his muscles and snapped him into immediate tension.

"Who's there?" he barked as he shoved up from the bed.

"It's me," a soft voice answered.

Lancaster drew in a deep breath and exhaled all the tension from his body. He could just see the pale glow of her beyond the faint light of the night lamp he'd left burning. "Cyn, are you all right?"

"I'm well, yes."

"Are you ready to talk?"

"No," she answered sharply.

He frowned into the darkness. "Are you planning to murder me then?"

"Probably not." Her voice came closer.

Nick squinted toward the sound as he reached for

the lamp. His fingers twisted the knob, pushing the wick a bit higher. Then he swallowed his tongue.

She was nude. Starkly, beautifully nude. And walking right toward him. "No," he said. "No, absolutely not."

Her eyes narrowed and she kept coming, breasts bouncing slightly with every step.

"I told you we wouldn't do this."

"And I told you we would." She came to a stop a foot from him and raised her arms out from her body as if to give him a better look.

He didn't need a better look. He could see everything quite clearly. The way her nipples tightened in the cold, offering a temptation for his tongue. The way her hips flared out at the perfect angle for his hands to grip. And the dark curls covering her sex. He could *feel* the way he'd slide inside her, the way her sex would resist with delicious tightness before giving way to the full width of him.

His cock, already half hard from the interrupted dream, pulsed to brilliant life at the thought.

"Go back to your room," he ordered in desperation.

Cynthia arched an eyebrow and took the one last step that brought her flush with his bed.

Lancaster scrambled back, but despite his best intentions, he couldn't stop himself from watching when she raised one knee onto the mattress. "Oh, Lord," he groaned at the brief glimpse of pink sex. "Cyn . . ."

Though he had enough restraint left to resist reaching for her, Lancaster couldn't make himself back farther away. He could only freeze like a cornered hare.

"Do what you did this morning," she said, her voice low and soft, like the finest kid leather on his skin.

He shook his head. "We must wait." But his eyes

wandered from her face to her breasts as she knelt before him like a supplicant.

"Take me, Nick."

On her knees. Begging.

A tremor took over his muscles. And then she reached for him as if she meant to spread her fingers through his hair. He grabbed her wrists to stop her, and his fight was finished.

His fingers curled tight around her bones. He felt her tendons press against his grip as she strained against him. His heart pounded harder, and the world and his worries disappeared.

He wanted this. He wanted it now, with Cynthia, good intentions be damned. They'd find that blasted treasure, and he'd marry her and all would be well, because he would make it so.

When he pushed her to her back, Cynthia gasped. He slid between her legs, and pressed his naked weight into her, watching her eyes widen.

"Oh," she breathed. A nice enough sound, but he suddenly needed her moaning, sobbing, screaming.

"Open your legs," he growled.

Cynthia blinked up at him. Her lips parted as she breathed harder, and her knees inched higher on his thighs.

"More. Wrap them around my hips."

She didn't obey him at first. He waited to see if she would trust him, or if she'd push him off and demand to know what was wrong with him. She should push away. He knew that. But when her knees rose up to his hips and her ankles slid over his thighs, Lancaster's blood surged in triumph.

Now his cock was snug against the cradle of her

body, held by the heat of her. He rocked his hips and her eyelashes fluttered. So did his heart.

Ah, God, she felt sweet and warm and soft against him. He kept rocking his hips in a slow rhythm, rubbing against her until he felt her wetness begin to ease his way. He slid easier, faster against her.

"Nick," she groaned as her hips tilted up, pressing her softness into his hard shaft. "Oh, God, yes. Oh, yes."

"Does that feel good, love? Is that what you wanted?"

"Yes." Her hands curled into fists under his hold. "Keep doing that. It's . . . It feels so . . ."

A bead of sweat trickled down his neck. "Tell me."

She shook her head. "It's so good. Please don't stop. *Please.*"

He wouldn't. He wouldn't stop. He'd keep her like this forever.

Her thighs began to tremble around him. She threw her head back. Though Lancaster was desperate to shift his hips and slide deep inside her body, he clenched his teeth and maintained the exact rhythm, the exact pressure that was making her jaw quiver.

A soft keen began deep in her throat. Her heels dug into his thighs. Lancaster's arms shook, but he managed to hold onto his control until her cries swelled into screams. Then he plunged deep and hard into her sex, shuddering as her flesh spasmed around him.

"Ah!" she cried out, her hips bucking up to meet his thrust.

Heaven. Or something better than heaven, something more earthly. A timeless limbo where right and wrong ceased to exist. He had no past, and there was no future; there was only Cynthia and her hot, tight sex around him.

He flexed his fingers and ran his hands down her

arms before dragging them back up to grip her wrists tighter than ever. He rode her slowly, trying to hold on, trying to keep them in this place forever.

"Cyn," he whispered. "I love you."

When she turned toward him, he caught her mouth in a kiss, and this was a whole other intimacy he wasn't used to. Kissing during sex. Drinking a woman down as he filled her up. This was sweetness to temper his bitter need.

Sweetness, love, and her arms shaking under his grip . . . These things shouldn't go together, but here they were, wound together and spiraling through him like a storm.

The pressure spun tighter and tighter, dragging him under, until he couldn't breathe.

He desperately wanted to spill himself inside her, fill her up, mark her with his very essence.

But they weren't married yet. "Not yet," he murmured. "Not yet."

"Nick," Cynthia moaned. And he wanted her to say his name over and over again. His *name*. The name no one ever called him anymore. He was real with her. He was whole.

"Nick," she breathed again, and he felt his climax begin to build with sudden, bright pressure.

"Ah, God. Cynthia. Cyn." Though it nearly broke him to do it, he slid free of her body when he most wanted to push deeper, and spent himself on her belly.

Despite that he'd been in Cynthia's room countless times already, Lancaster felt more than a little titillated to be standing in her chambers as she slept. He turned a slow circle, not focusing on any one thing. Just taking it in.

The gray dawn had only just begun to sneak past the cracks of the shutters. He felt as if he were underwater, wading through murky depths toward a glowing undersea angel.

Grinning at the newly romantic bent of his thoughts, he walked the last few steps to Cynthia's bedside. She didn't look like an angel when she slept, despite everything he'd read about women and the gentle bonds of Morpheus. No, Cyn looked a bit put out, as if she anticipated that he hovered near, about to disturb her rest. Her forehead crinkled, and her lower lip jutted out, tempting him to nibble on it. But he had a feeling he might encounter a fist against his ear if he tried that.

Touchy girl.

Somehow her moodiness relieved a pressure deep inside him. In London he was surrounded by acquaintances who seemed hidden beneath a clear, impenetrable veneer. They treated him either as a harmless amusement or a novelty to be indulged. Even his family . . .

The moment that his sheen had been stripped away, his parents had withdrawn from him with brutal speed. He'd been left alone to hurt or heal as he saw fit.

But he'd only been *fifteen*. A child. And that loneliness had nearly devoured him.

Watching Cynthia in the gray light, he dared to run a finger over the roundness of one naked shoulder. She frowned a little harder but didn't wake.

Holding his breath, Lancaster gave in to temptation. He eased himself down and stretched out next to her, atop the blanket, not quite touching her body. Her eyes flickered beneath her lashes. When they stilled, he slowly released the breath he'd been holding and let his body sink into the feathers.

She looked a bit more angelic up close, her expression blurred a little by proximity. Her skin looked like the finest silk, though he felt clichéd even thinking such a thing. Hell, he was ashamed to admit even to himself that her lips looked like cherries, flushed a deep red in sleep. A strand of hair curved over her cheekbone and cupped her chin.

He didn't dare brush it away. She might awaken and then he'd have to smile and make a joke and bounce up from the mattress with a jaunty air.

He didn't want to get up. He'd never slept with a woman before, and wasn't sure he ever could. If she reached for him in the middle of the night and brushed a hand down his back . . . Lancaster shuddered at the thought. At the very least, he might wake screaming. Worse, he might lash out.

It had seemed a simple problem to live with. He and his wife would have separate chambers. He knew now that Imogene would've welcomed such an arrangement, but he wasn't sure about Cyn. And now he wasn't sure about himself either.

This was peaceful. Here, watching the rise and fall of her chest, enjoying the faint jump of her pulse beneath the skin of her throat. His life felt suspended. He was underwater again, floating in a calm pool.

Minutes passed. How many, he couldn't say. He may have even dozed off for a time. But eventually the gray light brightened to a dull white, and it was time to wake her. They had treasure to find and a future to plan.

After one last deep breath, Lancaster pushed carefully off the bed and tugged his coat back into place.

He smoothed his hair down and rubbed the daze
from his eyes.

"Cynthia." He hoped to ease her awake, but his soft
tone failed completely. She didn't even twitch. "Cyn!"
Nothing.

Apparently he could've thrown himself into bed
beside her and not worried a bit.

"Cynthia! Wake up!"

Finally, she stirred, but only to groan and turn away
from his voice. Her hand emerged from the covers to
pull the blankets over her head.

Sighing, Lancaster wandered toward her desk. "We
need to get moving if we're to get out before noon."

"Mm," she grunted.

"Sweet as morning dew," he muttered back, idly
pushing around a few blank papers strewn across the
desk. "Out of bed, love. The—Good God above!"

The pile of papers had spilled forth a very interesting sketch. He squinted at it.

"What? What's wrong?" Cynthia asked in a raspy
voice.

Lancaster looked from the sketch in his hand to
the stick of charcoal rolling slowly toward the edge
of the desk. Then he looked back at the drawing.

A naked man, clearly aroused, who looked a bit like
a malformed, slightly lumpy version of *him.*

"Is this *me*?"

The sudden rustle of sheets drew his attention in
time to watch Cyn's eyes widen in his direction. When
her gaze darted to the paper in his hand, she popped
upright—the sheets clutched to her bosom, unfortunately.

"What are you doing?" she screeched.

"Waking you up. Cyn, you didn't tell me these were *your* drawings."

"Get out!"

"I'm sorry. I'd never have called them horrid and immature and—"

"You didn't call them horrid," she snapped. "Until now. Just get out! You've no right to be in my chambers. I'm not even decent."

"Um, Cyn . . ."

"Completely outrageous!"

"You wouldn't even *be* in your chambers if I hadn't carried you in here in the middle of the night. And you weren't decent then, I'll remind you."

"Oh!" she growled, her brow falling low as she looked frantically around the bed.

"Nothing to throw, dearest?"

He should have backed away when her eyes narrowed to slits, but in the end he was glad he didn't. Cynthia rose up in all her warm and rosy glory and leapt at him.

There was only one brief moment to brace himself before her heat wrapped around him.

"Good aim," he gasped as he spread his hands over her generous bottom. "Amazing, really."

Now that she was plastered to him, Cynthia didn't seem to know what to do with herself, so Lancaster decided to help out. He stepped to the bed, let her fall to her back, and helpfully followed her down to the mattress.

"Well then," he murmured, pressing her hands down as he nestled between her hips.

"You have no . . ." She stumbled over her words when he nuzzled his open mouth against her neck. ". . . no right."

He sucked gently at that spot before kissing a wet path down to one deliciously pink nipple.

"Oh, God," she cried out, her back arching her harder into his mouth. He sucked and nibbled until she was whimpering, her hips pressing pleadingly into his.

"I'm not sure we have time for this, love." *But what was time, really?* his brain countered helpfully. And if they *did* wait till later to leave, perhaps they'd avoid the curious stares of any late-returning fishermen who might spot them on the coast.

Her body was so unbelievably *hot* in the cool air of the room. Like a newly stoked fire.

Lancaster shook his head to dismiss his own misgivings, then reached one hand down to unbutton his breeches.

Breath held back by his tightly clenched teeth, he freed himself from his clothing and slid deep into her in one brutal thrust.

Cynthia opened her mouth in a wordless scream as he reared up to his feet. He tugged her toward him so that her bottom perched at the edge of the mattress.

Ah, sweet Lord above. He could control his thrusts perfectly from this vantage, and the pleasure of it skittered up his spine as he pushed slowly inside her and pulled just as slowly out.

Her hands fluttered as if she didn't know what to do with them now that he'd set them free. He watched her fingers clench at air as he slid deep inside her again. One of her hands twisted into the sheets.

Lancaster closed his eyes and told himself not to do what he wanted to do. But once the idea wormed its way beneath his skullcap, there was no setting it aside. And she'd like it. He knew she would.

When he opened his eyes, he found Cynthia biting

her lip, head thrown back in pleasure, and he reached for her.

"Cyn," he rasped, working her fingers free from the sheets. "Here." She didn't resist at all, even as he pressed her palm to one of her breasts. He slipped the other hand down her belly to lie snug against her curls.

Her eyes finally opened, glazed with the distance of pleasure.

"Touch yourself," he growled.

When she glanced down at her body, her eyes widened. Would she refuse? Would she draw back in horror? Of course she must. But then her fingers tightened on her breast and he nearly moaned with joy.

"That's it." Horrible lust surged up inside his chest, scraping his words to raw need. "Touch yourself while I take you."

Shock flickered over her flushed face, but she did as he said, and her fingers closed over her nipple.

"Ah," she gasped, arching into his thrust.

"Lord, you're beautiful."

She closed her eyes and turned her head away as her other hand cupped her sex.

Lancaster watched her fingertips ease closer to that little pearl of nerves. He thrust slow and careful, giving her time to tempt herself into touching just *there*. Just where their bodies met, where his cock fit so snugly into her wet sex.

Her fingers brushed his shaft, sending shudders down his thighs. Could she feel that? How hard he was for her? How wet she was for him? The miraculous perfection of this profane act?

She touched him again, more deliberately this time, and then she found the spot, and her body twisted. A strangled, desperate cry escaped her throat, and Lancaster gratefully increased his pace.

"You're beautiful, Cyn," he breathed. "Beautiful." And she was. Impossibly so. He hooked his arms beneath her knees to hold her firmly in place. And he watched her take control of her own pleasure.

That place inside him opened again, that place where he was real. Not angry or frightened or broken.

Pleasure began to gather too fast, compressing into a heavy weight at the base of his cock. It was too much, being inside her, watching as her fingers rubbed tiny circles into her sex. Her other hand spread wide over her full breast. Her head pressed hard into the soft mattress and her neck strained.

"Nick," she chanted. "Nick. *Nick.*" The words sounded like a prayer. For him. "Oh, that feels . . . so . . ."

He watched as her fingers dug into the flesh of her breast. Her other hand moved faster, faster, and Lancaster drove into her. Too rough. Too fast. But it seemed to ease the ache building up inside her, because Cynthia dug her heels into his arse and arched up for more. Hips jerking against him, she screamed.

He felt the grip of her muscles tighten around his cock and gritted his teeth until the spasms faded. When she finally began to relax, Lancaster let himself go. He fucked her hard. His hips slapped against hers as he pumped himself into the tight vise of her sex.

Pulling free at the last possible moment, he watched his seed splash against her belly and breasts, a sight so vulgar and exquisite that it stole his breath and replaced it with a swelling heat that filled his lungs.

Lancaster let his head fall back and just stood there, rigid, trying to hold on to the painfully strong pleasure pulsing through him.

"Oh, my," Cynthia sighed.

Lancaster breathed in and out and felt the earth's slow spin around him.

The sheets rustled. Her body shifted a fraction of an inch.

"Goodness! Is that your seed?"

His eyes popped open, giving him a view of the timbered ceiling. "What?"

He looked down to find Cynthia propped up on her elbows, staring at the mess he'd made of her.

"There's quite a lot of it."

"Er," he answered, face slowly heating to a furnace. He cupped his hand over his manhood. This was entirely unseemly. In fact, it crossed the line to complete and utter absurdity when Cynthia reached a finger out to slide over her stomach. Her forehead wrinkled in curiosity.

"Gah," Lancaster croaked.

"Nicholas Cantry, are you blushing?"

"Of course not!" He retreated a step.

"As many naked women as you must have seen, I can't imagine you'd find this shocking."

"Not . . . just . . . Pardon me." As he fled to his room to find a towel, he clearly heard Cynthia's snort of amusement behind him.

It was very strange to make love with a friend, he was finding. Strange and wonderful and . . . happy.

Chapter 16

"I think we'll find it today," Lancaster said for the third time.

Cynthia slanted him a doubtful look, but he kept right on smiling into the biting wind.

He could feel the promise of it in his bones, as if a secret layer of the earth vibrated just beyond his hearing. His skull hummed with the sensation.

When Cynthia remained silent, he went back to calculating the amount he would need to extricate himself from a marriage of convenience.

An ideal amount would be twenty thousand. Ten for him and ten for Cynthia. More would be wonderful, but he couldn't be greedy. Ten thousand would pay off nearly all his family's debts. Enough so that, with some reasonable economies taken, a few years' of income from his properties would pay off the rest. And Cynthia would have her own money then. She'd be an heiress. Free to marry him with no guilt or hesitation.

If it were more like five thousand pounds, the path toward marriage would be more difficult. But Lancaster was done with being easy. He should have been done with it years ago. With five thousand pounds, he could negotiate terms with his creditors. They might live close to the bone for a few years, but it would be worth it. The family would still be respectable enough to see his sister make a desirable marriage. His brother could continue his London lifestyle, albeit at a considerably lower level of luxury.

And he and Cynthia would still live happily ever after. Wonderful.

A seal splashed up from the gray water a few dozen feet from the shore before dipping underwater. When it poked its head up again and watched them with dark eyes, Lancaster took it as another good sign. Cynthia glanced toward the animal with no change of expression, but he supposed she'd seen a lot of seals in the past ten years.

"I'd like to apologize again for my ungenerous words about your sketches."

"Oh, just leave it. I know they're horrid."

"I wouldn't say horrid. You definitely show . . . emotion."

"Stuff it, Nick."

Sighing, he looked back out to find the seal watching them eagerly. "I think that seal likes me."

"Oh, for God's sake. It thinks you're a fisherman who'll begin tossing bait at any moment."

He tossed her an exasperated glare. "Why are you in such an awful mood today? You seemed perfectly happy this morning."

When she narrowed her eyes at the path ahead, he thought she'd argue, but eventually her brow smoothed out. A few steps later, she met his gaze and sighed. "I'm sorry, but you're making me nervous."

"How?"

"You seem to be deliberately trying to raise my hopes."

"About our marriage?"

"No! We won't be married, Nick. And that's another thing. You must stop thinking about that."

"Hard not to think about marriage after this morning."

"Oh, really? Do you think about marrying every woman you swive?"

"Cynthia Merrithorpe!" he barked, shock shifting to anger in the space of one heartbeat. "That wasn't swiving, damn you."

"I'm fairly certain it was," she snapped.

She couldn't think it meant nothing to him. He'd made clear he was in love with her. So was she trying to tell him it meant nothing to *her*? He stopped in his tracks and turned toward her, wrapping his hand around her elbow to pull her to a stop.

"I'm not going another step until I hear the truth from you. Are you in love with me or not?"

She gasped as if he'd just pinched her.

"Answer the question."

"I won't!"

"Why?"

She jerked her arm away. "Because it's not relevant."

"I've already made clear I'm in love with you."

"You are *not* in love with me. You think you're in love with me because I'm a novelty. I'm not like those London women, remember? I'm different. I don't give a fig about your debts or your standing or whether you can afford the latest fashion. I'm a *reprieve*, Nick. That's all."

Unbelievable. How had she become so cynical out here in the country? "That is *not* all, damn it."

"Oh, really?" She crossed her arms. "What is it, then? What makes me so much better than all those beautiful London women? What makes me better than a pretty girl in a pretty dress with a pretty inheritance? Nothing."

"Nothing?" he shouted.

"I'm a plain country girl with no education. I've no money and nothing to recommend me, not even beauty. Any of those London women would make you a better wife."

"*None* of them would. There isn't a soul in London who knows me. Not *one* person. Do you know why I wasn't frightened of your haunting? Do you know why I accepted it so easily? Because I was a ghost too, Cyn. I *am* a ghost. And you're the only one who still sees me."

Even the gulls seemed to stop squawking in that moment as his words hung in the air between them. He took a step back, shocked that he'd said them, but Cynthia looked far more shocked than he.

"What do you mean?"

He shook his head. "It's just . . . It's not like it is here. That's all."

"I don't think that is all," she whispered.

Lancaster stretched his mouth into a smile. "What else could it be? Just homesickness. A craving for the simple life."

"So you acknowledge that I am only a symbol of that simplicity?"

"I do not."

The wind whipped a thick rope of her hair free of its ribbon and dragged it over her mouth. Her eyes shifted to the sea for a moment as she tucked the hair behind her ear. It snuck free again to sneak across her cheek, but she ignored it.

When she met his gaze, he stiffened at the hesitation in her eyes. "Nick . . . What happened when you left?"

The wind seemed to scream against his ears all of a sudden. The cold bit deep beneath his skin as he watched her eyes fill with uncertainty.

"Nothing," someone answered in his voice. "I went to London. That's all."

"That's not what I mean. There's something else."

"No. Nothing at all."

"Don't lie to me. If you don't want to tell me, just say so. But don't *lie.*"

His lungs seemed too small. He parted his lips and tried to hide the fact that he was fighting for air. He meant to repeat his claims. To lie to her as he lied to everyone. But somehow he couldn't. Not with her asking him for honesty. "I don't wish to discuss it," said the voice that sounded just like him. His hands shook at the terror of offering the truth.

"All right." But her eyes grew more troubled, swimming with fear. "All right, but . . ."

He spun on his heel and began moving toward their goal. The sand crunched harder beneath his boots with every step he took. Cynthia called his name, but he couldn't stop, not even for her. He just set one foot in front of the other and kept moving away from his past. And hopefully toward his future.

Fifteen minutes later, Cyn's knees still shook. She didn't understand. Couldn't understand.

Was it true? Had he tried to kill himself? The idea repelled her. Partly because the idea of Nick dead made her gut knot in on itself. And partly because Nick *wanting* to die clashed with everything she knew about him. But he'd said he was a ghost. A ghost. As if he'd come back from the dead.

She wanted to pounce on him, throw her arms around him and beg him to tell her it wasn't true.

But Nick just kept walking, silence drawn around him like a cloak. And if she threw her arms around him, he'd push away in a panic. *Why?*

"This is where we stopped, I think." His voice was friendly to the point of distance. "I recognize that ridge just there."

She nodded and swallowed back the tears pushing against her throat.

"Right then. Let's press on." His smile looked unnervingly genuine. *There isn't a soul in London who knows me.* As they rounded a corner of rock, he winked and pointed up to a narrow crevice about five feet off the ground. "I'll take this one."

Ever since the incident with the animal skull, Cynthia had let him take the lead on any deep, dark holes. But she wouldn't have objected regardless. She couldn't speak. She couldn't behave as if nothing had happened, as Nick did. So she watched him scramble over loose rocks and haul himself over ledges, constantly checking for any deep spaces not visible from the sand.

She kept silent watch for nearly an hour, no longer sure if his good cheer was still feigned or had evolved into his previous genuinely fine mood. Regardless, she began to forget her anxiety and simply enjoy the show of Nick working, his hair mussed by the wind, breeches stretching tight over his haunches each time he stepped up.

He'd asked if she loved him. Of course she did. She loved Nick as she'd always loved him. His hair, his smile, his laugh. The way he brightened whenever anyone spoke to him. His impossibly warm brown eyes. The small kindnesses he offered without thought.

And now there was more. His strong hands and hot mouth. The crisp hair furred over his wide chest. And all the wicked things he did to her in the dark. And the light.

Of course she loved him. As if that made any difference at all. She'd loved him once before. She'd loved her father too, if those hazy memories could be believed. She'd loved her mother her whole life. And none of that love—none of it—had brought her anything but pain. Deep pain that stretched on for weeks and months and years until the ends frayed like worn cord. It never really stopped, it only spread out until the gossamer threads grew thin enough to overlook and deep enough to ignore.

So yes, she loved him. And there was nothing for it but to go on with her life. She could love him from afar, just as she had before. As long as she knew he would be all right.

But she no longer knew that.

"Cyn!" he called from somewhere far ahead.

Blinking, Cynthia realized she'd been staring at the foamed rush of water sneaking into a little pool between the rocks.

"Cynthia!" Nick waved to her from a perch about four feet off the ground. "I need your help!"

She'd have been alarmed if his wave hadn't

been so blatantly cheerful. Instead she felt a spurt of excitement.

"What is it?" she panted when she skidded to a stop before him.

"There's a cave up there. I can't get to it, but if I boost you up, you should be able to reach the edge."

She took his hand when he reached for her, and stepped up to join him on the wide ledge. The next flat surface was at least seven feet up.

Nick laced his fingers together and leaned over to offer a step up. That fall he'd taken a few days before had changed her perspective on heights, but Cyn gulped back her fear and settled her boot into the cradle he'd made.

"One, two, *three*." Nick tossed her up high enough that she could get a firm hold on the edge of a rock. Then he put the heels of his hands beneath her boot and pushed her higher. Cynthia simply rose up on the strength of his arms, until she could get her hands beneath her and hook a knee onto the surface.

Crawling quickly away from the edge, it took her a moment to realize what was right in front of her, but when she rose up to her knees, Cynthia froze.

"How does it look?" Nick called.

It looked . . . like a *cave*. A real cave, not some hollow in the rock pretending at cave-dom. Her knees shook when she rose to her feet.

"Cyn?"

"It's a cave!" she screamed, jumping up and down. Only a tiny bit though. The open air hovered a foot behind her.

"Good," she heard him call from below.

"No!" She spun around and edged forward so that

she could see him. "It's a real cave, Nick! You've got
to get up here."

His eyebrows flew nearly to his hairline. "Is there
something solid you can tie the rope to?"

After glancing around, she gestured for the rope,
then tied it to a narrow outcropping that climbed
nearly vertical at the mouth of the cave. Within moments, Nick was standing beside her, panting.

"You weren't kidding," he gasped. "That really is
a cave."

"I know!" Forgetting the tension that had stretched
between them all morning, Cyn grabbed his hand
and tugged him toward the opening. He tugged her
just as quickly behind him.

"Let me go first. We have no idea what it's like
in there."

Once they got past the bright reach of daylight, Cyn
was glad she'd conceded the lead. The roof of the cave
sat low, so that even she had to bend her head. Any time
her cloak brushed the ceiling, shards rained down, pep-
pering her shoulders with rock. She tried very hard not
to notice the spiders that scrambled away as her feet slid
on the rough debris littering the floor. If there were cobwebs, Nick was clearing them for her.

"Keep close," he ordered, tightening his hold on
her hand.

"Don't worry," she muttered back. The air around
them grew dimmer, the walls crept closer.

"Ow." Pebbles rained down as Nick rubbed the
crown of his head. "I think the end's ahead. Either
that or the floor drops out completely and that's why
I can't see anything."

"You're not making me feel better!"

His chuckle rumbled through the cave like a dragon

awakening. His foot slid loudly against the floor, and she hoped that meant he was feeling his way carefully and not tumbling over the edge. She squeezed his hand even tighter.

"Definitely the end."

Peeking over his shoulder, she could just make out the shape of his fingers resting against a pale surface. Her eyes adjusted as she stared, until she could see his fingernails too, and the pockmarked texture of the rock. A musty odor filled her nose as she turned carefully to look around her.

"Smells like something died in here," she murmured. "Do you see anything?"

"Not yet."

She watched in amazement as he began running his hands along little ledges without any hesitation at all. Aside from the spiders she knew were there, she suspected more bones. Or maybe something not quite dried out yet.

"Eek," she choked out, shuddering at the thought.

Nick glanced over at her with a smile. A smile that didn't waver when he reached out a hand to brush at the hair at her temple.

"What?"

"Nothing."

"*What was it?*"

"Mm. Just a cobweb."

Not believing him for a moment, Cyn brushed frantically at her hair. Then her dress. By the time she'd finished, she'd given herself a stern lecture about fear and foolish missishness. This was the likeliest spot they'd found in this whole damn shoreline, and she wasn't going to miss out because of spiders. Or decomposition.

Cyn threw back her shoulders, hit her head on a

low bulge in the ceiling, and headed for the opposite side of the narrow hollow. But before she reached for the wall, she tugged on her thick gloves. If it was any kind of treasure worth finding, it wouldn't be hard to feel even past salt-stiffened leather.

They worked in silence, aside from her occasional squeaks of panic whenever she felt something shift away from her searching fingers. *Just rocks,* she told herself. *Just pebbles.* But when she reached deep into a wide hole, the distinctive sounds of skittering claws clattered up from the dark.

"Oh, God," she whispered. "Oh, God. Oh, God." She took three deep breaths and then eased her hand back in. A mouse couldn't hurt her. Even a rat wouldn't do damage past the gloves. And she couldn't just move on. The hole was a good fifteen inches wide. The perfect hiding place.

She ran her hand down the concave wall of the hole, wondering if the grit that shifted under her fingers was sand or droppings.

"Here!" Nick shouted, scaring the stuffing out of Cynthia. She snatched her hand out of the hole so fast that she fell to her backside with a squeal. That squeal turned to a groan when rocks dug into her bottom.

"I've got something," Nick said, completely ignoring her moan of pain. "I've got something."

The scrape of metal against rock ricocheted through the tiny cave. Cynthia, on her knees now, held her breath and watched Nick's back as his arms shifted and tugged.

"Almost." Metal screamed, Nick grunted, and then hundreds of tiny rocks pinged against the ground. "Got it!"

She scrambled up to her feet.

"It's a box, Cyn!" He was moving toward the light as he spoke, and she hurried to catch up. "And it's heavy."

Her blood pounded against the walls of her veins, banging out a crazed pulse. They'd done it. They'd actually done it. "Let me see!"

Just under the edge of the mouth of the cave, Nick stopped and turned toward her, box balanced on both his palms. It was small, but solid, constructed of rough wood banded with iron and rivets. In short, it looked like a smuggler's chest of treasure. Inconspicuous and sturdy.

"Oh, Nick," she breathed, daring only to touch one finger against a metal corner.

"It's yours. Take it." His smile stretched to a grin that narrowed his eyes with its intensity. When she took the box from his hands, her own eyes widened. It *was* heavy. She hurriedly set it on the ground and tugged off her gloves.

"I told you I had a good feeling," Nick said as he knelt beside her.

"Stop saying that." She tried to toss him an exasperated look, but when she turned toward him he kissed her. A brief, happy kiss that was over nearly before it had begun. Still, she felt stunned by it.

"Go on," he urged.

Lips still tingling, she nodded and ran her hand over the cool metal bands. There was a loop for a lock, but it seemed to have been secured with string. Another hint, perhaps. How would an eleven-year-old boy secure his treasure?

Nick handed her a penknife, but he needn't have bothered. She'd barely put the knife to the string when it gave way. Too much moisture for too many years.

"Ready?" he breathed, and Cynthia lifted the lid.

Chapter 17

Gold glinted under the pale sun, throwing starbursts against the dull wood of the small chest. Those starbursts were absorbed by the flat darkness of tarnished silver and copper.

For a moment, for one glorious, joyous moment, his heart floated, buoyed by its own desires.

And then the sparkle of the gold lost its enchantment, and more details began to filter past his vision. The thick wooden walls of the chest, compressing the space inside to a few square inches. The relative scarcity of gold coins in comparison to silver.

But still . . . it *was* treasure.

Cynthia met his gaze, her eyes half excitement and half doubt.

Lancaster offered her a smile, eager to keep the hope alive for both of them. "We found it."

"We did."

"They look like old guineas."

"They do." She raised her hand, and then dropped it for a brief moment before reaching to touch the coins.

"You have your treasure." He recognized the under-current of his own words as he spoke them. Her treasure. There was money here, but not enough to share. Not enough to buy him out of his indenture. Even assuming the space dropped all the way to the very bottom of the chest, there couldn't be five thousand pounds here. There couldn't even be a thousand.

Coin slid against coin, the metal sound trying to convince him he was wrong. He hoped he was.

"How much do you think it is?" Cynthia whispered.

"Let's count it." The words tripped lightly from his tongue, as if he'd just proposed a picnic.

Nodding eagerly, Cynthia picked out a handful of coins and began to separate them into piles while Lancaster's heart flailed around, searching for its mooring. What could he do now? What could he do?

He tried to ignore the panicked flutter in his chest. *There may be more money than it seems,* he lectured himself. *How can you possibly tell with one glance?*

But the piles were growing, the gold guineas not keeping up with the rest of them. His heart was falling too fast, and the descent began to burn.

Cynthia cleared her throat and began to count, while he tried very hard not to see which pile she was counting, not to calculate the amounts as she added them. But there was no escaping the sum.

"If the guineas are worth twenty-one shillings . . ." she murmured. "And most of them are five-guinea coins . . . I believe it's three hundred four pounds and eleven shillings. Or thereabouts." Her voice wavered a bit at the end.

Lancaster sat down hard. She'd always been good at sums.

"Nick? Are you all right?"

"I'm fine, yes." Fine. Or completely devastated.

"You don't look fine." Her hand curled around his arm.

"I only thought it would be more, that's all."

"I did too." She sat down beside him and they stared at the coins together. "A thousand pounds at least? Maybe more? But it is a child's fortune, I suppose. Three hundred pounds. A respectable amount."

"Respectable," he agreed, "Yes. Definitely so. But," he added as if it were his only concern, "not enough to pay your stepfather's debts."

"No, not that much." Her hand played idly with the coin towers. "Perhaps it will be enough to buy my family some space, at the least, though I'm sure I can't imagine Richmond being so generous."

So it all came back to murder again, it seemed. The death of Richmond to protect Cynthia. But who would protect Lancaster? There were only so many creditors one could run over with the carriage. The sick thought made him laugh.

"What is it?"

"Nothing. Did you anticipate this? Perhaps you've an alternate plan?"

"No. I just . . . I guess I didn't think it through." Her words cracked a little at the end, but she shook her head as if she'd shake off the emotion too.

"We'll find a way, Cyn," he murmured, reaching for her limp hand.

Finally, his gut seemed to realize what had just happened. It dropped as if he'd just jumped from an impossible height.

This was the worst possible outcome. Not enough to pay off his creditors, not enough to marry her, not even enough to buy her free of Richmond and send her to America. Worse than not having found the treasure at all. At least then he'd have hope.

He'd promised something important to this woman. Despite that she hadn't believed him, he'd promised to find a way to marry her. Now what could he do?

She grabbed up the coins and began dropping them back into the tiny chest. With clumsy hands, he tried to help.

"There," she said with a determined nod. After closing the lid and dusting off her hands, Cynthia stood. "We can think while we walk."

Think. Yes, he needed to think. Conjure up a miraculous solution to this problem. Funny, a few days ago he hadn't even believed the treasure existed. Somehow he'd traveled from disbelief to total dependence, and now he was lost.

"I'll go first," he murmured, dropping down to his knees to ease his legs out into thin air. "Toss the chest down to me before you follow."

Was it possible he'd been here only a week? No, it wasn't possible. Because when Cyn dropped the chest and then scooted her legs out over the ledge, he didn't gasp in shock at the view of her exposed limbs. Her hiked skirts were already a familiarity. A pretty reminder of the intimacies shared the night before.

How, in the space of one short week, could he have wandered from old acquaintance to renewed friend to reckless lover? And how could he move now toward fond memory? He couldn't.

Cyn inched toward him, her boots scissoring at the rope, trying to catch it between her feet. Lancaster got beneath her and wrapped his arms around her knees to give her some leverage. As she slid lower, he let his arms slide higher, until his cheek was pressed to her bare thigh, her legs clasped tight in his arms.

A small voice floated in like a lapping wave. "Blimey!" it whispered.

Lancaster froze, Cynthia's skirt bunched on his shoulders. "Oh, bloody hell." He couldn't turn to look, so he just eased Cynthia lower as she shimmied down the rope. One of her boots banged into his knee. "Don't turn around," he ordered, but it was too late. He looked up to see Cynthia's neck crane toward the beach.

"Bloody hell!" she yelped, and Lancaster finally dared to look.

Four boys stood frozen in the sand, mouths hanging open as if they'd been stopped in the middle of a song. They ranged in size from tiny to lumbering, but each one seemed entranced with the sight of Cyn's thighs.

"Drop!" he muttered, and Cynthia let go of the rope. "Pull up your hood."

She reached for the cloak just as the tiny one pointed. "That's Miss Merrithorpe," he said, then added helpfully, "The dead one."

Two of the remaining pack crossed themselves with shaking hands while the third turned and bolted, ruining any hope Lancaster might have had of gathering them all around and threatening to sell them to pirates if they breathed a word.

"It's a ghost," the rather portly child cried out, but the little one shook his head.

"What would a ghost want with climbing down ropes?"

Gads, when had children gotten to be so sensible? Damned observant monkeys, the lot of them.

"She's not Cynthia Merrithorpe," Lancaster said quickly. "So of course she's not a ghost."

"Begging your pardon, milord, but if she's not Miss Merrithorpe, then I'm not Henry Johnson."

"Listen. Henry, is it? This woman is my companion from London."

The boy's jaw edged out. "I ain't heard nothing about a London lady around here."

"You don't think Miss Merrithorpe—assuming she weren't lying dead at the bottom of the sea, I mean— would find herself alone on a deserted beach with a gentleman, do you? Completely improper, and Miss Merrithorpe was a lady."

The boy looked incredibly doubtful at that. Apparently the delicate flower of femininity argument wouldn't work in Cyn's case. "Well then, Henry, what would Cynthia Merrithorpe want with a crumbling bit of cliff anyway?"

Sly intelligence narrowed the boy's eyes, and Lancaster tried not to cringe. "But what in the world would a London doxy want with those cliffs, milord?"

The other two boys began backing away.

"Grab him," Cynthia whispered too loudly, and all three spun around and ran.

"Damn it," Lancaster muttered as he made a short attempt at giving chase. The boys were fast and less hampered by the pull of the sand. Well, all except the big one, but Henry Johnson was the problem and he was already halfway to Neely. *"Damn it."*

Cynthia stopped at his back. "Henry is too smart by half. He always has been."

"I'll say. Well, I suppose that clears up any question of what our next move must be."

"Oh? What's that?" Her hand touched his shoulder, so he turned toward her, forcing it to slide off.

He met her gaze and didn't even attempt to look light or happy. "We're leaving Cantry Manor. Today."

"I'll pack the last of the cherry compote too. It'll go well with the brown bread." Mrs. Pell was a blur as she darted from the pantry to the table and then to the shelf above the stove.

"I'm sure this is entirely unnecessary," Cynthia grumbled. Of course, Nick chose that moment to stride in from the hallway.

"Don't be ridiculous. If your stepfather gets word you're here, he has every right to take you by force. If we're not here, he can't do that."

"I'll be twenty-one in nine days."

"And you're free to return here in nine days. But for now, we're going."

"Where?" she cried.

Nick stopped his pacing and met her gaze. "Do you know the Duke of Somerhart?"

"Who?" She felt her face cool with shock. "Of course not. A *duke*?"

"Somerhart isn't too far from here. About a six hours' drive."

"And . . . But . . . We cannot simply waltz up to a ducal estate and beg protection!"

Nick stared thoughtfully at the floor. "He owes me a favor."

"A *duke*? That makes no sense. What could you possibly have done for a duke?"

His eyes crinkled in a smile. "I helped him find his runaway bride. Well, she wasn't his bride yet, in truth.

But they married shortly thereafter, so I gather it all worked out."

"But . . . This seems a rather large favor to ask anyone, much less a man of such standing."

"He was a broken man, Cyn. Tormented by unrequited love." Something about his own words made him chuckle, and the laughter made Cynthia want to yell.

He'd taken full control of the situation, brushing aside every argument she'd made for calm. They could at least wait and see what happened.

"Where's Adam?" Nick asked.

"He's not back yet. Which is exactly my point! We don't even know what those boys might've said."

"Stop being so obstinate. One boy we might have been able to coerce into silence. But four boys? It's hopeless. I don't doubt someone's sprinting to your stepfather's door right this moment, eager to be the one to carry the story."

The fact that his words were true didn't make them easier to swallow. She'd meant to leave Oak Hall and the village of Neely behind. She'd meant to sail much farther away than the Somerhart estate. But now it felt too rushed. Her last night here in Cantry Manor and she hadn't realized it. Her last evening in the kitchen with Mrs. Pell, and now she couldn't even remember what they'd prepared. Her last walk along the sea. Last glimpse of the village.

How could she leave without even a fare-thee-well?

"I'll simply hide in the passageways if he comes. I lived with you for days and you never even *heard* me."

"Cynthia," Nick scoffed, dismissing her objections with an exasperated shake of his head. "Have you packed yet?"

She clenched her teeth together to keep from screaming. "Yes, but I'm not going anywhere until Adam—"

The kitchen door flew in, propelled by gangly limbs. The face that followed looked a bit different than it had when he'd left.

"Adam!" she gasped. "What's happened to your face?"

"They said you was a trollop!" he cried, then pressed his fingers to his split lip. His eye seemed to be swelling as she watched.

"Oh, Adam!" Cyn moved aside for Mrs. Pell who was already approaching with a cold rag. "Lord Lancaster here told them I was a trollop from London! There was nothing to defend."

"I didn't like it," the boy answered, voice conveying the finality of the statement. He did spare a scornful look for Nick.

"I said lady companion! But I take it from your gallant action that tongues are wagging."

"Aye. They are." Adam snuck a hesitant look at Cynthia from under Mrs. Pell's arm. "I told my mum I'd be gone for a while. Maybe a week or two."

"No," Nick said flatly.

Mrs. Pell cocked her head. "Be good for the boy, your lordship. Get out and see a little bit of the world."

"We are about to become *fugitives*, Mrs. Pell."

"Quite an adventure for a young man, milord."

Nick scoffed. "An adventure in questionable conduct!"

"Oh, fiddlesticks," the housekeeper snapped. "What other kind of adventure is there?"

When he looked at Cynthia, she shrugged. She saw

no reason to deny the boy a trip to a grand estate, but Nick looked filled with doubt.

"What did your mother say, Adam?"

"She said to be careful, take good care of Miss Merrithorpe, and do as Lord Lancaster says without question."

A brief tremor of some strong emotion rippled over Nick's face, but it passed so quickly that Cynthia couldn't place it. "I find it hard to believe your mother supports this," he muttered.

"She trusts you, milord."

"Well, she shouldn't. She knows nothing about me."

Cynthia wasn't the only one studying Nick's face now. Mrs. Pell stopped her work to watch him. When he caught them both looking, he scowled and threw up his hands. "Fine. You may ride with Jackson and learn about driving the carriage, would you like that?" Before the boy could answer, Nick stalked toward the hallway. "I'll get the trunk."

Mrs. Pell snapped the towel in Adam's direction. "Get your things, boy. His lordship won't wait on the likes of you."

Cynthia turned back to the jug of cider she was securing for the trip, but Mrs. Pell's familiar hand invaded her vision and covered Cynthia's fingers. "You need to marry him, sweeting."

"Pardon?" Flash-flooded with guilt, Cynthia jerked her hand from beneath the housekeeper's. "I don't know what you mean."

"Aye, you do."

Cyn couldn't stop the blood from rushing to her face, so she turned to slip the jug into her satchel. "No, I don't."

"I came to wake you this morning."

The simple calm of those words shot through her like a bullet. Her body seized up and wouldn't move as she recalled what had gone on in her bed that morning.

"This house is old, but the walls aren't that thick, sweeting. Lucky for all of us, I didn't open the door."

"I . . ." The edges of her vision went a bit gray, but she wasn't so weak that she would faint in the face of a choice she'd made. "I seduced him. He tried to say no."

"I'm sure he did. And I'm pleased you followed my advice."

"I didn't." Cynthia forced herself to turn and face Mrs. Pell, shocked to find that the older woman's eyes held not a hint of disapproval or even embarrassment. "It wasn't about marriage."

"Well, it will be now, I'd imagine."

"It won't. He needs to marry money. Why can no one acknowledge that simple truth?"

Mrs. Pell wrapped a hand around Cynthia's elbow and tugged her to a chair. "Because life is not so simple. Sit down."

Cynthia sat, relieved to take the weight off her shaky legs.

"I came to Cantry Manor in 1813. You'll remember my son, Tom. He was a tiny baby at the time, and now a grown man living in India, of all places."

"Yes, I know. Your husband died at sea."

"That was a lie. I've never told anyone the truth. I wasn't a widow, and there was never a husband." She swept a few crumbs off the table as if she hadn't just said something spectacularly shocking.

"Pardon?"

"Tom's father was my sweetheart. I didn't come from a wealthy family, but we were respectable all the same. We owned the local inn and my da' rented horses as well. When I turned up pregnant, there was no doubt I'd marry. No shame in an early birth, you know, so long as you've signed your name at the church."

Stunned into silence, Cynthia nodded.

"He was the local vicar, so—"

Her throat abruptly unlocked. "He was *what*?"

"So I would have led a comfortable, respectable life as his wife. But when I told him I was pregnant, he slapped me." Mrs. Pell's hands finally stilled, and she stared hard at them. "He slapped me and called me a grasping whore. Apparently he thought he'd at least work his way up to the local squire's daughter, increase his social standing with a fine marriage. But he was caught and that was that. He would marry the innkeeper's daughter instead."

"Oh, Mrs. Pell. That's awful!"

"It was awful, and I couldn't accept it. I didn't have to spend my whole life in service, Cynthia. I chose it, because I couldn't bear the thought of that man spitting on me every day for the rest of my life. I'd thought he loved me, and I wouldn't settle for less."

Cynthia clasped her hands around Mrs. Pell's. "But you see, I don't want to be that to Nick either. I won't be the one to bring him low."

"He's already been brought low, child, and it had nothing to do with you, did it?"

"We don't know that's true."

"Then ask him. There are some things in life more important than money. I'd wager Lord Lancaster already knows that."

"Knows what?" his deep voice asked from behind

her. She could tell by the slight echo of the words and the sound of his boot heels that he was still in the hall and likely hadn't heard anything else. Thank God.

Mrs. Pell, more cunning than Cynthia had suspected, smiled and pushed to her feet. "He knows that if he doesn't keep my lovely girl safe I'll box his ears."

"Ah, yes. He does know that. Are you ready, Cyn?"

"I am." And yet she just sat there, dreading the moment to come.

Nick cleared his throat. "Well then. I'll let you say your good-byes. Though I'm sure we'll be back in a matter of days."

Cynthia forced herself to her feet, crying even before Mrs. Pell's arms came around her.

The housekeeper tutted and murmured wordless sounds as Cynthia choked out inelegant sobs. "Come now. None of that."

"Come with me to America," Cynthia whispered hopelessly. They'd had this discussion too many times. Mrs. Pell didn't even answer, she only shook her head.

"But you'll be all alone here."

"That's how I like it. What in the world would I do in a place like New York? I can't even fathom that number of people."

Cynthia sniffed into her shoulder.

"Perhaps you won't go at all. We'll see. Now be careful and be kind. And send letters. Lots of letters."

Cynthia was still crying hard as Jackson closed up the carriage with a curious look at her messy face. But strangely enough, as they rolled past the distant vista of Oak Hall, her tears dried and she stared emotionlessly out at her old home.

Chapter 18

Nick's face was blue in the twilight glow of the sky. Blue as if he were dying.

They'd eaten their dinner long before, and though the sun was setting, they still faced another hour's drive before descending, unannounced, upon a ducal household. Up to that moment, Cynthia had spent the hours staring rapt at the passing countryside. She'd never been so far from home and could hear her own excitement expressed in the rapid chatter that floated down from Adam's seat above.

But it was darker now, and they were all tired. And she couldn't stop staring at Nick's twilight face.

Had he tried to kill himself? If he had, she couldn't leave him as she planned, not if he really thought himself in love with her.

His eyes closed, adding to the morbid vignette. When his head fell to rest against the seat, the darkness of the scar peeked above his collar.

A burn. But how did one burn one's whole neck?

Her stomach clenched at the obvious answer.

The scent of approaching rain filled the carriage,

somehow adding to the pressure in her head. She couldn't stop the words that swelled in her throat and couldn't think of any way to soften them. "Did you hang yourself, Nick?"

His eyes opened and looked at the ceiling of the coach before sliding slowly down to meet hers. "Pardon me?"

Cynthia touched her own neck, troubled by the delicacy of the skin there. "Did you try to kill yourself?"

The warm brown of his eyes cooled to the color of frozen dirt. "Why in the world would you ask me that?"

"Because you have a scar that circles your neck. Because you never came home after your trip when you were meant to. Because servants talk and they say . . . they say that you *hung* yourself, Nick."

"It's not true." He leaned back again and closed his eyes, as if the conversation were over.

"How did you get that scar?" she demanded.

"I already told you. It was a burn."

"A burn from *what*? A cravat soaked in boiling oil?"

His mouth actually twitched up in a smile, and Cynthia knew he wasn't really Nick at that point. He was Lord Lancaster, who could smile through a discussion of his own brush with death.

"Tell me the truth," she pleaded, and the smile dropped away. "Something changed you, Nick. And we were friends, and I have a right to know what happened."

He met her gaze again, glaring. "You have no right to ask me. It was a decade ago. And I do not discuss it. Ever."

"You will discuss it with *me,* damn you."

When he sat forward the tendons on his neck tightened with anger. "I've told you I didn't try to kill myself." His voice rose to a shout. "Is my word not good enough for you? Do you think I'm lying? Telling falsehoods to cover up perversion and weakness and cowardice?"

"I . . ." She'd never been afraid of Nick. Never imagined that she could be. But for a brief moment she saw something flicker behind his eyes. Something dark and powerful with rage. "Of course not," she whispered. "Why would I think that?"

Shaking his head, he ran a rough hand over his face. "Why would you not?"

"Nick . . . I only want to know what—"

"I've got to get out of here." He banged a fist on the roof, and the carriage, already driving much slower, eased to a stop.

"Wait!" she cried as he launched himself out the door. "Where are you going?" By the time she'd stuck her head out, he was disappearing into the dim, heels crunching on the lane. She watched until she couldn't hear his steps, then glanced up to the coachman's box to find two faces staring down at her. Adam's eyes were wide with trepidation.

"Why's his lordship so angry?"

"He's well," Cyn replied, ducking back inside, still tasting the lie in her mouth. He wasn't well. Not at all. *What had happened to him?*

She had to believe him, didn't she? But what could the explanation be? She swiped at a tear caught on her lashes and sat down to await Nick's return and whatever that might bring.

* * *

Rain dripped down his nose. Lightning flashed somewhere in the south. It was nearly full dark and he was stalking through the rain like an angry child.

And he'd been as foolish as a child to think that Cynthia would never ask about his scars. Still, he hadn't known there'd been rumors among the servants here in Yorkshire. London, yes, though his parents had taken care to hire only three servants that first month, and all of them recommended for their discretion.

Did you try to kill yourself?

No one had ever asked him that question. Not even his parents had asked, though he'd pled and pled with them to believe he hadn't. But now, after so many years of living with it, he was no longer sure of anything.

Had he meant to die? At some point, he had. At some point, it had seemed a great and blessed relief. Once his body had given up its struggle, dying had become peaceful. Rather like walking alone in a dark rain.

When Lancaster looked up from the muddy road he realized his anger had faded. Now he was only exhausted. And wet. The faint pinpoints of the carriage lamps glowed ahead, and he picked up the pace and headed toward them.

With only a dozen feet left to go, a vibration began to penetrate his legs. He stopped and cocked his head, quickly picking up the sound of approaching hoof beats. Adam jumped down from the seat.

"Who's that?"

"I'm not sure," Lancaster muttered. "But tell Miss Merrithorpe to stay hidden and close the curtains."

Adam did as he was told before jogging over to stand beside his master. Jackson stood up on his box and drew out a rifle, and Lancaster nodded his approval before turning to face the coming rider.

The man slowed a good twenty yards from them and approached at a careful walk. He was alone, and Lancaster's shoulders relaxed a bit. Not a band of highwaymen then. And he could tell by the straight line of the man's back that it wasn't Cyn's stepfather either.

The rider stayed silent, so Lancaster held his tongue as well.

At first, the glow of the carriage lights only touched the horse, a big bay with a crooked white star that reached up to one eye. Then the rider's boots were illuminated, then his legs, and when he dismounted, finally, his face.

A demon's face, despite that it was neither ugly nor sinisterly beautiful. Lancaster slid one foot back before he stopped himself and stood straight.

This must be Bram, because the face . . . the face belonged to Richmond.

Skin crawling, he made his body stay still. He did not back away. He did not lunge forward. He did not let his stomach complete its somersault and toss its remains upon the dirt. Lancaster only watched those innocuous, perfectly bland features come closer. The only difference was the eyes, and he suddenly understood what the villagers had meant. Richmond's eyes had sparkled with joviality in one guise, and glittered with heat in another. But Bram's eyes . . . they were dead as dried wood. Not cruel or angry or sad. Dead.

When those eyes shifted to Adam and stayed there, Lancaster let himself move. He curled a hand over Adam's shoulder and pulled him back from Bram. "Back to your post, Adam," he murmured, his gut tight as a drum. He didn't want this man's gaze on the boy.

Adam threw him a puzzled look but eventually

turned and shuffled back to the front of the carriage. Bram watched him go.

"I assume you did not stop to chat about the weather," Lancaster said.

"Are you Lancaster?" the man grumbled.

"I am Lord Lancaster, yes."

The dead gaze flicked down Lancaster's body, then shifted to the carriage. "Miss Merrithorpe in there?"

"Do I know you, sir?"

"No, but I've heard about you."

A wash of cold, separate from the drizzle, snuck beneath Lancaster's coat to shiver over his skin. *What did that mean?*

"Lord Richmond wants his bride back."

"Does he? I can't imagine what that would mean to me."

"You've been seen with her."

He raised his brow in mock surprise. "The girl is dead, or so I've been told."

Bram took a step toward the carriage, but when Lancaster shot out a hand to catch his arm, the man backed up and pulled away. As if he liked being touched as little as Lancaster did.

"As you haven't seen fit to introduce yourself, I'll be on my way." With those words, he expected Bram to offer his name, perhaps volunteer that he worked for Richmond in whatever capacity that was, and then pepper Lancaster with further questions. But Bram did none of that, he simply watched Lancaster for ten seconds, then twenty. He watched him with his dead eyes, then turned and remounted his horse.

He didn't ride off, he only waited. It seemed they were about to be followed.

So be it.

* * *

There was a garden sculpted into the ceiling.

Cynthia craned her neck, trying not to look like a complete rustic while still getting a view of the plaster ivy. And the roses. Each individual petal visible even from fifteen feet below.

"Nick," she whispered. "We shouldn't be here."

Nick, pacing the length of the reception room, didn't seem to hear her. He hadn't noticed the ceiling at all as far as she could tell. Likely he lounged about in homes like this as a matter of habit.

"He's sure to toss us out on our ear, showing up unannounced in the middle of the night!"

"It's eight P.M.," he muttered.

"What about the duchess?"

"What about her?"

Cynthia clenched her hands hard together. "How am I to speak with a duchess?"

Nick finally glanced toward her. One side of his mouth lifted. "She seems to have a good grasp of the English language."

"What? What does that mean? Is she French? Mercy, she must be so elegant."

"No, she's not French. Cynthia, I'm teasing you."

"Well, stop it. Can't you see I'm terrified? Maybe she isn't here."

He stepped closer to pull her hands apart and stroke a thumb over her wrist. "As far as I can tell, Somerhart never leaves her side, so I'd imagine she's here. But there's nothing to be afraid of. Emma is . . . Well, she's rather exceptional, but very kind."

"Emma?" she said. *Exceptional?* she thought.

"Her Grace, of course."

"Her Grace," Cynthia muttered, practicing. "Your Grace." What if she forgot? What if she called her "my lady" or, horror of horrors, *Emma*? "Oh, why did you tell me her *name*?"

"I apologize." Nick chuckled. "I knew her before she was so lofty and imposing."

"She is imposing?" She realized even before he began to laugh that Nick was teasing again. Incensed, she stalked across the room to the fireplace to stare at the plaster vines that climbed up to the mantel.

At least there wasn't silence between them anymore. At least he was laughing. After rocking the carriage with his abrupt entrance, he'd explained that Bram was following them to the Somerhart estate, but he could only go so far onto the duke's land without permission, after all, and there was nothing to worry over.

Then he'd smiled and apologized for his earlier rudeness in polite words that invited no question.

But she'd forgotten that worry now. There was a larger one looming. A duke. The grandest of all grand gentlemen. And he had no previous connection to Cynthia, no inclination to set aside his gentlemanly honor and offer help. She belonged to her stepfather for nine more days, and the Duke of Somerhart would be obligated to send her back to him, or at least jot out a letter inquiring if he wanted his daughter back.

"Nick, please," she tried one more time. "I think we should continue on. Stay at an inn. Perhaps you could call on His Grace in the morning. Test his mood. I—"

When the door opened, Cynthia regretted the pique that had sent her stomping across the room. Now she was separated from Nick, alone and adrift in terrifying waters as a footman bowed an elegant couple into the room. The woman was rather . . .

normal looking. Not six feet tall. Not adorned in a white-powdered wig. On first glance, she was very young and almost plain. But she carried beauty with her in the confidence she wore like a gown.

"Emma!" Nick called, striding forward to bend low over her hand. The woman smiled and pulled him into a hug. The man at her side scowled.

Cynthia had thought the woman lovely enough, but the man—the duke, surely—was as beautiful as Lucifer himself. His black hair might have made her think of the devil, but when his pale blue gaze fell on her, Cynthia decided it was the eyes. So cool and measuring. She realized she'd taken a step back when her shoulder touched the mantel.

In that moment, she'd have given anything to find herself somewhere else. Even facing Richmond, she'd at least known where she stood. He was her enemy. He was evil. But the Duke of Somerhart . . . this was shaky ground indeed. This man was, at best, a dangerous ally.

Past the rushing in her ears, Cynthia heard the word "introduce" and watched all three of them turn toward her. She waited in vain for the ground to swallow her up—perhaps there was an underworld of plaster roots and hollows where she could hide for days—but the floor stayed solid beneath her.

Nick winked in support, and Cynthia forced herself to step forward and meet the trio in the middle of the room.

"Your Graces, may I present Miss Cynthia Merrithorpe of Oak Hall? Miss Merrithorpe, Her Grace, the Duchess of Somerhart, and His Grace, the Duke of Somerhart."

Trying in vain to remember how deeply she was to curtsy, Cynthia sank as low as possible, as low as she would if presented to the queen. Her ugly boots stuck out beneath her skirts.

"Don't fall over," the duchess said. "Though I daresay that would make a story to laugh over in future meetings. Regardless, up you go." A hand wrapped around her elbow and tugged her up.

"A pleasure to meet you, Miss Merrithorpe," she said, linking her arm through Cynthia's. She turned them both to face the duke. "Smile at the girl, Hart. Then you can go back to scowling at Lancaster."

"Charmed," he offered, flashing a smile that showed the enchanting side of the devil.

"A pleasure, Your Grace," she managed to say.

His smile fell away when the duke looked to Nick. "Well, Lancaster, lovely traveling companion aside, what brings you so unexpectedly to Somerhart?"

Nick offered his wide London grin. "I think the lady could use a refreshment before we delve into deeper subjects. Care to offer one?"

"Nick!" Cynthia gasped, horrified by his rudeness. He couldn't quite smother a choked laugh, and when she glanced toward their hosts, she realized why. Both of them stared at her with raised eyebrows.

So much time had passed since she'd been in polite company. Months. There were rules to be observed. Important ones. Nick was Lord Lancaster to her here.

"I . . ."

Nick didn't look horrified at least, but he took everything with such ease. "Miss Merrithorpe and I have known each other since she was in pantaloons. We are very nearly cousins."

"Cousins, hm?" the duchess replied. "Then as Lancaster is very nearly family, we must treat you as a cousin, too, Miss Merrithorpe. How lovely."

"When," the duke snapped, "has he been anything even close to family?"

"Well, not your family, perhaps. Stiff stodges the whole lot of them. Excepting your sister, of course. And Aunt Augusta."

"Why, thank you." Despite his grumbling, the duke moved to the sideboard and poured four glasses of red wine. "All right then," he murmured as he handed them out. "Civilized enough for you, Lancaster?"

"Nearly."

"Sit then."

They all took a seat near the low fire. The duke could not possibly have been expecting visitors. Cynthia could hardly fathom a household where fires burned in empty rooms.

"I've come to collect on my debt," Nick announced without preamble.

Somerhart snorted. "You are the one who specializes in debt, not I."

"You know what I mean."

Somerhart inclined his head. The duchess murmured something about posturing, but both men ignored her.

"Miss Merrithorpe requires a discreet home for a few days."

Those blue eyes cut toward her. "How so?"

Cynthia turned to Nick in alarm. What would he say? Why had they not discussed this beforehand?

"She reaches her majority in nine days."

"I see." What Somerhart saw clearly did not please him.

The duchess, however, brightened. "Are you fleeing a disastrous marriage?"

Cynthia's whole body twitched with tension.

The duchess's eyes brightened further. "Are you eloping with *Lancaster*?"

"No," she answered, at the same moment Nick said, "We shall see."

The duke's eyebrow rose again. "I see. But I'm not sure my debt obliges me to suffer the wrath of an entire enraged family. Two families even. Or . . ." He looked to Nick. "Perhaps four."

Four, Cynthia thought. Yes, that was exactly it. Four families ruined if they married. "Of course, Your Grace." She stood, forcing the gentlemen to stand as well. "We should never have asked it."

"*We* did not ask," Nick interrupted. His London face disappeared, replaced by gravity. "I did. And family wrath or not, I'll ask you to take her under your protection. The suitor in question is Lord Richmond."

"*Richmond,*" the duchess gasped.

"I thought you might be familiar with his reputation."

"Oh, at least," she said. "He was one of my father's *dearest* friends. If one believes that jackals have the capacity for friendship. A more despicable man I've never met."

Cynthia's face heated. She could feel the disgust in the room coalesce, as if it were something solid. Something *she* had brought here.

"Well, there's no question then," the duchess said. "You shall stay."

Somerhart crossed his arms. "I suppose you must stay as well?"

Nick bowed with a little flourish. "Your generosity knows no bounds."

The duchess stood and took Cynthia's arm. "Come, I'll show you to your room. And you must call me Emma, for it seems we are more like cousins than I suspected."

Stunned by the quickness of the current she found herself in, Cynthia let herself be swept from the room. The men stayed where they were. She was to be discussed. She understood that. She only wished she knew what would be said.

"You can imagine my confusion," Somerhart said as soon as the door closed behind the women. "Emma and I were just discussing our upcoming trip to London. For your *wedding*."

"Ah. Confusion. Yes."

"I take it you've broken your betrothal."

"I'll call on Miss Brandiss in person as soon as I return to London."

"That won't go over well. With her family or your creditors."

"I'm aware."

Somerhart took a seat and crossed his legs. "I was given to understand that Lord Richmond had become . . . incapacitated."

"If you mean that someone castrated him, yes I'd heard that as well. I don't know what he's about with Cynthia. All accounts are that he's no longer capable of fathering children, but perhaps they were wrong."

Somerhart grimaced and took a hasty sip of wine.

"His man followed me here. I plan to send my carriage on in the morning to try to throw the scent. If you'd like me to go with it, I will." Relief washed over him when Somerhart waved him off.

"I'll not lose a second of sleep over the likes of Richmond. At worst, I can hold Miss Merrithorpe's family off for nine days. No point in being a duke if one can't abuse one's power on occasion."

Lancaster raised his glass in the man's direction

before downing it. "How is your accumulation of power proceeding? I knew about your railroads, but I've only recently heard talk of your shipping enterprise as well."

Somerhart grunted. "Despite the dealings with parliament, I find the railroads simpler. The shipping . . . I swear these damned Americans expect to be seduced into a contract. The only person I'm interested in seducing is my wife."

"What's that?" Lancaster grinned. "They want you to be *charming*, Your Grace?"

"As if I have time for that," the duke spat out in disgust.

"I could give you lessons."

"Somehow I don't think they'd take."

Lancaster inclined his head in polite agreement.

"If you care to exercise your one remaining asset on someone else . . . We've a bit of a fete planned two days out. You're welcome to join in and trot out your charm if you like. Emma's invited the Osbournes and a few dozen of her favorite opponents."

"Opponents?"

"At the tables. She misses gambling, though she denies it. Claims she's merely helping the stable hands learn math when she plays them for biscuits."

"Oh, good Lord." Lancaster laughed.

"I've never had enough patience for it, whether it's biscuits or crowns I'm betting."

As soon as Somerhart uttered the word *crown*, Lancaster forgot his amusement and sat forward. A gambling party. And Cynthia had 304 pounds that needed to be more. Perhaps the solution had just fallen into his lap.

"Thank you, Somerhart. I'd love to attend."

Chapter 19

His feet swung slightly as if there were a breeze in the room, as if the rope were a child's swing instead of a noose. The creaking of it filled his ears, but the sound spun farther away the longer he hung. His hands dropped from the rope.

"Nick." He opened his eyes to find Cynthia standing in front of him, glaring up. "Did you hang yourself?"

Did she expect an answer? He pointed to the rope. I can't speak.

"Well, you should be ashamed of yourself, Nicholas Cantry."

So he should. Deeply, horrifyingly ashamed. He stared down at her, relieved that her face would be the last he saw.

But then a door opened behind her and Richmond entered, completely nude, hand cupping his bollocks. His skin was fish-belly pale, his gut soft and doughy, just as it had been ten years before. Lancaster watched in horror as Richmond, fully aroused, approached Cynthia from behind.

Lancaster kicked his legs, tried to raise an arm to point, but Cynthia just shook her head in disgust. Then Richmond dropped his hand and reached for Cynthia, blood dripping from his fingers. When Lancaster looked down to see the

*man's bollocks were a mangled, torn mess, he opened his
mouth in a silent scream.*

"Nick!" Cynthia called again, rapping a little harder
on the door.

The doors in this house were damned solid. A hint
of a noise drifted through. A muffled curse. The faint
rustle of bedclothes.

She knocked once more. "Nick, it's almost time for
dinner!"

She couldn't go downstairs by herself. Her nerves
were a jangling mess of wires and barbs. Guests had
been arriving all day, and Cynthia had only just begun
to relax into the idea of being in a duke's home. Even
after two days, she still jumped like a frightened mouse
whenever His Grace entered a room. The duchess,
however, no longer scared her at all. She was enticingly
mysterious though, and Cynthia wondered what her
guests would be like.

At the thought of the mill of lords and ladies she
was about to face, Cyn raised her fist to knock again,
but the door finally swung open.

"I take it you had a good nap?" The words were out
of her mouth before she registered Nick's pale face
and sweat-damp brow. "Are you ill?"

"No. Just sleeping too soundly."

"It's nearly time for dinner."

He rubbed a hand over the nape of his neck. "I'd
best dress then. Thank you for waking me."

When the door began to close, Cynthia huffed and
slipped past him into the room. "Nick, I'm terrified. I
don't think I should attend."

He shut the door with an irritated snap, then leaned

against it with his arms crossed. "Whatever are you talking about?" His teeth chattered a bit over the words.

"Perhaps you should get back into bed. Are you sure you're well?" She started to reach a hand toward his brow, but changed her mind at the way he stiffened.

"I'm only chilled and I'd like to dress, so if you could excuse me . . ."

"Would you simply dress then? I have seen it all quite clearly before. Though *not* in the past few days, I might mention."

He scowled at her as he passed. "Agree to marry me and I'll agree to see to your needs again."

"Arrogant cur," she muttered. "And I would recommend against your taking naps. They seem to leave you in a foul mood."

"After catching a glimpse of that portrait you started of Emma last night, I found myself incapable of sleep."

"Lout."

Ignoring her, he shucked off his robe and tossed it on the bed. Cynthia forgot her irritation, and lost herself in the sight of his naked back as he rifled through the wardrobe. His buttocks tensed and relaxed in a fascinating rhythm as he shifted and moved. His muscles created hollows that begged her fingers for a thorough study of the contours of his body. And his thighs looked so hard, nothing like hers. Solid muscle dusted lightly with fur. She'd never touched his thighs, but now her mouth watered with the lust to do so. Her sex melted.

But Nick's uncooperative mood foiled her fantasy. He pulled a starched shirt over his head and the hem fell to cover him all the way to the tops of his thighs.

Cynthia sighed.

"Are you ogling me?" he asked over his shoulder.

"Yes."

He tugged on trousers with a smirk, facing her fully as he buttoned them closed. "My. I do believe Somerhart's a tad slimmer than I."

"If I had an extra set of stays I'd let you borrow them."

"Oh, I've got my own," he said with a wink. "That's why I wanted you to leave, damn you." His eyes sparkled as he took a starched cravat from the wardrobe, and Cynthia's stomach let go of its worry. He looked better. The sweat had dried and the blood had returned to his face.

His eyes dipped down her body. "You are breathtaking."

"Really?" She ran a reverent hand down the deep gold silk of the dress. "You seemed to be breathing quite easily for a while there."

"An illusion." His gaze lingered on her décolletage. "I assure you I am quite weak."

Cynthia raised her chin. "Your weakness would have been better served before you dressed."

Winding the dark blue cravat around his neck, he kept his eyes on her. "I'm not sure you are entirely decent, Cyn. Even aside from the danger of a chest cold, I don't like it at all."

She glanced down to the rise of her breasts above the gown. She'd spent a good fifteen minutes studying them in her room. "Emma told me my breasts were perfection."

"And so they are. Too much perfection."

She tugged at the neckline. "Stop it! I am nervous enough without you making me feel like a cow past the milking hour!"

"Have mercy, Cyn," he choked out before collapsing against the wardrobe in laughter.

She tugged again. "Is the dress inappropriate? Emma had it taken out just for me, and I'd hate to be ungracious, but I don't think I should go. I *won't* go."

"Come now." He walked toward her, ends of the cravat still hanging free. As he drew closer, she could see that the blue was darkened with stripes of coal black. She wished she knew how to tie a neck cloth so that she could fuss over him.

"Cynthia, you are beautiful. Too beautiful. And every man will fall in love with you tonight, and I shall be quite distraught."

"I don't think it wise to draw attention to myself. The duke has already stuck his neck out for me, and I can't imagine why he would allow me to waltz about tonight as if nothing is wrong. Someone shall tell my stepfather and—"

"Your stepfather has already written."

"What? Why did you not tell me?"

"You were out in the gardens with Emma." He turned to the mirror and began to execute an elaborate knot that looked as if it took years of practice. She could not keep track of the turns and twists.

"Well, what did it *say*?"

"It was excruciatingly deferential, as I'm sure you can imagine. 'I appreciate Your Grace's unbounded good will in taking in a wayward young girl,' and so on. Seems your stepfather would like to come and retrieve you at His Grace's earliest convenience. I believe Somerhart responded that his household would be fully occupied with social activities until late next week."

"Did he?" she chirped.

"And I don't expect your stepfather has the where-withal to impose himself uninvited on a prince of the realm, do you?"

She allowed herself the hope of one small smile. "So this could work? It could honestly work?"

"It could."

"And if we lose all the money at the tables? What then?"

"If I lose all the money at the tables . . ." Cravat forced into an elegant sculpture, Nick slipped on the black coat he'd borrowed from Somerhart. "Don't worry. I will see you free of him."

"What does that mean?" she pressed, more than a little distracted by the picture he presented. Here was the Nick who'd spent the past ten years among the highest reaches of the *ton*.

"Come." He held out his arm with a wink. "Let's away."

She kept her hand at her side. "I am not like these people, Nick. You said so yourself."

He touched her cheek, fingers spreading to cup her jaw. "You are better than these people, Cyn, and they will love you." When he pressed his lips to hers, she stayed still and breathed him in. Their time together was rushing toward a close. She could feel the breeze it created in its passing. *I love you,* she thought. *I love you.*

But she only nodded silently and took his arm.

He was winning.

Lancaster looked at his pile of coin, slightly larger than it had been at the start of the evening.

He'd avoided the games of pure chance like hazard. He'd also rejected whist as it left him dependent on the judgment of a partner, and he simply wouldn't leave Cyn's future in the hands of an acquaintance. And in his final effort to turn luck in his direction, Lancaster had studiously avoided any table where the Duchess of Somerhart was playing. That woman was a miracle at the tables. A miracle for herself, at any rate. A curse for others.

But the game of *vingt-et-un* was serving him well. His holdings had increased to 550 already, though nervousness had made his mouth dry as a bone.

Lancaster collected his winnings and set off in search of a glass of watered whisky. A muzzy head would do him no good tonight.

Before he'd taken three steps, he spotted Cynthia smiling politely at Lord Osbourne. She didn't look quite at ease, but less than abjectly terrified now. Thankfully, Emma had sat him across from Cynthia at dinner, but all his encouraging smiles hadn't seemed much help. She'd looked ready to bolt at any moment. Or toss up her accounts.

When he spied her laughing at one of Lord Osbourne's jokes—they were new to her at least—Lancaster decided to leave her be. The only solution was to let her navigate the party on her own. He knew this, because he'd felt that terror himself on his first forays into London society.

Not only had he felt hyperaware of his lack of city polish, but he'd been sure he was marked in some way. A secret script feathered over his skin. A scent that permanently marked him as defiled.

But no one had noticed, not even those men known to prefer the company of their own sex.

Lancaster had watched them carefully those first few months, looking for some sign that he was a member of that forbidden club. And of course, there was the constant, exhausting guard against pursuit or attack.

In the end, Lancaster had found that those men were like any other men, no better or worse. Just the same. And as stories of Richmond had filtered into his social circle, he'd come to realize a sad truth. Richmond didn't favor boys over girls. It wasn't about sodomy or Greek love. Richmond simply liked the taste of innocence.

With the memories clinging to him, Lancaster gave up his search for temperance and plucked a whisky from a passing footman. Emma caught him mid-swallow.

"I hope you're not drowning your sorrows."

He shook his head. "No. Celebrating. I'm doing moderately well."

"Well, that fifty pounds you entrusted to me has blossomed into nearly two hundred."

Though he'd meant to take another sip, he slowly lowered the glass. "You're joking."

"I'm not. I purposefully played against Wolfson. He's a spectacularly awful player and he can well afford the losses. You're welcome."

"Emma!" he said. "Have I ever told you how mad I am for you?"

"Not explicitly, no. But don't let Hart or Cynthia overhear that. *They* might actually believe it."

He winked and raised his glass in a toast.

"Care to tell me what happened between you and Miss Brandiss, by the way? I assume it wasn't a love match."

"Not between her and me, no."

"Ah, I see. Well, if she cannot love you, then she

doesn't deserve you, Lancaster. The whole of the *ton* is in agreement that you are easy to love."

His cheeks heated at her words. "I . . . Um . . . Regardless, it seems I find myself continuously involved with women who do not love me. Quite pitiful, actually."

Emma cocked her head. "Cynthia loves you."

He wanted to grab her hand and ask what she meant and how she could know and what Cynthia had said to her. But he had his pride.

Actually, it wasn't pride at all. It was the hard realization that it didn't matter if she loved him. The girl had been born with a spine of pure iron. If she was determined not to marry him, she wouldn't. Her heart would have no say in it.

"Well," he said, "thank you for that small kindness. And for the larger kindness of spinning straw into gold. And for the unrepayable gift of keeping Cynthia safe."

Her eyes wandered toward a table that had grown raucous with laughter. "I would sooner cut off my own hand than see a young woman turned over to that man. I have witnessed his games, you know."

"As have I."

Emma turned back to him with a grim smile. "Then we are resolved."

By the time he'd wandered off from Emma, the whisky had finally hit his blood. Between the whisky and the winnings, he was hardly even bothered at all when the third person of the night mentioned his wedding.

"Best be heading back to London soon!" chortled Sir Chisholm. "You'll miss your own wedding if you're not careful, you great lout!"

He really wasn't on the sort of terms with Sir

Chisholm that would invite him to call a viscount a lout, but he patted his shoulder anyway, and escaped without a word.

Yes, he had best be heading back to London soon. He couldn't very well cry off the engagement on the eve of the wedding. Though facing Imogene and her father would hardly be pleasant, Lancaster couldn't wait to have it over. He wanted to be happy. And breaking the bad news to the Brandiss family would be a start.

"Lord Lancaster!" a familiar voice called in a very unfamiliar way. He turned to see Cynthia hurrying toward him.

"Good evening, Miss Merrithorpe," he said with a bow.

She looked disconcerted for a brief moment, then offered a curtsy with a twinkle in her eye. "Good evening, milord. And how is your luck holding tonight?"

"Well, thank you. Tolerably well."

Still smiling politely, she reached for his hand, and pinched the skin of his wrist between her fingernails.

"Ow!"

"Pray, Lord Lancaster, could you be more specific?"

For a moment, rubbing his stinging wrist, he considered teasing her further, but she was nearly vibrating in her slippers, and the tremors had made their way to her breasts. Much as he enjoyed the view, there were far too many other men around. He leaned closer, keeping his eye on her exposed flesh. "We are winning, Cyn."

When she drew in a deep breath, the dress strained at the seams. So did Lancaster's brain.

"Are we?"

"Yes. We've over seven hundred pounds now."

"Oh." She latched onto his elbow and leaned toward his ear. "Oh, Nick, I'm so relieved."

"Yes." Her breasts brushed his arm, then pressed even closer. "Perhaps I should get you a shawl."

"I shall start to moo if you say another word."

But he was distracted from his teasing again by the flush in her cheeks, and her pink lips, and the soft, soft skin that curved down her neck. He wanted to nibble there, work his way down to those generous breasts . . .

Lancaster glanced up and his heavy eyes focused on the nearest face. Lady Osbourne, who was watching him quite strangely. Lancaster stood straight and eased his arm away from Cynthia's chest.

"If my luck holds, another hour of play perhaps. Are you enjoying the party?"

"Absolutely not," she answered, but she smiled when she said it.

"Cynthia . . ." She was so lovely tonight, and he'd already told her, but what if she hadn't believed him? "Cyn . . ."

An outraged voice floated above the crowd. A bad turn of a card perhaps. Cynthia glanced toward the noise.

"After we've paid your stepfather," he started, but the voices grew louder. They seemed to be coming from the entry hall.

"What is it?" Cynthia whispered, anxiety threading through her voice.

"A player in over his head, I'm sure." Except he was no longer sure. He put a hand on Cynthia's arm. "Stay here."

Moving slowly at first, he picked his way through the guests. But as more people swayed toward the front hall, a sense of urgency overtook him. He edged past close-leaning couples, and glided around larger groups. By the time he got to the crowd gathered at the entrance to the hall, he simply pushed his way through.

And found himself face to face with a nightmare.

Chapter 20

A decade had passed since Lancaster had seen him. Richmond did not frequent London. Not enough innocence to be had in town, perhaps, while the country offered a generous bounty.

The past ten years had not been kind to the man. He looked helpless and frail. But Richmond had never appeared a monster. He'd been the consummate wolf-in-sheep's-clothing. All "hail fellow, well met" in public, before he turned into a demon behind closed doors.

Now he didn't seem capable of even the smallest evil.

His pleasant face sagged at the edges. He hunched slightly forward, fingers clasped over the handle of a cane. The hand holding it still looked strong though. It still looked thick and ugly. Lancaster felt frozen as he stared at that hand, remembering.

He wasn't aware that his ears had ceased to function until they began to pick up sound again. Richmond's voice, hard with scorn, berated the butler. Two large footmen stood at his shoulders, preventing Richmond from walking farther into the house.

Stepping forward, Lancaster broke free of the

crowd at his back. As he moved closer, he saw Bram standing at Richmond's back, his face impassive, as if he were staring at an empty meadow instead of a chaotic argument. Bram's gaze touched on Lancaster for a moment, but no recognition flickered there.

"I won't be kept waiting like a damned whore," Richmond growled. "Escort me to a private room now." His voice skipped down Lancaster's chest, scraping at his skin.

For so many hours of his life, for whole days, that voice had been the only sound in Lancaster's ear. That voice laughing and grunting and cursing. That voice issuing cruel demands and whispering vile thoughts.

When Richmond's face angled toward him, Lancaster almost retreated. He almost turned and walked away. He could not do this.

Richmond frowned at him as if he couldn't place him. His eyebrows dipped lower as he tried to puzzle it out. Had there been so many then? Too many to recall? Lancaster's stomach clenched at the thought.

Then Richmond's mouth bloomed into a friendly, harmless smile. "Hello there, boy. You look well." His eyes dipped over Lancaster's body. "Very well indeed."

Boy. Lancaster's hands squeezed to fists. "Get out."

Richmond's brow rose. "Are you speaking on behalf of His Grace now? I had no idea you were such intimate friends."

"Get out." He stalked closer.

"Not until I've retrieved my property."

"She is not your property, you bastard." Lancaster lunged for him, leapt like a hound for his throat, and he managed to get his fingers into the soft flesh beneath Richmond's jaw before hands grabbed at his arms.

"Milord!" the butler gasped. "Please!"

Lancaster dug his fingers deeper and watched Richmond's eyes bulge with alarm. His cane cracked into Lancaster's shin. Bram looked on, impassive.

The hands finally pulled him off.

"Lord Richmond," Somerhart's voice drawled from behind Lancaster's back. "I don't remember your name on the guest list."

"Where is she?" Richmond rasped, hand pressed carefully to his neck.

"Perhaps we should retire to my study. Lancaster, would you join us?"

Fingers still curled tight, crushing an imaginary throat, Lancaster glanced dazedly behind him.

Somerhart's hand was on his shoulder, so Lancaster turned and stepped out of his grasp. The faces of the crowd were pale ovals etched with open mouths and wide eyes, all staring at him. "Very well," he said and started toward Somerhart's study, the past trailing behind him like the shadow of a flame.

"Richmond is here," Emma said in a low voice as she led Cynthia out of the ballroom. "In my *home*." Her voice vibrated with fury, or perhaps that was just the shocked trembling of Emma's bones.

"It's Richmond?" The words came calmer than she expected. "Where?"

"In Hart's study. My husband wanted to end the scene, I suppose, but I'd have preferred that he toss that dog out on his ear."

"I'm so sorry," Cynthia murmured.

"Don't be ridiculous." She stopped at the mouth of a long hallway. "Would you like to join them? I understand if it would make you too nervous, but they are discussing your future, after all."

Yes, it made her nervous. It made her gut churn with acid to think of being in the same room with that man, but she had faced him before. Alone. "I'd like to join them, if you'd be so kind as to show me the way."

Emma smiled. "Good girl. Follow me. We cannot let gentlemen determine our futures, can we?"

"God, no," she muttered. "I'd sooner toss myself to the wolves. No offense to His Grace, of course."

"They are peculiar creatures," Emma offered with a wink.

Cynthia's smile fell away when she realized they'd stopped before a tall, imposing door. Emma reached past her to ease it open, and Cynthia was rather relieved when the duchess followed her into the room. Dark wood reached all the way to the ceiling, and deep brown furniture added to the overwhelming masculinity of the space.

Two pairs of men stood at opposite sides of a low table. There were chairs behind their knees, but none seemed inclined to sit. When she closed the door, Nick's head snapped toward her, his face radiating disapproval.

"Ah, here she is," Richmond purred. Cynthia didn't look in his direction.

"You should leave," Nick snapped.

"No."

"I don't want his eyes on you."

Richmond chuckled at Nick's words, and the air sizzled with tension. Crossing his arms, the duke leaned against his desk and offered Richmond a cool stare.

"Miss Merrithorpe is currently a guest in my home, and she isn't going anywhere, I'm afraid."

Richmond sneered. "Even a duke can't keep a man from his daughter."

"You are not her father."

"Cambertson means to retrieve her."

Somerhart shrugged. "My communication with Mr. Cambertson is none of your concern. If you are done here, Smith will show you the door." ·

"I am not done here," Richmond snapped. "My need for an heir outweighs this chit's need for independence. My cousin is in line to inherit and he is entirely inappropriate."

"*Inappropriate?*" Nick barked.

"This girl has been promised to me, and she has violated the contract of our betrothal with her childish drama. Her father will retrieve her and we shall be married tomorrow." He snapped a paper from his coat. "I have the license here if you care to examine it. In a few hours time, she will be my wife."

Nick stepped so far forward that his shins pressed into the table. "You will never lay another hand on her, you sick fuck."

"Oh, she will not mind," Richmond drawled. "There have already been hands laid on her, as I'm sure you're aware." He arched a mocking eyebrow. "I hope she did not try to convince you *I* was the one to breach her. I have been a perfect gentleman."

Faced with the barrier of the table, Nick simply leapt atop it and flew toward Richmond, who backed quickly behind the desk.

"You shut your mouth about her," Nick growled. He looked like an animal, back curved and teeth bare as he pushed both fists against the desktop. Cynthia was very afraid of what he might do next, and even the duke watched Nick with uncertainty, moving around to the side of the desk and holding up a hand for calm.

Nick leaned across the desk, eyes locked on Richmond's face. "I will kill you."

Despite that he'd backed up so far his shoulders pressed into the curtains, Richmond smiled. "Seems I've heard those words from you before, boy."

Though she'd been moving toward them, Cynthia's step stuttered. What could he mean?

"Bram," Richmond barked, and the man moved to his side. "I believe we are overdue for a call on Cambertson. I shall see you again soon, Your Grace."

Cynthia hurried forward and was nearly to Nick's side when Richmond passed. Nick kept his head down and his fists to the polished wood. The air sounded torn from his throat with every breath, as if he were a horse run too hard.

What had Richmond meant? When had Nick threatened to kill him before?

Just when she thought the confrontation over, just as she was drawing a deep breath of relief, Richmond stopped and spun slowly on one heel.

Illogically, he leaned closer to Nick, well within reach of his hands. He leaned in until his face was only inches from Nick's ear. And then he whispered something. Something that sounded horrible and made no sense.

"I hope she squeals as prettily as you did, boy."

Everything shifted so quickly that time seemed to slow to accommodate each movement in the room.

Nick's head snapped back as if he'd been slapped, and Richmond drew away with a smirk, confident he'd landed a fatal blow. Past the line of Nick's profile, Cynthia caught sight of the duke's face just as a terrible realization lit his eyes. She could recognize the thoughts popping like tinder behind his gaze, because those same thoughts exploded behind hers.

Richmond. Nick. Pain. And suicide. *I hope she squeals as prettily as you. . . .*

Paralyzed by shock, Cynthia was still staring at Somerhart when his expression flattened to alarm and he began to dive forward.

"Wait," she murmured, not understanding until she looked at Nick's face. It wasn't him anymore. He was a desperate, mad animal, teeth bared in a feral growl. Skin drawn tight over the bones of his face. And he was moving toward Richmond.

His fist landed on Richmond's jaw with such a loud crack that Cynthia's stomach turned in protest. Nick followed the man's falling body down to the floor, one of his elbows landing in Richmond's soft gut.

As the sound of retching choked from Richmond's throat, Nick hit him again and then again. It must have been only seconds, only a few heartbeats of time, but it seemed forever before Somerhart reached them and pulled Nick off. Even Bram was moved to help, stepping over his master as Nick fought to get free.

"Let me go!" he screamed, struggling as if he fought for his life.

"Lancaster," the duke snapped. "Lancaster!"

"I'll kill him!"

"I know. But not in front of the ladies, if you please."

Those words seemed to trip a lock, and Nick gave up his fight with a startled glance in Cynthia's direction. Though his chest still rose and fell with frightening rapidity, his face lost some of its madness. He stopped struggling and set his feet flat to the floor to support his weight.

When Somerhart let go his grip, Nick rolled his shoulders as if putting things back into place. Then he stood straight and smoothed his coat.

Richmond groaned.

"I will see you at dawn," Nick said without looking at the man sprawled on the floor. "And we will end this insanity."

"No," Cynthia breathed, expecting some echo of that sentiment from the others in the room, but no one else protested.

Somerhart jerked his head toward the door. "Get him out of here."

For a moment she thought a phalanx of footmen would enter the room and drag Nick away, but of course he was speaking of Richmond. Bram pulled him to his feet and led him out.

Her strange paralysis faded, and Cynthia reached for Nick's arm. "Nick," she breathed. "Nick?"

His eyes were dark and blank as slate when he turned to her. "I'm sorry. Would you pardon me for a moment?" he said before he walked stiffly from the room. She started after him, but was stopped by a touch on her elbow.

She followed the hand to an arm and then up to Somerhart's grim face.

"Leave him," he said. "Just for a time."

Coward that she was, Cynthia nearly melted with relief. Terror was gobbling her up inside, fear of the truth she might hear, and if she could hold it at bay for a few moments, she would.

Emma appeared at her side and wrapped an arm around Cynthia's waist. "What happened? What did Richmond say?"

Somerhart gave a sharp shake of his head while Cynthia tried to swallow her tears.

"You can't," she choked out. "You can't allow this duel."

"I won't stop it."

Emma's brow fell in confusion. "On your land, Hart?"

"If need be."

Cynthia grabbed his hand. "But he could be arrested or . . . or hurt or *killed*!"

"Miss Merrithorpe . . . he is hurt already."

"I know that!" she cried, and finally the tears came. She was folded up in the faint citrus scent of a duchess's arms and, knowing she didn't need comfort as much as Nick did, Cynthia cried harder.

Chapter 21

Like a lost child following crumbs, Cynthia had gone from footman to footman in an attempt to trace Nick's path. But the path had finally led to a side door to the gardens and all she could do was stand in the open doorway, arms crossed against the cold, waiting for him to reappear. He hadn't.

In despair, she retreated upstairs to change into her nightdress and await Nick in his chambers.

An eternally long hour passed before his door opened. She sprang up from the bed to stare at a ragged Nick.

"You should be in bed," he murmured, voice hoarse and low. "Your bed."

"No." She poured a glass of wine and pressed it into his cold hands. "Here."

"Thank you."

She refilled the glass when he emptied it, then poured one for herself. She'd been afraid to drink during his absence, sure she would overindulge and fall asleep. If she fell asleep she'd wake to find he'd never returned, just like ten years before.

Nick sat hard on the bed and stared at the fire as he took another long draw of wine.

"Will you reconsider meeting him?" She knew the answer already, and did not flinch when he shook his head.

"I can't."

"Very well," she said as if she weren't filled with fear. Silence fell as her mind twisted itself, knotting around all the horrid things lodged inside it. The thoughts were sharp rocks pushed deep in her brain.

Nick tossed back the dregs of his wine. "Ask whatever question it is that has you staring at me."

"More?" she asked, though that wasn't the question at all. When he nodded she handed him her glass and refilled his for herself. After a few sips, she felt braver and took a seat next to him on the bed.

"Was Richmond called Trevington before he inherited?"

"Yes."

Yes, of course. *Trevington.* The man who'd come to Cantry Manor and taken Nick away. It had been Richmond, all those years ago.

Nick turned his back to her to look at the fire. She waited for him to say something more, but he said nothing. Despite the fear climbing up her gut, Cynthia swallowed hard and asked, "What happened?"

"I don't want you to know."

"The truth can't be worse than my speculation."

"I'm afraid it can be."

"Nick . . ." She wanted to touch him. Wanted to hold him. But she was beginning to understand the reason he always moved her hands away. "What did he do to you?"

"What do you think he did to me?" he snapped, and then dropped his head into his hands.

"I'm sorry," she whispered. "I'm sorry. I should never have involved you. I should never have come to your house."

"God, Cyn. Don't apologize. Don't ever apologize. It's all my fault. I knew what he was, what he was capable of."

She watched the edge of his jaw tighten and jump in the firelight. "What is he capable of, Nick?"

Nick's hands dropped to his knees and he lifted his head to stare at the fire. "He took everything from me, Cyn. Everything."

"Do you remember how agreeable I was?"

She stayed quiet behind him, and he was thankful for that.

"I try to go back and mark a point in time where I could have changed things. My family met him by chance when we went to York, do you remember that?"

"I do," she whispered. "I was so envious."

He'd brought home a little shell box for her which, now that he thought about it, had been a singularly uninspired idea. But York had seemed so exotic, perhaps because he'd been allowed to attend a play and two dinner parties. Richmond had been at the play too.

"He introduced himself to my father, and soon enough they were fast friends. 'Your son needs a bit of polish before you think of moving to London,' he told my father. My mother was overjoyed. We all were. The chance for me to travel, to make important friends, and to solidify our relationship with someone like him."

"I remember," she whispered.

"I liked him. He was generous and witty and he made me feel important. Treated me as a future peer of the realm. That first day we left, we only rode for a few hours. We stayed at an inn. He poured me ale all night. And he noticed that I stammered every time the young tavern wench came near. He sent me up to our room and sent her as well."

His face heated at the memory. He'd been frightened and painfully aroused, and she had been soft and very friendly. "It was a test, I think. Because he came up soon after. And I thought, 'Well, this is a thing that gentlemen do.' He watched us, me and the girl. Then he had her also. Much . . . rougher. And I think if I had said no, if I'd asked him to leave or left myself . . . It was a test to see if I could be bent to his will. And I could."

"How could you have known?" Her voice rose, defending him from himself.

"It does not matter. That's who I was. I was *easy*. I liked everyone, and I was eager to please, was I not?"

"Stop it," she hissed.

"It is *true,* damn it." He stood and grabbed up the fireplace poker to jostle the logs. When he touched them, they disintegrated into coals. Though he meant to set the poker down on the tiles, somehow it clattered as if he'd thrown it.

"What did he do to you?"

"He took me to his home. There was no tour." *I've a bit of business to attend. Make yourself at home.* "And he seemed *surprised* when I resisted. He wanted me afraid, but not defiant. He wanted me to beg, not yell." *On your knees, boy.*

Lancaster rolled his shoulders against the feel of a

hand gripping his neck, winding into his hair. He opened his mouth and drew a breath just to know that he could. "After three days he seemed to realize I would not break. No matter how many times . . . no matter what he did. I kept telling him I'd see him hanged. Drawn and quartered. First he said no one would believe it. Then he said that everyone could see me for what I was. A ganymede and a foul pervert. No one would be surprised. Finally, he claimed to have made a deal with my father." Tears stung his eyes, then burned away in the blast heat of the red coals.

Cynthia gasped, her soft sorrow filling her ears. "That's monstrous."

"'Your family needs the money,' he said, 'And your father promised you were a biddable child. You don't wish to disappoint your father, do you'?"

"Nick . . ." Whatever she'd been about to say dissolved into a sob.

"I didn't believe it. In the end, he panicked, I think. He'd expected acquiescence. He thought I'd be cowed and silent. And there were already rumors, apparently, and he couldn't risk more. So he hung me."

He glanced over his shoulder with a twisted smile. "There is your answer. You finally got it out of me." He had to make a joke, because the sound of the rope creaked in his ears.

"You didn't try to kill yourself," she breathed, hardly believing it even as she spoke.

"I didn't. But . . . I wanted to die, so perhaps it is all the same."

"No." He hadn't meant to kill himself even after all that, and that knowledge freed some cold, tight grief from her heart. She could not imagine a world without Nick in it. And if he had made that happen . . .

"It's not the same," she insisted, pushing off the bed to move closer. She needed to touch him so badly, but she now grasped why he flinched at every brush of her hand. Instead of touching him, she stood close and held her hands at her sides, palms up so he could see that she meant to leave him be.

"It's not the same, Nick. When I ran from Richmond, I had a plan. I'd thought it through so carefully. I ran all the way to the cliffs in case someone was watching. I even leapt over the edge and landed on a ridge five feet below. It all went according to plan.

"But when I was hunched there on that rock on my hands and knees, I stared over the edge. I looked at the stones below and I thought, 'This is too hard. I am too tired.' I felt as though I'd struggled for years, trying to free myself from my stepfather. I just wanted some peace. I watched the blood drip from my lip and disappear into the sea and I knew it would've been over in seconds."

Nick dropped his hands from the mantel and turned to her. Her skin shivered with relief when he wrapped her in his arms.

"I couldn't do it," she whispered, "because of my sister. Not because of me."

"You didn't do it," he said. "And you wouldn't have. I know that."

His heart beat so loud against her ear, as if insisting that it would never stop. "How did you survive?"

His chin shifted against the top of her head when he spoke. "I don't know. He cut me down too soon. That was part of the deception, I think. The villain recast as hero. 'I found him and cut him down and tried to save his life.' But I gather that suffocation takes a long time, and I was skinny enough to delay the process."

Cynthia squeezed her eyes shut and mouthed a silent prayer against his chest.

"By the time he realized I was breathing, the doctor was nearly there. And then it was over. My parents were sent for."

Desperate to wrap her arms around him, Cynthia fisted her hands in his waistcoat instead and held tight to his clothing. "I don't want you to risk your life tomorrow."

Nick sighed and his chin rested heavier on her head.

"But if you must, then be sure you kill him, Nick. I want him dead."

Her angry words surprised a bark of laughter from him that boomed through her ear.

Cynthia pulled away. "I'm serious."

He smiled down at her. "I have every intention of killing him. I should've done it long ago."

"He deserves to die. How could he have *done* that? You were so . . ." She didn't realize she was crying until Nick pulled her back into his arms.

"Shh. It was long ago. And I am healed."

"You are not healed. I want to help you, Nick."

Nick shook his head.

Forcing her tears to stop, she stepped back and kept her hands locked onto his crumpled waistcoat. "Tell me what to do."

He shook his head again. "Nothing. I don't need help. I'm well."

"You won't let me *touch* you."

"I'm sorry, Cyn." He put his hands over hers and stroked them down to her arms. "I just can't."

His hands squeezed tighter, pressing her wrists together. A shock of recognition traveled up her bones.

This was lust to him. This was need. The way he held her when they made love. The way his hands restrained her.

And he might be hurt tomorrow, or worse.

She took a deep breath to keep the sobs at bay. "I want to make it better, Nick."

His hands wrapped around her arms seemed to ease him. He calmed enough to smile, though it trembled a bit at the corners. "You do make it better."

"You need something from me, don't you? You've tried to hide it, but I feel your hands tighten around my wrists. I feel you hold me down." As she said it, the words became the truth, so easy to recognize.

"No." He dropped her hands and jumped away. "That's not what I want."

"It is." When she wrapped a hand around her own wrists, his eyes followed. "I want to make you forget him."

"You *can't.*"

"For a moment, I can." A shuddering sob broke free before she could stop it. "I *can.*"

Resolved, Cynthia reached for the tiny buttons at the top of her nightdress. She moved slowly so he could stop her if he wanted, but Nick stayed still.

"Let me," she begged. "You want to know I won't touch you? I won't. I swear I won't. Hold me down. Keep me still."

Nick took one step back, but his gaze fluttered over her working fingers. "Don't ask me to."

"I *want* you to. I'm not afraid of you, Nick. You won't hurt me." She pulled her arms free of the sleeves and let her gown fall.

His eyes devoured her, his breath came hard and fast.

Ruthless, Cynthia held her arms out in front of her and pressed her wrists together the way he had. "Tell me what you *want*."

"I want to . . ." Desire burned in his eyes as he watched her arms, but that hunger was edged with horror. "I want to restrain you." He closed his eyes for a long moment, and when he reopened them, his tortured gaze met hers. "I want to bind your hands."

She nodded. "Do it."

"It's not right, Cyn. You're not a . . . a *whore*. I won't use you like that."

Dropping her hands, she stepped forward until she was nose to nose with him. "You listen to me, Nicholas Cantry. You claim to love me? How dare you claim to love me and then hide this side of you? You refuse to do something with me that you would do with a *whore*? With a *stranger*?"

His mouth tightened with anger. "Better with a stranger than you. It's ugly and wrong."

"Not with me. Not between us. Lose yourself in me." She rose on her tiptoes and placed her lips just above his jaw. Her breasts rubbed the wool of his coat. "Tie me down, Nick," she whispered. "Tie me down and have me and forget everything else."

Chapter 22

Close to tears, Nick placed his hands carefully on her shoulders. Her skin was so soft. Her body so delicate compared to his. He shouldn't want this from her.

He spread his fingers over her shoulder blades and whispered into her hair, "I won't hurt you."

"I know."

Even as he told himself to turn and walk away, leave the room and leave her be, he stroked his hands all the way down the glorious curve of her back.

If he tied her up, he could lose himself, just as she said. He could forget Richmond and fear and reaching hands and concentrate on pleasure. With *her*.

Knowing it was wrong despite her words, he still couldn't stop himself. Not with her naked and warm and asking for exactly what he wanted most. "I swear I won't hurt you."

He opened his mouth over her exposed neck and sucked gently just above her shoulder. Sighing, she arched her neck in encouragement. That acquiescence sealed his fate.

He'd told her the awful truth. All of it. And now he needed the taste of it out of his mouth.

Trying not to think what he was doing, Lancaster let her go and walked to the wardrobe. He pulled two plain black cravats from the small stack and carried them back to Cynthia. "Give me your hands."

Lacing her fingers together, she lifted her arms to him. He laid a strip of black fabric over her white skin, and his cock swelled to needful life.

"Tell me to stop," he whispered as he wound the cravat 'round and 'round her wrists. He waited for her to stop him, and prayed she wouldn't. *Please let me,* the beast inside him begged, and Lancaster hated it. But he knotted the cravat and trembled at the slithering sound of tightening fabric.

Once Cynthia's wrists were tightly bound, he picked her up and carried her to the bed. She looked down at the knot and then up at him, calmness a soft veil over her face. His own hands shook as he tugged her arms high above her and began to tie the second knot, the one that would bind her to the bedpost.

His heartbeat filled his throat as he pulled that last knot tight. Then he stepped back and looked at the vision he'd created. Her arms were stretched tight above her, leaving the rest of her body vulnerable to his eyes. She arched her back as if to encourage him, and her nipples tightened to ruched buds.

Anticipation swelled so hard and fast inside his body that his skin ached.

Lancaster stripped off his coat and waistcoat and tugged so hard at his shirt that two buttons popped free. Only seconds passed before he was free of all his clothing, and he couldn't wait another moment to feel her.

Free to do just what he wanted, Lancaster stretched his body over hers and pressed his full, naked length to her heat. Cynthia gasped, but he couldn't breathe at all past the joy of her skin. Nuzzling the spot just behind her ear, he let himself feel. Just feel. Every inch of her touched him.

When he could breathe again, he eased himself lower, edging his knees between hers, dragging his lips over her collarbone. He sucked her nipple into his mouth, and drew at it. Gently at first, but she was whimpering and writhing beneath him, and soon he was sucking hard at one nipple and plucking the other with his fingers.

Too rough, but she gasped with pleasure. And so did he.

The women he'd tied up before had meant nothing to him. They'd been nameless vessels for his secret needs. He hadn't wanted to linger or explore.

But Cynthia had been right. With her it was something new. It wasn't ugly or sick. It was a chance to know her body, to worship it in ways he'd never dared with another woman.

He shifted again, crouching over her so he could run his tongue down the skipping puzzle of her ribs. Her stomach sucked in hard, and he smiled to find that she was ticklish. When he rubbed his cheek to her belly, she jumped again.

"Sorry," he murmured. "I need to shave."

Cynthia laughed.

My God, he'd never imagined this, but as he dipped his tongue into her navel, she yelped, and Lancaster realized that lovemaking could be . . . fun.

He chuckled against her and breathed in the warm female scent of her skin. Gooseflesh bloomed over her.

"Are you cold?"

"No," she breathed. "Not at all."

Thank the Lord. It would've broken his heart to cover any part of her. He nibbled his way over to the jut of her hipbone and traced his tongue there. How different she was. So curved and soft and sweet. So perfect.

He scooted lower, and settled his shoulders between her spreading thighs.

His hands trembled at the sight of her sex, pink flesh peeking between curls. He would taste her there. Something he'd never done. It had always felt too . . . *defenseless.* Kneeling before someone, waiting to feel a hand in his hair.

When a shiver overtook him, he shook it off and refused to think of it. Cynthia's hands were tied, and he could do what he liked.

His hand fit perfectly over the curve of her mons. He smoothed the hair down and watched it spring back up.

"What are you doing?" Cynthia asked.

"Petting you."

She giggled, her belly shaking with the laughter. He petted again, drawing his fingers farther down as he did. Her laughter stopped on an in-drawn breath. He slid the tip of one finger along the seam of her body.

"Look at you," he breathed in amazement. Her foot slid against the sheets, and the delicate petals opened. Lancaster was mesmerized as he traced the shape of her.

A tiny moan drifted from her mouth as he stroked her. Her wetness licked at his skin.

Lancaster leaned forward and kissed her.

Heat was the first thing he noticed. Then the sweet

ocean taste of her against his tongue. He licked the wetness his fingers had found, and licked again when she gasped and moaned. When he touched his tongue to that little pearl of nerves, Cynthia's hips jerked away.

"Nick!" she groaned, as he curled his arms beneath her thighs and held her still. Yes, he could do what he wanted, and he wanted this.

It was over too soon. He had only just begun to settle into his task when Cynthia screamed and arched. He felt the spasms of her climax against his lips and licked at the eager wetness.

Though he was painfully aroused, he felt strangely suspended in the moment. Languid and patient as he kissed her plump thighs. He could stay here forever, pleasuring her. Tasting her. Feeling her thigh tremble against his cheek.

But he supposed it might be excessive to keep her tied to his bed for the next few hours. He didn't like to think of her hands getting numb or her wrists aching.

Cynthia sighed his name again when he rose over her. Her eyes were sleepy and dark. She looked perfectly content to be tied to the bed.

He smiled even as his heart beat harder at the sight of the black fabric. His stomach slid against hers as he lowered himself. His cock slipped easily inside her tight sheath. "I love you," he murmured. "I love you."

She arched beneath him, one hand wrapping around the binds that held her. His entire belly tightened at the sight.

This was his fantasy, the one he'd never dared to think could be real with her. His darkest needs, and she embraced them.

His strokes were deep and true. Cynthia pressed her heels to the mattress to meet his thrusts. Her teeth bit into her tender lip as she whimpered and arched beneath him.

"Yes," he whispered, watching her arms pull at the restraints. Her fingers curled to tight fists. He took her harder and watched her fingers flex in shock. "Take me," he growled.

Each of his thrusts pushed a little cry from her throat.

A perfect moment, and yet not perfect.

"Cyn." He slowed to a stop.

"Mm?"

"Look at me."

She opened her eyes, and Lancaster let his body rest against hers. He kissed her gently, over and over again. "If . . ." He paused to think if he could do this. She'd let herself be tied down. He could do this. "If I untie you . . . would you touch me?"

The distance cleared from her eyes. "You don't need to do that, Nick."

"I do. I need to. If you would just be slow?"

"Yes, of course."

He slipped free of her body and knelt to untie her hands. "And don't . . . don't touch my hair, all right?"

She was still for a long moment before she finally nodded. Then her hands were free.

Nick fell to his back and pulled her astride him.

"Like this?" she gasped.

"Yes," he said, "like this."

She lowered herself onto him carefully, eyes widening with every inch, but she kept her hands on her own thighs.

His cock strained as if desperate to fill her completely.

"You have no idea how beautiful you are." Another

new experience, and though butterflies danced in his stomach, he wasn't afraid. Even when her hand fluttered down to his chest.

She flattened one palm against his skin, then the other. He closed his eyes and pressed his hands over hers, pushing her fingers into his flesh. She was touching him, and still he could hold her and know he had nothing to fear.

"Yes," he breathed as she began to ride him.

He let her set the rhythm, let her find the pace. She dug her nails into his chest, and he startled at the pleasant pain of it. And when he finally spent himself inside her, Nick's cheeks were wet with tears.

A knock invaded her slumber, just before the sound of a door banging into the wall woke her fully.

"They've snuck away," a female voice said from the dark.

"What?" Cynthia clutched the blanket to her chest. "Who?"

"Our men. Hurry. Get dressed. I've brought your clothes."

"The duel!" Cynthia cried out as memory hit her full in the gut.

"Yes, yes. Hurry."

She hesitated for a moment, aware that she was very naked in a gentleman's bed, but the circumstances were obviously clear to Emma. She'd brought clothing, after all.

Decision made, Cynthia jumped from the bed and pulled on the chemise that Emma handed over. Five minutes later, she was dressed and rushing after Emma as she led Cynthia through a maze of hallways and steps.

They finally reached the front door and stepped out into a dawn of gray and fog. A curricle awaited them, and Emma leapt into the driver's seat.

"Do you know where it is?" Cynthia called over the crunch of the gravel.

"I eavesdropped when that Bram returned to negotiate the details. I don't think we'll make it."

Cynthia held on tight as they raced straight out onto the lawn and started up a low hill.

She'd meant not to fall asleep at all, but after such an exhausting day, she hadn't stood a chance. Had Nick slept? Would he be too tired for good aim and a quick trigger?

The curricle crested the hilltop, and Cyn braced herself for a frightening scene, but the hill was bare, and Emma pushed on toward the valley below.

Cynthia spied one horse tied near a dense copse of trees. Just one horse. What could that mean? She spied another mount as a great flock of birds burst from the trees below. Cynthia jumped as if she'd heard a shot fired. "Oh, God. Oh, God."

"We're almost there, Cyn. Don't fret. He'll be fine. I'm sure of it."

"Yes," Cynthia prayed. "He must be." She couldn't imagine a world without Nick even if they were separated by an ocean. She'd only just gotten him back. Nothing could happen to him now.

They finally reached the flat plain of the valley, and Emma whipped the horses to a reckless gallop. It seemed an eternity before they reached the pale green trees, and another eternity before they drove around the edge of them and saw the men standing there. Even at that distance, even in the dim and misty light, she could pick out Nick's body. The elegant way he turned. The line of his wide shoulders.

The other man raised a gun. Nick didn't move.

"Oh, no," she sobbed.

Emma's hand bounced against her knee. "No matter what, do not distract him."

Aim! She screamed inside her head. *Shoot!* But Nick stared at Richmond as if he were impervious to fear or bullets.

The curricle began to slow. A crack tore through the tranquil morning and rent Cynthia's heart in two. Richmond's gun smoked, and Nick was still standing.

Finally Nick's arm rose. He took his sweet time sighting his prey. Richmond took one step back, but it was no use. Nick pulled the trigger, a sharp blast exploded through the air, and Richmond was falling.

Before Emma could stall the horses, Cynthia had jumped down. She wanted to hug Nick and then charge over to Richmond's body and spit on it. But Nick still held the pistol, raised and pointed straight at Bram.

Cynthia skidded to a stop on the wet grass. It wasn't over after all.

"Keep Cynthia back," Lancaster said to Somerhart before walking toward Bram. Richmond lay on the ground at his feet, blood trickling sluggishly from the hole in his neck.

Lancaster was tempted to shoot him again. It didn't seem possible that the creature who'd caused so much torment could die so easily. It should have been harder than that.

But he needed his last bullet.

He tightened his grip on the pistol and aimed it at Bram's head. "Are you his heir?"

"No. I come by way of the housekeeper."

"You're his son."

Bram glanced down. "I was."

Lancaster hesitated. "You grew up there? In his home?"

"I did." His face was blank as ever, and Nick felt sick at the sight of it. This was what a man looked like when he was raised by Richmond. Not one emotion crossed his face. No thought flickered behind his eyes. He was gone as if he'd never existed.

But Lancaster kept the pistol pointed at his heart. "What about Miss Merrithorpe?"

Bram shrugged. "What about her?"

"Do you mean her harm?"

"She's nothing to me now."

The answer tightened his shoulders. "What was your interest before?"

"Richmond wanted an heir and couldn't get one on her himself. He promised me two thousand pounds."

"For what?" Lancaster bit out. The muzzle shook.

"A successful breeding."

"You fucking *bastard*." The world began to buzz around him.

Bram lowered his hands while Lancaster's knuckles whitened on the grip. "Shoot me if you mean to. I don't care. Dead or alive, I'm free of him now."

Shoot him. He wanted to. This man had planned to rape Cynthia. In Lancaster's new rulebook of crimes and punishments, Bram deserved to die just for that. But his blank eyes showed he'd died long before.

I'm free of him now.

This man might be a monster too. Who wouldn't

be, after a lifetime in Richmond's home? But how could Lancaster be sure?

He didn't know what to do, and in the end, Bram simply turned and walked away.

It was over. They were all free of him now, for better or worse.

Chapter 23

Cynthia was wiping tears from her cheeks.

Lancaster watched from a distance, fighting the urge to rush over and rescue her. She hugged her mother one last time before the woman pulled herself wearily into a carriage and waved good bye.

As soon as the carriage began to roll away, Lancaster walked toward Cyn.

After her initial grateful relief that he hadn't been injured in the duel, she'd spent the morning glaring her outrage that he'd snuck from bed without waking her. As if he would have voluntarily exposed her to danger and bloodshed. But regardless of her previous mood, he couldn't leave her alone now.

Her shoulders rose and fell in a deep breath. "Are you well?" he asked.

She wiped her cheeks and glanced back at him. "Yes."

"She seemed . . . overwhelmed."

"Yes, but she was happy to see me alive, and she didn't try to persuade me to return home."

"Good."

Cynthia turned back to watch the carriage roll away. "I gave her half the money. I told her to keep it to protect herself or Mary if this sort of thing arises again, but she may turn it over to her husband as soon as she sets foot in Oak Hall."

"There's not much more you can do."

"I know. It makes her feel safe to have a husband who's so certain in all he does. Even . . . even after what's happened. She apologized for not stopping the match but she said I've always been strong. Stronger than Mary ever will be."

"You *are* strong. But that's not an excuse to give you up to the world like that."

"I know."

He reached for her hand and held it tight until she nodded. "All right then," she murmured. She set her shoulders straighter. "What happened with the magistrate?"

Lancaster shook his head. "He seemed oddly satisfied with Somerhart's explanation. Only asked me to remain here for two or three days in case there is further inquiry."

"Thank God."

"I suspect it would be more appropriate to thank Somerhart. Seems he was right about the power of a duke's word." Setting aside his worry over the day's events, Lancaster offered her a small bow. "If you have a moment, I thought perhaps we might walk in the gardens. The rain is holding off, it seems."

Cynthia nodded and they strolled toward the gardens together.

"Are you well?" he asked in a low voice.

"I already said I was."

"But after last night . . ."

She flashed him an exasperated smile. "I am quite sturdy enough to withstand even your most earnest assault, dear Viscount."

Lancaster choked on his own breath and nearly tripped over an uneven brick on the path.

Just like that, all her sadness was gone, and Cynthia laughed until tears leaked from her eyes. "You are so very arrogant."

"I certainly am not! And *you* are outrageous."

"I am that. And I am also very well, thank you for asking again."

He watched from the corner of his eye as she smiled down at the path. "You are not . . . disgusted?"

"I am not even scandalized."

Well, that was one thing. Lancaster tried to pretend he felt only mild relief when, in fact, he was reeling as if he'd held his breath for hours.

"I did not mean for you to see what happened this morning."

"Yes, I know."

And that was it. There was nothing else awful to say. But he still had a difficult task ahead of him. He led Cynthia to a stone bench and sat with her.

Daffodils had begun to bloom and the scent of green leaves tripped to them on the wind. It was springtime, and he must return to London. "About our future . . ."

"Nick, I won't deny that I love you. I do. I always have. But love cannot make a future for a family. It can't be everything. Your family is depending on you to marry well, and I am nothing short of a disastrous match. I won't destroy your future. I won't."

He'd known what she must say, and yet he still

wanted to grab her and kiss her and shake her for good measure. "So you will go to America?"

"I will."

"All right," he answered, and Cynthia seemed startled by that. Good. "Though perhaps you might wait a time. You could be with child, you know. *My* child."

He watched as she pressed her free hand to her belly in a moment that made his heart thump, but then she shook her head. "No. I . . . My belly is already aching."

Lancaster shook his head in puzzlement.

"It means I will bleed soon."

"Ah." These things were a bit of a fascinating mystery to him. "You're sure of that?"

"Yes. It's the same every month."

"I see."

Her face flushed, and Lancaster cleared his throat. "Have you written to your aunt?"

"Um. Yes, I have." She darted a puzzled look at him. Oh, she meant to go, but she'd expected a fight.

"Emma says that she will help you choose a paid companion. I hope you'll consider her recommendation. She's canny about people."

Her forehead creased. "Of course," she snapped, then lapsed into silence.

They sat quietly for a long while watching the daffodils bob their heads in the breeze. Or Lancaster watched them. Cynthia glared as if they'd betrayed her in some way.

Finally, he cleared his throat. "I will come for you, you know."

She turned to face him. "Pardon?"

"I won't marry someone else. Ever."

"Nick, you must!"

"No," he said flatly. He studied the way her delicate

fingers fit between his. "In all honesty, I'd hoped there would be enough gold in that treasure to buy both our families free of our debts. Without it . . ." He shrugged. "I'll find a way. I've sacrificed for my family already, Cyn. I paid for their comfort and their future on my knees, and I shan't do it again in my marriage bed."

Her hand jerked in his grasp. "But that story wasn't true. That was a lie. Your father would never have . . . He'd never have . . . Tell me you don't believe that."

The pain had never left him, and it bloomed again, recalled by his memories. "No, it wasn't true. But it became true. Richmond paid for our home in London. He paid for a new wardrobe for my parents and for me. Paid for lessons so that my sister could learn to dance and my brother could learn French. He bought us easy entrée into the *ton*. My father took his money in exchange for silence. In exchange for the services I had so thoroughly rendered."

"That's not true," she whispered, her voice twisted by tears.

"In his defense, I suppose he did not want to believe his son had been tortured and raped and nearly killed by a man he trusted. A hard thing for a father to bear. Easier to believe Richmond, who said I had made an unnatural offer and then tried to kill myself over the shame of it when he pushed me from his bed."

Her nails bit into his skin now, and it was such a relief to focus on that physical discomfort.

"But you know, my father could never look at me again. Either I was a degenerate coward or he had betrayed me. Neither possibility could be borne, I suppose. So when I say I will not do my duty by my family," he heard his voice rise and could not stop it.

"I mean that I owe them *nothing* more than I've already given."

That dark, wet beast inside him roared its pleasure.

Cynthia eased her arms slowly around his waist, and he held his breath and let her. When her head pressed into his chest, he wrapped her tightly to him. "Don't cry. I'm not trying to abuse your pity to have my way."

"Hush," she ordered, the stern word too watery to be effective.

"I only tell you so you know I mean this. I will not marry for money. You were right. I deserve happiness as much as the next man. And I know how to have it."

"How?"

"It may take a while, Cyn. A year. Maybe more. I was using you as an excuse to flee my duties, but you are not the start of this. You will be the *end*. Will you wait for me?"

He leaned back to meet her gaze, but she didn't answer.

"Will you trust me?"

"I . . ." she stammered. "How? Anything could happen in a year, Nick!"

"All right then. Don't trust me. But I will come for you, so you'd best not make promises to some American gent." He touched a finger to the one tear that still clung to her cheek. "You'd best leave room for me."

"I don't understand!"

"Let me prove myself to you."

She shook her head. "You don't need to prove yourself to me, Nick."

"You've said I only think I love you because you are a reprieve from my duties. But you are not a reprieve, Cyn. You *are* strong. And you are brave and passionate.

You're my best friend. You know the boy I used to be, and you see the man I am now, and still you love me."

"Nick . . ." She swiped at her eyes and clenched her trembling jaw. "You are so easy to love. There are women with ten thousand a year who will love you. Do not settle for less than you deserve."

"I deserve to be happy, Cyn. I will find a way. And I will come for you. And then I will court you properly, not . . . as I have done."

Her snort was rather damp, so he handed over his handkerchief. When she'd finished blowing her nose, she gave him a shaky smile.

"If that was not done properly, I'm not sure I understand the workings of it."

He growled at her joke, but in truth he was light with relief. "There's another reason you'd do well to wait for me. What other man could love a woman with such an indelicate sense of humor? And then there are the awful drawings of unclothed men to consider."

She shook her head.

"If I find you entertaining an American beau when I arrive, I shall have to accidentally mention your portfolio."

Cynthia didn't laugh, but her tears had stopped, so Lancaster pulled her to her feet to continue their tour of the garden.

He would do this the right way, even if it tore his heart from his chest with yearning. And she would wait. She'd said she'd always loved him, after all. So she would wait. He was almost sure of it.

Lancaster stared into the amber glow of the whisky and wondered at what he was about to do. The changes he would make . . . they would change him too. But he felt different already. Hopeful. And some of his rage had dripped out onto the grass along with Richmond's blood.

When the study door opened behind him, Lancaster stood and turned to Somerhart. "I was hoping you'd stumble upon me. Do you have a moment?"

Somerhart poured himself a whisky and dropped into the opposite seat. He nodded.

"You were right about the magistrate. He's sent 'round a note to tell me I'm free to leave. Seems he was easily satisfied with your version of events."

"I'm a duke, Lancaster. My truth *is* the truth."

"Even when it's not."

Somerhart shrugged. "Richmond did fire first."

"You forgot to mention that it was a duel."

"So I did." The duke laid his head back.

"The crown may not be so easily dissuaded."

"We'll see. But I'm fairly sure the crown will be glad the title has been passed. And who will protest? The new earl? Everyone is well rid of that animal."

Lancaster looked back to his drink. "Thank you, Your Grace."

"You're welcome. I gather I'm free of my debt now?"

"Of course. I am forever obligated to you for—"

"Ah, Christ, I should hope not. Let's end this here, shall we? Cheers." He drained his glass and set it down hard on the table.

Lancaster swallowed down his own whisky, but he couldn't leave the subject so easily. "My apologies also. For bringing him here. And for what you overheard."

Somerhart lifted his head and met his gaze. He stared for a long time. "I will likely never say this again, so listen closely. You are a more complicated man than I took you for, Lancaster. If you weren't so disgustingly charming, I might actually like you." As Somerhart's head fell back to rest on the chair again, Lancaster looked at him, shocked speechless. He wasn't even sure what Somerhart had meant by all that.

"So," Somerhart murmured, "are you planning to leave this afternoon?"

"Yes. I hope you'll watch over Miss Merrithorpe for me. She's not accustomed to travel or . . ."

"I'll arrange passage on one of my own ships and escort her to her cabin myself. If you don't change your mind and come riding back before sunset, that is."

Lancaster's stomach clenched at the thought. He didn't want her to go, but Cynthia had dreams too, and he'd see her live them if he could . . . and continually pray that her dreams of the future involved him.

"I won't stop her," he murmured. "But speaking of ships . . ." Lancaster steepled his fingers and leaned forward as Somerhart cracked an eye open to look at him. "I have a proposition for you, Your Grace. Something a bit . . . unorthodox."

Hours later, he left for London with an excitement about his life he hadn't felt in years.

Chapter 24

"Oh, look," her cousin Lenore cooed. "There is that nice Mr. Morgan. Do you think he's brought his son?"

Cynthia leaned forward to see the stage past her cousin's feathered hat. "Perhaps. But Lenore, do be quiet, I am trying to hear the music."

Lenore sighed. "You are so very clever."

She patted the young girl's arm. "I am not clever at all."

"You're so interested in *everything*."

"Lenore, I know almost nothing about music or art or theater. That is why I'm so interested. You are already used to such things."

"I suppose. Oh, there is Mr. Echols! His eyes are such a lovely shade of blue."

Cynthia tried turning back toward the stage.

"Do you think it would be an exaggeration to call them periwinkle?"

Cynthia closed her eyes and gave in to exasperated laughter. "No. He does have exceptionally pretty eyes."

Lenore continued her chatter, overwhelmed, as always, with the excitement of her first Season. Of course it was Cynthia's first Season too, but she was neither seventeen nor eager to meet the gentlemen passing by.

She'd met plenty of them already during her three months in New York. American men were interesting. Bold and brave. Bright and shiny. But none of them had kind brown eyes that sparkled with secret laughter. And none of them knew her at all.

These American men heard her accent and thought she was refined. They heard a silly rumor that she was the cousin of a duke and invited her to the finest homes. On occasion she'd had to fight the urge to raise a glass at dinner and inform everyone she'd been sleeping in an attic just weeks before.

Now she slept on a deep feather mattress under pure white sheets in a bedroom larger than any she'd ever had. Somehow she hadn't imagined her American relatives would be wealthy.

In truth she hadn't realized America would be quite so obviously prosperous. It was more than she'd thought it would be.

The music and parties and the frighteningly crowded streets made her heart skip with joy. It was even hotter in the sun than she'd imagined, and there were far more people in this city than seemed physically possible. She loved it all.

And she missed Nick horribly.

Sighing, she nodded at something Lenore had said. Her cousin reminded her of a colt, all enthusiasm and long limbs and energy. Like the bustling city itself. And Lenore was just like her mother, who'd taken Cynthia in with the intensity of a whirlwind.

When Cyn had purchased three new gowns, more than ten boxes had been delivered, the order somehow multiplied in the waiting. When she'd ordered a pair of sensible black slippers, boxes of shoes had arrived in sets of rainbow colors. Pink and blue and green and violet.

She'd objected at first but eventually had given in under the sheer force of her aunt's good will.

It made Cyn wonder what her father must have been like.

And it made her wonder what Nick would think of the dresses.

The bright yellow silk of her gown slid like water through her fingers. What would it feel like to Nick's hand? The neckline scooped across her chest, offering just a hint of the curves beneath. Would his eyes follow the line of silk and remember how he'd opened his mouth over that very path?

"Cynthia, would you care for a lemonade?" Her uncle's voice made her start in shame. A glance around showed they'd reached intermission, and Cynthia rose to her feet, flustered.

"I'm sorry, Uncle. I must have been daydreaming."

"A favorite pastime of yours lately." His smile added kindness to the words, a stark contrast to the tone her stepfather would have used. Not that her uncle was perfect. He drank too much in the evenings and could be dreadfully rude to the servants.

He was as imperfect as the rest of his family, in fact, but perfection would have been a bit much to bear. Her aunt was a spendthrift who showed no interest in conversation that didn't involve clothing or gossip. Lenore was following very closely in her mother's footsteps, and her older brother seemed intent on gambling away his yearly allowance before September.

But they were kind and openhearted and seemed to

want nothing from her but company. Yet Cynthia had become increasingly poor company over the past weeks.

Nick had written only twice, and he'd said nothing at all in either letter. Platitudes and observations on the weather. What could that mean? Had he changed his mind? But he'd signed each letter with a carefully worded flourish. *All my love, and everything I am, Nick.*

She'd picked over those two letters, and when they'd offered nothing at all, she'd recreated their last few days together at Somerhart. Upon reflection, she realized he hadn't promised to write her faithfully. He hadn't promised to write at all. He'd declared his love and asked for her trust and promised to come for her. And that was it.

Her first month in New York she'd been impatient. The second month she'd been angry. But now she was afraid.

Every moment she was afraid. At dinner, at plays, and now, as the crowd swept her along toward the lobby of the theater, she was afraid.

She hadn't encouraged him at all. Not one little bit. Even after he'd laid his heart bare and showed her all the broken pieces, she'd drawn away at the mention of trust. But how much trust must it have taken for Nick to tell her such awful truths? How much trust to set aside the only future he'd ever imagined and leap blindly toward something better?

Surely she could have dared a small step in his direction.

Shame filled her at her cowardice. She *was* afraid. Doubts filled up the space in her heart she'd thought would be filled with happiness in America. So many doubts. What place did she have here, aside from the place she'd filled in England? She was a marriageable lady, nothing more.

She was not a pawn here, at least, but still a vaguely inanimate thing that would one day be picked up from her current life and set down in another.

And it was enough now to have comfort and contentment with her aunt's family, but what of next year or the year after?

With Nick she felt real. A person with a past and thoughts and a tendency for naughty wit. A daughter of society who'd once slept in an attic and knew how to pickle onions. A woman who'd been tied up for a gentleman's pleasure.

Cynthia blushed as she stepped into the theater's opulent lobby. With Nick she felt real, but what if he was gone again, swept from her life like dust? What if Imogene Brandiss had realized her stupid mistake? What if she had thrown herself at Nick and begged his forgiveness? He'd never been able to tolerate a woman's tears.

Lost in her miserable imaginings, Cynthia walked right into her uncle's back. Startled, she glanced around. Glittering ladies hovered in groups while black-coated gentlemen swarmed around them. Cynthia followed her uncle as he headed toward the bright blond hair of Lenore.

"Cynthia!" Lenore cried. "Where have you been?"

"In the box where you left me."

"I thought you were right behind me, silly. Come over and meet Miss Lee. You already know her brother, Mr. Ethan Lee. They have the loveliest little cottage on Cape May. Please say you'll invite us again. It was ever so precious. And Cynthia's never been to Cape May!"

The young man at Lenore's arm bowed over the chatter swelling from the young girls. "It's a pleasure to see you again, Miss Merrithorpe. I hoped I might encounter you this evening."

"You're too kind, Mr. Lee. Are you enjoying the show?"

"It's lovely, but it must be quaint compared with the culture you're accustomed to."

"You'd be surprised."

"I hoped to . . . I hoped it would not be a burden to you if I called on your family tomorrow. The last time we met, you said you were reading that Maria Brooks poem, and I took it upon myself to purchase a copy of my own. I'd love to know your thoughts on the language."

"Oh, I . . ." What was she to say? She didn't wish to encourage him, but he was a nice man. There could be no harm in talking with him. "Of course," she stammered out, just as she remembered the rather intense passion of the last pages.

"I'm honored," he breathed, raising her hand for a polite kiss that went on longer than she'd expected.

Her brain squeaked, *Oh, no,* just as Lenore cried out, "Cynthia!" She jumped and felt a flash of shame climb up her neck. Mr. Lee let go of her hand, but when he saw her blush, his eyes sharpened with pleasure.

Cynthia had the impulse to turn and flee. *Tell him about the nude drawings and he will run away,* Nick's voice suggested from inside her head. But she wasn't entirely sure he was correct.

A year, she thought with sudden sadness. She might not see him for a whole year.

"Cousin, do you know who's here?" Lenore gushed, giving Cynthia's arm a little shake.

"Mr. Morgan's son?"

"No! An English gentleman!"

Another one? She'd been foisted upon every English "gentleman" who'd passed within ten miles of Manhattan over the past few months. Two of them had been Scottish. Americans didn't seem to know the difference.

Lenore seemed shocked each time she found that Cynthia had never met the gentleman in question. *But England is so small,* she'd say.

"I hear he's an actual *lord,* Cynthia! You must know him."

"I've told you I know virtually no one, Lenore. Honestly." Another wave of sadness washed over her, dampening her earlier pleasure in the evening as Lenore and Miss Lee put their heads together for a bout of excited whispering. "I seem to be beset by a headache. Do you think your mother would let me take the barouche home and send it back for you?"

Mr. Lee held out his elbow. "Let me help you find her, Miss Merrithorpe."

"Thank you." She put her hand gingerly on his arm, careful not to brush her side against him.

"Oh, Cynthia! You mustn't! Miss Lee says that she saw him when he walked into the theater and he is *ever* so handsome, *and* . . ." She drew in a long, shuddering breath. "Miss Whitman told her he is a *viscount*! Can you even imagine such a thing?"

Mr. Lee chose that unfortunate moment to swing her around toward the crowd. Her stomach turned too, moving in the opposite direction. The feather in her hair tickled her jaw. A viscount? "Wait," she murmured, as the room took its time settling around her. "A viscount?"

"Miss Merrithorpe, do you need to sit down?"

And then she saw a reckless swirl of familiar gold hair, and that head turned toward her so slowly she wanted to scream.

Brown eyes locked on her, and Nick's mouth

bloomed into a wide smile of pure joy. Her heart fluttered into complete silence.

"Miss Merrithorpe?" Mr. Lee whispered. "Are you faint?"

Nick's eyes slid down to the place where her hand touched her companion's arm. She fought the urge to jerk away.

"Would you get me a lemonade?"

"Of course!" Mr. Lee answered. "Only let's find you a chair first."

"No, I'm fine. Only a bit warm."

When she looked back toward Nick, he was gone. Her heart slammed back to life inside her chest, rushing to drive too much blood into her head. Where was he? Had she only imagined him there, like a desert mirage? What an unbearable thought.

Panicked, she scanned the room, but the crowd was packed too tightly around her. "Oh, no. Oh, no."

"Cynthia." Lenore's hands grabbed her arms from behind. "Cynthia, I think it's *him*. With Mother!"

"Where?" She spun around and the crowd parted to reveal *Nick*. He strolled across the lobby, hands clasped behind his back as he leaned politely down to hear her aunt's words. His gaze flashed up to Cynthia, sparkling with mischief.

"Nick," she whispered.

Lenore glanced at her. "What?"

"Nothing."

"Oh, this is so exciting!"

Cynthia nodded. It was. It was so exciting she thought she might collapse right there in the middle of the lobby. But Nick looked perfectly composed as he stopped before them.

"Lord Lancaster," her aunt gushed. "I am so pleased

to introduce you to my daughter, Miss Rossburg, and my niece, Miss Merrithorpe. Girls, this is Viscount Lancaster." Her voice rose in a little trill at the end.

"An honor, Miss Rossburg," he said with a bow. Lenore bounced into an exuberant curtsy.

Then he turned to Cynthia. "And I have actually had the pleasure of making your niece's acquaintance in England, Mrs. Rossburg."

Cynthia stared, openmouthed.

Nick cocked his head to the side. "Perhaps she doesn't remember me?"

The air whistled through her throat as she bobbed a stiff curtsy. "Lord Lancaster."

Lenore hopped on the balls of her feet. "This is so exciting!" she repeated.

Her mother nodded. "This *is* exciting! Lord Lancaster, I insist you join us for dinner tomorrow evening."

He bowed again, perfectly calm and charming as if they hadn't been separated for 110 days. Cynthia drank in the sight of his smile.

"Mrs. Rossburg, I'd be delighted. What a kind people you Americans are, to take interest in a lonely stranger."

Her aunt giggled like a girl while Cynthia's shock twisted into irritation. A lonely stranger? What kind of poppycock was this? And why was he acting like a mere acquaintance? "Lord Lancaster," she snapped, but Nick held out his arm for her aunt's hand.

"If you would indulge me by writing down your direction, Mrs. Rossburg, I'm not yet familiar with your lovely city. Miss Rossburg. Miss Merrithorpe. A pleasure. I'll count the minutes until tomorrow."

And he led her aunt away without a look back.

Cynthia stared in shock. Then she panted in rage. The bells chimed, calling the patrons back to their seats. Cynthia stood stock-still among the flow, fists clenched. When she caught a glimpse of Nick moving away with a group of gentlemen, she stormed toward him.

She caught him just before he stepped into a stairway, and wrapped her fist around his sleeve. "What do you think you're about?" she whispered.

He turned gracefully toward her, a delighted smile already in place. "Miss Merrithorpe! What a lovely surprise!"

"Nicholas Cantry, you either explain yourself or I will stand right here in front of you and scream out the vilest curse I can think of."

"Oh, my. What would that be, I wonder? Something truly shocking, I suppose." He held up a hand when she drew in a deep breath. "Calm down, Cyn." He leaned closer. "I'm courting you."

"You . . . *What?*"

"I'm courting you properly, remember?"

"Remember?" Heat rose up her face, and when it reached her eyes, they overflowed with tears. "I sent letters, and you hardly wrote anything back, and it's been months since I've seen you, and I was so frightened. I *missed* you, Nick."

"Ah, love. Don't cry." His eyes lost their bright charm and went soft and warm. *"Please."*

Her face crumpled.

"Here, Cyn." Nick tugged her gently to the side, leading her to a narrow alcove that would shield them from the inattentive, at least. He pressed a handkerchief to her face, nearly smothering her before Cynthia batted his hand away.

She wiped her eyes and scowled. "You've made my *acquaintance?*"

"What did you want me to say? That I've known you biblically?"

"Well . . . What are you doing here? What has *happened*?"

"I'm sure we'll have time to speak tomorrow." He glanced toward a passing man who sent them a curious look. "We are being inappropriate again. Come, let me return you to your family."

She stopped him with a hand on his arm. "Wait. Come to my window tonight. It's in the east corner on the second floor—"

"I certainly will not."

"There's a balcony. If you—"

He stepped back. "I treated you shamefully before. I was betrothed to another woman and without any prospects and I dishonored you. I shan't behave that way again."

"Don't be an idiot!"

Outrage flashed briefly in his eyes. He bowed. "Good evening, Miss Merrithorpe."

Before she could protest, he turned and disappeared into the theater, and all she could do was blow her nose and calculate how many hours would pass until tomorrow's dinner.

Bastard, she shouted in her mind. He was a thoughtless, cruel bounder. A heartless cad.

And he was *here.*

Pressing a hand over her wide grin, Cynthia slipped out of the alcove and floated back to her seat.

Her gasp echoed through the room so loudly that everyone turned toward her. "I'm sorry," Cynthia managed, then patted her throat as if she'd swallowed her wine too quickly. Nick watched her carefully.

Had he just said he was part-owner of a shipping company?

Her uncle grunted. "I thought you Englishmen had an aversion to honest work."

"So we do. Rather shameful, I admit. But even the lordliest among us believes in investment. The majority owner of Huntington Shipping is the Duke of Somerhart."

"I'd heard that," her uncle said.

Her aunt perked up. "Is there any chance the duke might come for a visit?"

Nick's eyes watched Cynthia with rare seriousness as she hovered at the edge of the crowd. He'd invested with Somerhart? Where had he found that kind of money? It made no sense.

She had so many questions, and he was so very carefully keeping his distance. She stalked him, drawing closer.

Her aunt had invited three other families, of course. No point in having a viscount to dinner if you could not show him off. The others crowded around Nick, and she could not edge closer. When she caught his gaze again, she narrowed her eyes at him.

In England, she'd been so confident in her position. She'd nobly refused to marry him and ruin his family. But something was different inside her now. She was in America. A new land that let her see things in a new way. People made their own destinies here. Why shouldn't she?

Here, they believed in the pursuit of happiness. They believed in a greater destiny. And both her happiness and destiny were with Nick. She was sure of it.

He'd called her strong and brave when they were in England. She hadn't believed it then. But standing on the deck of that ship, sailing across the ocean, she'd felt brave. With the salt wind whipping her skirts and the sun glinting off thousands of miles of water, she'd felt strong.

And now she felt like a vengeful goddess, resolved to have her way. Perhaps that had something to do with the dowry her aunt had gifted her with. "It's only what your father would have wanted," she'd said.

A thousand pounds.

Not a fortune, but here in America, they could turn it into something. Or perhaps she would invest in Huntington Shipping.

Cynthia threw a suspicious glare in Nick's direction. A part-owner?

Whatever her suspicions, her glare lasted only a moment. Then she was caught up in the movement of Nick's hands as he said something to amuse the people gathered around him. He laughed, throwing his head back to reveal his throat. She couldn't see the scar, but she thought of it.

It would be better for him to marry a rich woman. His life would be better. But who would understand him the way Cynthia did?

Dread rolled through her gut when she thought of how careful he was with his body. How protective. Another woman wouldn't understand that. She might touch his hair and hurt him. She might not want her hands held down, might degrade him for doing so.

How could Cynthia willingly give him over to someone else?

She couldn't. She set her jaw in determination.

"Shall we proceed to the dining room?" her aunt

announced with a clap. "Lord Lancaster, I've put you with Miss Merrithorpe so you won't feel quite so beset by strangers."

Triumph roared to life in Cynthia's chest. Finally, she'd have him in her clutches. Armed with her excuse, she approached. "Lord Lancaster. A pleasure to see you again. It's been an honor to watch you from across the room."

"Miss Merrithorpe," he said warily. But then his eyes focused on her mouth. "Your beauty amazes. As always." He held out his arm.

She'd planned to torment him this evening if she could, but when Cynthia curled her hand slowly around his forearm and spread her fingers wide, pleasure wound through her gut so quickly that it hurt. She was the one tormented. Still, Nick closed his eyes and inhaled.

When she'd caught her breath again, she whispered, "I need to speak with you privately."

He shook his head. "That wouldn't be proper."

"I am not proper and well you know it."

Alarm showed on his face as he glanced around, but no one was paying any mind. She took deliberately small steps to draw out this private moment.

"I have questions," she insisted. "If you won't come to my room, meet me in the library after dinner. I'll excuse myself from the drawing room. No one will miss us."

"I won't risk your reputation. We'll have plenty of time to talk when I come for tea tomorrow."

"I don't wish to speak of bonnets and books!"

Nick leaned slightly toward her. "I am a new man, Cynthia. I am determined to no longer take the easy way. And if there is anything in my life I mean to do correctly, it is this. I will be in New York for a full month. Please allow me to do this properly."

For a brief heartbeat, she felt sympathy for him. Understanding. And then she looked down to his hand, to the tanned skin of his wrist and the golden hair that glinted against it. She'd waited so long already. She was strong and brave. She was resolved.

"I have a beau."

"Liar."

"You'd better not dawdle. He could propose at any moment."

"Too bad you're in love with me. Poor fellow will be heartbroken."

Well, what was she to say to that? She wouldn't deny loving him, not even to hurry him up. But she knew his weakness. She knew how to get him alone.

Cynthia edged her chin up, inching her mouth nearer his ear. "I declined to wear drawers this evening, Lord Lancaster."

His shoe seemed to catch on the smooth wood of the hallway, and Nick nearly tumbled to the floor. He caught himself and jerked upright, face flaming. "You never wear them. It's hardly a surprise."

"I do wear drawers now. Pink ones. Finished in lace and embroidered with naked harem girls."

"That's not true!"

"Come to my room tonight and I'll show you."

She was smiling when he held her chair at the dinner table. And Nick couldn't keep his eyes off her.

Damn her. Damn her all to hell.

Lancaster paced across the bedroom of his rented suite.

She'd done her best to torment him all evening. Flashing him naughty smiles. Leaning toward him each time she spoke to the lady on his opposite side. She'd even trailed her fingers up his thigh once, and it had felt . . . good. Exquisitely good.

Flirting with him. Mocking him with her eyes. And speaking about her *drawers*. In *public*.

When Lancaster had arrived in London, when he'd finally had some distance from Cynthia, he'd been horrified by his own behavior. To have so recklessly given into his lust with a sheltered young woman. To have even considered it when he was engaged to another. To have endangered her reputation and future . . . He'd behaved reprehensibly.

After coming to that clarity, Lancaster had resolved to behave with the utmost honor to prove to her that he could. To prove that she could trust him in every way.

It had seemed an easy vow out on the ocean. But now he was near her again and he'd missed her so much and she was so damned lovely. His body felt a husk. Dried out and wanting to be filled with *her*.

When she'd cried for him in the theater it had taken everything he had not to pick her up and whisk her to his carriage and . . . and what? Ravish her? In a carriage on a city street?

This was not going the way he'd planned.

Lancaster resumed his pacing, faced with an ugly truth. He couldn't resist her. She'd run her fingers up his leg for a count of four seconds, and he'd suffered in too tight trousers for a full thirty minutes.

Just the memory of it and he was suffering again.

He glanced at the clock. It was nearly eleven-thirty. Her last words to him hung like an ax over his head.

If you do not find a way to my room by midnight, I will find a way to yours.

She wouldn't really go traipsing about the city in the middle of the night, would she? Except that he had mentioned his hotel in passing over dinner. And Cynthia *was* damned stubborn.

"Bloody hell," he muttered, looking to the clock again.

He had to go, if only for her safety. And when he was near her, he couldn't resist.

Oh, this was not going to go honorably at all.

Cynthia glared at the clock. Eleven fifty-five and no Nick.

She'd suffered a great conundrum an hour earlier when she'd come to her room. Call the maid to dress her in her finest new negligee so that Nick would see her at her best? Or assume he wouldn't come and remain in her formal clothing? Her bright blue dress probably would not have been practical attire for climbing down the balcony, but it would've been better than the pale peach silk she wore now.

Damn him. She was going to have to sneak into the Ledbetter Hotel in her nightdress.

She stalked over to her bed to snatch the matching wrap off the mattress. Not that it covered much.

She was reaching for her cloak when her door opened. Her balcony door.

She froze, hardly believing he might be there. But then Nick walked in, his face tight with fury and his trousers ripped at the knee.

He pointed at the cloak in her hand. "You were actually going to do it, weren't you?"

"I said so, didn't I?"

Nick took a step toward her. "You manipulative, stubborn, impossible woman. I am trying to court you honorably and decently and you—"

"Oh, stuff it, Nick." Cynthia dropped the cloak to the floor and shrugged off her wrap. When his eyes swept down she knew exactly what he was seeing. The pale silk did nothing to disguise the shape of her nipples or the dark thatch of hair between her thighs.

His eyes glittered.

Cynthia reached for the material at her hips and began to inch it up.

"Stop!" he whispered furiously.

"I want you."

"We have to wait."

"No."

"There are things we need to discuss. Serious things that I wished to ease into—"

"Oh, for God's sake, just ask me to marry you and be done with it!"

Nick gasped, his mouth falling wide with shock. Then he cursed. Then crossed his arms. Finally he pointed at a chair in the corner of the room. "Sit down."

"No."

"Sit down or I will change hotels and you won't see me again for weeks."

"Hm." She studied his face, trying to gauge his level of commitment. He did have a different sort of determination about him now.

Nick tugged at his cuff and offered her a casual smile. "I've another trip to America scheduled in four months. Perhaps I'll see you then."

"Oh, blast," she huffed and flounced into the chair,

making sure her gown rose enough to expose her ankles.

First, he checked to be sure her door was locked—as if she wouldn't have thought of that. Then he paced to the open balcony door and looked into the midnight sky for a long while.

Finally, he turned back to her. "I went to see Imogene Brandiss and her father the moment I set foot in London. I did not even stop at my home. I want you to know that."

"Was it difficult? Was she relieved?"

"It was . . . as difficult as would be expected."

Cynthia cringed. "I'm sorry."

"But she looked thankful, I think. I hope. And it was done. Of course, then I had to break the news to my mother."

"Oh, no." She'd been so consumed with her yearning for him, she'd forgotten all the difficulties he'd been suffering. "She must have been . . . disturbed."

"Yes, she was. But there was more difficult news for her to bear. The news I wish to discuss with you also."

Cynthia sat up from her slump. "What is it?"

"First, I've taken some economies. I've cut my brother's allowance by more than half and sold my mother's London home—"

"Ouch."

"And I've petitioned the crown to remove the entail from my own town home. It's a great monstrosity and will likely bring in an impressive amount if the crown agrees. I'll pay off my debts and invest the money in improvements on my other properties and in a few years, my income should improve. As for my mother . . . I'll rent a home in London for my family during the Season, and they may retire to the country as always during the winter."

"I see. And where will *you* live during the Season?"

He glanced at her through his lashes, then down to the floor. "This is what I wished to discuss with you."

Her pulse increased at his nervousness.

"I will not . . . I will not lead the life I had expected. Or that you had expected." He sighed and ran a hand through his hair. "It's a difficult subject."

"Nick, where in the world did you get money to *invest*?"

"I didn't."

She waited, but Nick said nothing. "*Please* tell me so we can get past this."

"All right." He paced for a moment, brow furrowed, jaw jumping with tension. "I made a proposal to Somerhart. He offered me a five percent stake as part of my compensation."

"Compensation? I don't understand."

"I, um . . ." Nick cleared his throat. "I have taken a position."

"A *position*?"

"I don't expect you to accept it. It's nothing a woman of your elevation should have to tolerate. If you can't . . ."

She waved his words away. "What kind of position? What in the world do you know about shipping?"

"Nothing. I am to be charming."

Cynthia cocked her head. "You are always charming."

"Yes. And now I am to charm people into doing business with Huntington Shipping. For a profit. And a share in the company. I'm to charm my way into being the most coveted guest in New York society. Boston as well. Perhaps Savannah."

"You're not serious?"

"Yes." He set his feet wide and stood straighter. "I'm afraid I am. I have every intention of increasing Huntington Shipping's profits by threefold within the year. This is the path I've chosen, Cyn. If the idea is distasteful or—"

"It's perfect!"

He pulled his chin in. "What?"

"You cannot possibly fail."

"Well, don't say *that*."

Unable to contain herself, Cynthia leapt from the chair and ran into his arms. "It's perfect!" She pressed kisses to his chin and jaw and finally—finally—Nick's arms were around her. "I'm so proud of you. Ask for my hand," she urged.

"I will not have the same social assurance I once did. There's already disapproval over my breaking the engagement with Miss Brandiss. Creditors are howling for my head. And there is talk about why I might have killed Richmond. If it gets out that I am *employed* . . . We've put it about that I'm part-owner, but that is only a half-truth, I suppose."

"Let them talk." She sucked at a spot on his neck while he tried to set her away. "I'm an American now. We expect ambition in our men."

"My mother has taken to her bed and will not speak to me."

Cynthia laughed. "So long as she does not blame me for it."

"I will have to travel, Cyn. Not always. I have my duties as viscount, but—"

She kissed his neck. "Take me with you?"

"Yes, of course I will."

"Ask me," she whispered.

"Cynthia." Nick eased one hand up to cup the back of her head in his hand. "Are you sure you understand? It's not an honorable position for a man of my standing. Or a lady of yours."

"Nick, this is . . . Oh, you are so very clever." She smiled up at him.

Nick must have seen the truth in her eyes, because he finally nodded and pressed his lips to her temple, then lightly to her mouth.

"I am not clever. But I will work so hard to make you proud."

"You do make me proud."

His mouth moved to her ear, so that his words seemed to breathe straight into her. "Marry me, Cyn. Be my wife. Bring me joy."

She'd thought herself impatient to hear this. Ready to marry just to get it over with and have him to herself, pragmatism be damned. But at those words, her heart stopped and swelled so large she couldn't breathe.

"Cyn? Say yes. Please."

She'd loved this man her whole life. Having him would be too much. But it was a sacrifice she'd have to make.

"Perhaps. Will you pose for my sketching?" she asked.

"Er, of course," he answered, shuddering only a little. "I'd be . . . honored."

She grinned up into his precious, familiar face. "Then yes," she said. "Yes."

That simple word seemed to wipe most thoughts of his pesky gentleman's honor from his mind. He kissed her hard, and ran his hands over her hips and pressed himself against her belly. When she pulled her negligee up and off, he muttered something about insulting the trust of her aunt and uncle. When she cupped her breasts in her own hands and told him she was lonely, he protested that they would be married within days and he could behave decently until then.

But when she lay on her bed and pressed her wrists together, stretching her arms above her head, Nick didn't say a word. He was far too busy nibbling his way down her stomach to speak. And Cynthia was too busy being dishonored to care.